Praise for

Captive

"*Captive* is not 'dumbed down' history—it is intelligent, chronicling a specific time and event in history, seamlessly balancing real and supposed and the enduring human spirit. The human aspect of the story—feelings of love, loss, separation—is something we can all relate to in spite of differences in time, race, and culture. I felt transported back in time, witnessing what happened. And even though I knew historically what was coming, I had goose bumps, anxiously wondering what would happen next!"

—Kara Fossey, Groton Historical Society

"*Captive* is a 'you are there' experience and I am held 'captive' by it—anxiously awaiting the next book. I feel like John chewing on that last piece of dog foot, waiting for another bone."

—Patricia Ann Magnell Seib, retired Executive Assistant to the Director of Southwestern Fair Commission

CAPTIVE

BASED ON A TRUE STORY

CAPTIVE

P. GIFFORD LONGLEY

Edited by Kalyn McAlister
Cover design by Kristen Verser
Interior design by Blake Brasor

Independently published in the United States of America

ISBN: 978-1-54959-912-5

1. Fiction, Biographical
2. History, United States, Colonial Period (1600-1775)
11.03.02

DEDICATION

In loving memory of my father,
Dwight Francis Longley,
who never knew of this story.

I know, O Lord, that a man's life is not his own;
it is not for man to direct his steps.
Jeremiah 10:23, NIV

ACKNOWLEDGMENTS

At the peril of forgetting a key contributor to the effort of writing this book, I mention those to whom I offer my thanks:

To my wife, for her patience rivaling that of Job—not only in enduring the years of distraction associated herewith, but also for her constructive criticism, creative ideas that had a real impact to the text, and for her simple willingness to listen when others may have been driven away from this obsession of mine. She is truly my partner.

To my daughter, Rachel, for her editorial commentary.

To my son David, for his insight into human nature as affecting the formation of the consistent character of the antagonist.

To my son Daniel, for his support and encouragement.

To my niece, Rebecca Friedman, for her scholarly translations of portions of the character dialogue into archaic French.

To my friend Fred McCormick, for his excellent literary criticism, which influenced in no small way the structure of this work.

To the Christian Creative Writing Workshop, and to its founder, Robert Williams, for their words of positive encouragement and venue that welcomed the reading of portions of this manuscript, spurring me to complete a first draft.

To Barb Welch for her belief in this work and for her kind recommendation to the publisher.

To the subjects of this work, especially my forebears and the citizens of Groton, who endured the terrifying and awful consequences of the Indian attack on July 27, 1694, worked through their pain to piece their lives back together and, by faith, pressed on.

To those who participated in compelling my seven-greats grandfather to return to Groton, without which I might not be here—or at least I would be very different.

And to my Lord, who protected all those that came before me, formed me, loved me, called me, *died for me*, guided me, and gifted me with the knowledge, wherewithal, and pure privilege to tell this story so that others might share in it.

—P. Gifford Longley

FOREWORD

In the tiny town of Groton, Massachusetts, located about thirty-five miles northwest of Boston, there is a street called Longley Road. Along the eastern edge of that road is a car-sized, granite boulder with these words etched into its face:

NEAR THIS SPOT DWELT
WILLIAM AND DELIVERANCE LONGLEY
WITH THEIR EIGHT CHILDREN

———————

ON THE 27TH OF JULY 1694
THE INDIANS KILLED
THE FATHER AND MOTHER
AND FIVE OF THE CHILDREN AND
CARRIED INTO CAPTIVITY
THE OTHER THREE

———————

GROTON HISTORICAL SOCIETY
1946

Of the three children of William and Deliverance taken captive by the Indians that day were two daughters and a son, the twelve-year-old John. After his capture, John lived with the Indians more than four years, adapting to their lifestyle. And when he was ransomed by his relatives, he preferred not to leave his captors, doing so only after he'd been compelled.

John would eventually return to Groton, embrace once again his English culture, marry twice, father eleven children, serve the town in various official capacities, and serve as deacon in the church the last twenty-eight years of his life. Three of John's sons would live to fight in America's war for independence, along with more than twenty of his grandsons.

John Longley is my seven-greats grandfather, and this is his story.

—P. Gifford Longley

NOTICE TO THE READER

While most of the names appearing in this book belong to real historical figures, it must be understood that this is a work of fiction, not biography. A simple recounting of the reliable known facts surrounding this story, without reference to the volumes of supporting historical documents, would necessarily be limited to a few pages of text. But this story deserves more than the simple facts found in those existing accounts. It deserves a telling of the perspectives of the characters, their passion and pain that surely must have accompanied those facts—thus my selection of this literary form.

In anticipation of this work, I researched the historical records related to the characters and setting for more than four years. Key places I visited in preparation include the Town of Groton, the Groton Historical Society, and the Massachusetts State Archives. The historical records I was able to gather and/or review would fill some two dozen volumes. My sources included probate records, where I was able to transcribe seventeenth-century handwritten documents, wills, and such; several modern histories on the early settlement of New England; nineteenth-century historical books on Groton written by Caleb Butler and Dr. Samuel A. Green; and a few family genealogies. Most notable among the genealogies was *The Sesquicentennial History of the Town of Greene, Androscoggin County, Maine: 1775 to 1900, with Some Matter Extending to a Later Date,* by Walter Lindley Mower, 1938. That private publication, which listed the name of my grandfather, the author's cousin, was the key to unlocking the lost history of my past, revealing to me the identity of my previously unknown ancestors, in particular, John Longley—dubbed "the captive" to distinguish him from other relatives who have also borne that common first name. Without that book, this one would not exist.

Some of the information that I encountered in the different sources contained contradictions, particularly as related to the generation that preceded the captive. In such cases, I relied on the earlier documents as my data source, notably, the last will and testaments of the captive's grandparents and the documents naming his custodians, Thomas Tarbell and Sarah Rand. Where the records were silent on certain issues, I filled in the blanks with conjecture, logically considering the culture and times.

The storyline of *Captive* is founded on facts from the record, including the ages and names of the captive and his family members; the geography and history of the town of Groton and certain key persons then living; and the role of Taxous and Madockawando in support of the French during King William's War, specifically their plotting and conducting of the raid on the Oyster River Plantation and Groton. Key elements of the storyline that some might label "legend" are similarly founded on the historical record, including the circumstance of the capture and massacre of the family and the ransom and conversion of Lydia, which is the subject of another work of fiction written for children, *Lydia Longley, the First American Nun*, by Helen A. McCarthy.

The climax of the story, the ransom and reason for the return of the captive, is amazingly devoid of historical facts, even legend. Only four facts appear in the record: 1) his ransom was paid; 2) he chose not to return; 3) he was somehow made to return; and 4) he returned. Here is where I took the greatest liberty to invent a plausible explanation to fit these facts—the subject of *Compelled,* the companion volume to this work. Thus, it is this aspect more than any other that requires that these combined works be labeled fiction and not biography. And while there are other aspects in this account that may be unsubstantiated in the record, including what the persons involved and affected by the events were thinking, such, in my view, ought not be difficult to reasonably infer, human nature being what it is.

—P. Gifford Longley

INTRODUCTION

Groton, Massachusetts, in the seventeenth century is a small village at the outer edge of the English colonial frontier, located thirty-five miles northwest of Boston, within the territory governed by the Massachusetts Bay Charter. The Groton settlement, known first by its Indian village name of Petapawag, meaning "swampy place," is established as an English town on May 23, 1655, when the petition of a few English settlers is awarded by the Massachusetts general court. But, due to the "remoteness of the place" and a lack of a sense of community by the few English dwelling there, Groton's town business is not regularly conducted until December 24, 1662.

Among Groton's original proprietors is William Longley, Sr. who, with his fifteen-hundred acres, is the third largest landowner. Having come to America in 1638 as a young married man with his wife, Joanna, William had first settled in Lynn, Massachusetts. After living in Lynn a quarter century, William had pulled up his stakes to start over here in Groton in 1663 at the age of forty-nine. William, who had emigrated from Firsby, Lincolnshire, England, had entered the colony as a "freeman," an indication of his high social standing, good education, and right to vote. William and Joanna had produced all of their children in Lynn: two sons, John and William, Jr.; and five daughters, Hannah, Mary, Elizabeth, Lydia, and Sarah. In these harsh times of high childhood mortality, each of William's children will be fortunate to reach adulthood, marry, and produce children of their own.

Arriving in Groton as a man of station, William, Sr. takes on important public roles, including town clerk, selectman, and constable. His influence among the townsfolk is strong as he is opinionated, outspoken, and driven—all character traits that also make him a dominating force in his household.

John Longley, William's oldest son, is also listed among the original proprietors of Groton, and he has his own substantial five-hundred-acre land holdings. John is twenty-four when he first comes to Groton, living apart from his parents and siblings.

William, Jr., the sixth child in the Longley family, comes to Groton as a boy, still living under the care of his parents. Here he matures and follows closely in the footsteps of his father. William marries as a young man, but his bride dies in less than year, after the birth of his first child, Lydia. William soon remarries to Deliverance, the daughter of neighbor, Benjamin Crispe. William and Deliverance have two children together, William (III) and Elizabeth, before moving from the family estate to their own twenty-five acre tract north of the village. At their new farm, they have their fourth child, Jemima, followed by John, Joseph, Nathaniel, and Zachariah.

Being on the frontier, Groton sits uneasily at the edge of the native culture. The 1660's are a time of transition in relations between settler and native, four decades into the peace and commerce they'd established in Plymouth under the leadership of the great sachem, Massasoit. During that time their two populations have gone in opposite directions. New England's native peoples, estimated to have numbered ninety thousand in 1600, have dwindled to a mere fifteen thousand, decimated by European diseases. The English, on the other hand, have swollen in number, driven by waves of new immigrants. By 1675, the English outnumber the natives three-and-a-half to one.

In 1661, Massasoit dies as his culture is under siege. The European lifestyle has made unwelcome inroads into native society and religion. Additionally, the English set strains on the environment, and in their thirst for land, seize the best where, for centuries, the natives had freely lived, farmed, hunted, and fished. Some of these land transactions amount to simple theft, turning many longtime trade partners against each other, and bringing suspicion into every interaction.

Rising in angry protest to this mistreatment is the second son of Massasoit, Metacomet, who takes for himself the English name of King Philip. Philip rallies the natives to strike back, against the injustices of the English. And when a band of his men attack a small village in southeast Massachusetts on June 20, 1675, events are set in motion that will bring war to all of New England.

In the spring of 1676, King Philip's war comes to Groton, and the town is attacked three times. The last assault is the most devastating, as all the buildings are burned. The village is abandoned and the settlers flee toward Boston. Over the next sixteen months the war will continue to sweep through New England, such that half of its ninety villages and towns are touched by violence, many burned to the ground. As for the English population, some one-and-one-half percent are killed in the conflict, double the rate of American deaths in the Civil War and more than seven times that of World War II. But the natives suffer a staggering toll, with mortalities of twenty percent.

King Philip's War ends with the signing of the Treaty at Casco in 1678. An uneasy peace is felt throughout New England, especially in the remote and undeveloped north and eastern regions. And though peace exists on paper, the violence of war is now permanently etched into the psyche of both English and native—each suspicious and fearful of the other, many moved to hatred. It is with this mindset that the settlers return to rebuild Groton in April of 1678, compelled by the government to do so, or forfeit their land.

After the outbreak of a new conflict between England and France in 1688, King William's War, violence spreads to their colonies. Two new Indian attacks are launched on Groton, seemingly unrelated acts of terror, randomly executed for profit. Both occur in the remote northern parts of town where it is possible to enter, conduct mischief, and afterward readily flee, without drawing the attention of the local militia. The first occurs in 1690, in which Simon Stone is wounded and his property pillaged. The other occurs September 13, 1692, killing James Blood—whose first wife, Elizabeth (now deceased), was the daughter of William Longley, Sr.

And now, in the summer of 1694, six years into war, Groton remains a remote village at the edge of hostile wilderness. More difficult challenges lie ahead for Groton's citizens, and they are unaware of the further terror that awaits them.

Uncle John "Jack" Longley

Born in 1639 in Lynn, Massachusetts, John is the first child of William (Sr.) and Joanna (Goffe) Longley and the first Longley born in America, named after his grandfather, John Longley (1586–1639), a priest in the Church of England. Though John receives no formal education, as his grandfather and father had, he is schooled in the home and learns to read and write. He reaches adulthood in Lynn and makes a number of friends there who nickname him "Jack." In 1663, Jack moves to Groton and establishes his farm south of the village, just a mile up the Lancaster highway from his father's property. There Jack meets and marries Hannah Elvey, and they produce three children.

But Jack's union with Hannah is not welcomed by William, Sr., who feels he has married low, and tensions brew between the two over that and other matters. Since Jack is one of Groton's proprietors, he is active in the town's early official business. But with time he withdraws from town matters to avoid his mounting differences with his prominent father. Yet as bad as relations become between the two men, Jack's mother retains her positive influence on him, as she is always kind to him while being openly devout. Thus Jack comes to realize that his own faith is a great help to him through the many difficult circumstances he faces, and he never departs very far from it.

In March of 1676, after Groton is destroyed by the Indians, Jack and his young family relocate back to Lynn, moving in with an old friend. In Lynn, he purchases a woodworking business and establishes himself. A few months later, Hannah dies while giving birth to their fourth child.

Being yet estranged from his father, Jack does not return to Groton at the end of the war in 1678; except for a brief visit, he remains in Lynn. A year later, Jack meets and marries his second wife, Priscilla ("Cicely"), who soon produces his fifth child in November of 1680. Within weeks of the birth, Jack's father dies, the two never having been reconciled.

In the spring of 1682, Jack's mother remarries to her neighbor and in-law, Benjamin Crispe (father of William, Jr.'s second wife), and Jack returns to Groton for the ceremony. Soon after, Jack sells his Lynn business and returns permanently to Groton to be near family and to help tend to his mother and Benjamin, who have become advanced in age. But after little more than a year, Benjamin dies. Widowed again, Joanna relocates to Charlestown to live with her youngest daughter's family.

The next decade is a particularly difficult time for Jack and Cicely, contending with the death of her only child and then watching the other four mature, marry, then leave home. By the start of the summer of 1694, Jack and Cicely, now past middle age, feel alone in their home, looking for purpose and fulfillment.

The Captive: John Longley

Born in June of 1682, John is the fifth child of William, Jr. and Deliverance (Crispe) Longley—her fourth birth. John eventually has seven siblings in all, four brothers, two sisters, and a half-sister, Lydia. John's education begins in his home at an early age, and he is an excellent student, just as his father had been. John's father is a large presence in the household, active in community affairs, serving as a selectman and town clerk, and following in the footsteps of John's influential grandfather, William, Sr.

John and his siblings grow up on a farm where they each perform chores to help the large family while their father remains preoccupied with town business. But John is a different sort of person than his father, athletic, fit, and advantaged with height over other boys his age. And because John loves the great outdoors, he sets his mind on completing his schooling and chores so that he will be free to roam Groton's woods and meadows with his friends, play games, fish, hunt, explore, and use his active imagination. Young and impressionable, and with so much opportunity available due to his wide array of skills and interests, John's future pathway is by no means established.

Around the time of John's twelfth birthday, and with the advent of summer, he is invited by his Uncle Jack to come and work in the woodshop on his property. Each morning, the young John rises early, feeds the livestock, and then rides his horse three miles south through the village to his uncle's place. After work, John returns home, performs his chores with his older brother Will, and then eats a light supper with the family. With the late summer evenings, John enjoys playing games with a few close neighbors before dark, after which he reads by the lantern before he goes to bed.

On weekends, John is constructing a shelter in the woods, in a secluded spot situated on the eastern part of his father's lot, about a half mile from the house. John borrows a few tools from his uncle's shop for the project, and he uses them with skill and care. He boasts in applying the new trade he is learning and savors the opportunity to creatively construct his own special retreat.

Lydia Longley

Born January 1, 1673, Lydia is the oldest child of William Longley, Jr. by his first wife Lydia Pease, who dies from complications brought on by the birth. She grows to love her beautiful stepmother, Deliverance, who marries William before Lydia turns two and who cares for her as though she were her own. Lydia is just three years old when Groton is burned by Indians during King Philip's War, so she is fortunate not to remember the terror of that event as she matures into a young woman. Lydia shows she is smart, resourceful, and confident by taking to her education in a way that is less than common in her male-dominated culture. Lydia happily sails through her teenage years enjoying good friendships but clings to tomboy tendencies. As she reaches the age of twenty-one in the tiny town of Groton and her feminine charm finally begins to bloom, she has imagined love but has not courted.

PART ONE:

Taken

THE STORM

Thursday, July 26, 1694

Just before midnight, a strong, hot wind rose up and began to push the tops of the tall trees over. The breeze subsided, the branches straightened themselves back upright, and then a stiffer gust shoved them sideways again, causing the trees to teeter drunkenly under the gathering roar of the sudden, summer gale.

John, who had been sleeping restlessly atop his bedroll on account of the heat, was awakened by the din. The boy sat up and looked at his dog, Skip, who was silhouetted against the faint light of the lamp. Skip, also alerted by the sound, lay there quietly awake, but panting. Skip was a good watchdog, so seeing the animal's calm attentiveness took away any sense of worry or insecurity that the boy might have otherwise had.

The gusts continued to strengthen as the walls of the shelter strained, but held. A sudden crash shook the roof. With a start, John scanned the timbers overhead. He stretched forward and reached over Skip, retrieved the lamp, and turned up the wick to brighten his view. He measured the log rafters overhead but saw no telltale signs of damage. Surely it had just been a branch that had been snapped off by the wind.

John leaned back on his bedroll and tried to relax, enjoying a genuine sense of satisfaction of just being there—there in *his* shelter. He interlocked his fingers, cupped his hands behind his head, and confidently let his eyes roam all around the interior of the space, feeling then a sense of pride—pride in his little lean-to, which he'd made with his own hands—product of his decisions, his design, his craft. It was a good size all right, eight-foot square, yet not so big that he couldn't single-handedly move the logs into place; the ones at the bottoms of the walls, some more than twelve-inch caliper, those had been rather heavy. And the shed roof, that had been manageable, lifting into place those smaller trunks that he'd felled. And he'd cleverly overlaid them with sheets of birch bark, which should work well to keep out the rain. And as for the tallest side of the square shelter, this he kept open, facing conveniently at the path. He studied the four corners, how carefully he'd fitted them together—squared and notched, solid, and unyielding to the mighty winds that were trying just then to push the walls over, yet to no avail. Those joints were doing all the work, he knew. Uncle Jack had taught him well, taught him his newly acquired carpentry skills. And these now gave him comfort.

But just as his presumption swelled near to overconfidence, a powerful blast stormed in through the unprotected opening, snuffed out the lantern, and plunged his little fort into darkness. John leaned forward instinctively and felt for Skip, who yet lay peacefully at his feet. This restored his suddenly fragile confidence.

He patted the animal's head and spoke to him as if to calm himself with the sound of his own voice, "I don't know if it's gonna rain. It has to. Don't ya think?"

John often discussed things with his trusty hound and didn't hesitate to engage him in a little midnight meteorological dialogue. Then leaning to the side, he peeked out the front of the shelter and tried to measure the sky. But strain as he might to discern it, everything was black, and not a single star or any other detail was to be distinguished. He could only hear and imagine the thick forest canopy swirling above them. *Surely there will be rain*, he concluded,

P. GIFFORD LONGLEY

but he could neither hear thunder nor see any lightning. This storm was like no other he'd experienced before—the strong, furnace-like wind, but without any indication of rain. He eased himself back down on his bedroll, with his sweat pouring out from every surface of his body. Yet the breeze was simply too hot to bring him any relief.

Whelmed by the heat, he pondered again his decision to sleep there at his project—his first overnight since he'd finished it. He'd seen how the weather had been so oppressive and humid all week. He'd been near desperate *not* to be up in the loft yet again, there beneath the steamy thatch roof with only that tiny window for fresh air. He knew Lydia, Betty, and Will must have been feeling awful at that very moment, lying as still as possible atop their covers, begging for comfort, hoping for slumber to dull their senses.

It was a good thing that Father had consented to his request, permitting him to use the shelter. And he was especially glad for it now. After all, the shady forest surrounding him was more than a few degrees cooler than the meadow back where the house sat, exposed and sun-baked. And though Mother had objected to his sleeping there, he was, after all, twelve—old enough to be alone. Father surely would have slept there when he was that age. Obviously that's why he'd approved, overruling Mother's worries. And having this trusty watchdog at his side—he stroked Skip's head—that had made his decision easy and quelled the sum of Mother's protests.

Thus being pleased with his circumstance—*One rather superior to that of my siblings*, he thought—John lay back down. With his body exhausted, he drifted off into a fitful slumber.

After a while, the young man was awakened again, this time by the low rumble of distant thunder. Not knowing how long he'd been asleep, he impulsively felt for Skip, who yet lay at his feet—alert, panting to try and cool himself, but otherwise still. Another rumble came, and then a great gust blew past the lean-to's opening. This one was noticeably different, distinctly smelling of rain. He sat straight up enjoying the change, relishing the evaporation of his sweat as it flew from his bare chest and arms. Then the sounds of the forest began to change. Rain was falling.

When the showers first started, only the tops of the trees felt the precipitation. But in just a matter of minutes, the fat, heavy drops began to patter on the roof. John savored the immediate cooling effect. Moments later the torrents came as the upper canopy of foliage became saturated and the waters poured straight through to the forest floor. Billowing winds followed, which sent a wave of spray swirling in through the open side, this delivering a shock of cold and damp that brought Skip to his feet. John knew he'd better secure the opening.

Groping in the darkness, he seized the folded tarpaulin that had been his pillow. It wasn't easy to hang the cover in the dark, especially against the contentious wind. He stood and braced himself against the gusts and gripped the canvas tightly as it flapped and fluttered like a sail in the wind. He fumbled with the lashings, groped for the hooks, and at last managed to secure the upwind side. The other edge followed more easily as he stretched it taut. He settled back down on the floor, greatly satisfied that he and Skip were now shielded on all four sides against the summer gale.

John returned to his bedroll and listened to the storm sounds, the great sheets of rain pounding the bark roof like myriads of fingertips tapping on a drum, and the tarp flapping and shuddering against the wind's onslaught. He contemplated his situation, fearless in his youthful naiveté, feeling poised by his careful planning. Of the various sites he'd considered for this fort, this one was proving to be the right choice, one that displayed his growing wisdom that was founded on his superior powers of observation. He'd set it on a high point along the trail and installed a wooden floor, which, though it had been so much more labor to install, had raised them up above the ground. The path by now had become a torrential stream, yet he and Skip were staying dry.

The rolls of rumbling thunder, once distant, at last drew closer, and the lightning finally came. The bolts illuminated the lean-to, penetrating the canvas with their brilliant, phosphorescent glow.

P. GIFFORD LONGLEY

These flashes briefly revealed the silhouette of Skip, still serenely resting at his feet, for nothing seemed to rankle his trusted companion. The lightning intensified.

Crack! Boom!

The ear-splitting clap of thunder came simultaneous with the blinding flash. This timing had meant that the bolt had been very near, but how close? John made a mental note to investigate in the morning. He leaned forward and huddled close with Skip through several more frightful minutes of the intense and brilliant flashes and booming cracks and echoes, and then he observed that these did almost instantly and unexpectedly begin to fade, as though smoothed by an unseen hand. After a few minutes more, the wind and the lightning subsided, slowed, and stopped. But the rain continued, falling straight down in the quieting forest as the rumbles trailed off into the distance.

He noticed how the air had changed, having become much colder. He groped in the darkness and found his shirt, donned it, and lay back down, shivering from the sudden raw clime. He pulled part of his blanket up and over his feet as Skip came and huddled close by his chest. After a few moments of listening to the soothing shower, he was lulled back asleep.

A third time the young man was roused, this occasioned by Skip's growling. Barely awake, John mumbled, "What is it, boy?" He knew the ordinary forest sounds wouldn't rouse Skip, so a sense of fear pulled him toward full consciousness. His ears strained to detect the disturbance, whatever it had been. But outside of the enclosure was a deathly quiet. He realized the rain had stopped.

Skip's growling intensified. John placed his hand on his companion and felt the tenseness in the canine's muscles. Skip turned to face him. The dog's eyes were glowing golden in the dark, and this sent a disturbing chill up his spine. The animal turned back toward the opening and stared at the blank tarp, raising up, crouched and reared, as if ready to pounce.

"Easy, boy," John whispered in soothing tones, rubbing Skip's erect ears. "It's just some animal. *Calm down.*" He knew that packs of coyotes frequented the woods, sometimes even bears.

The dog's uneasiness persisted as he stretched forward and sniffed along the bottom edge of the tarp. Then, nosing under, he forced his head outside and bolted from the shelter. The sound of his running paws was heard fading quickly down the trail to the left, in the direction opposite from the farm.

John sat up immediately. He felt for his stockings and shoes and pulled them on. His fingers fumbled at the tarp's lashes. Freeing the canvas, he escaped outside and onto the path.

It was lighter now—lighter than it'd been before the rain. He could actually distinguish the way, though barely. He paused for a second and bent to tie his shoes as he peered down the trail.

No sign of Skip.

He stood upright again and listened and gave a skyward glance. A light wind stirred the branches overhead, and he could see stars up through the openings in the leaves.

His attention returned back down to the trail as he whispered, "I wonder what Skip is after?"

As if to reply, the cold night air glanced his cheek, causing the hair on the back of his neck to stand up. The thought that he might be in real danger dawned on him with force, but he knew that Skip faced the same hazard; and the dog must be in need of his help. He resolved to proceed with care and took a few steps forward.

Straight ahead, toward the east, a bright light revealed itself ever so briefly. It was eye-level, perhaps a bit higher, but far off down the path. Then it vanished.

Startled, he thought, *There's nothing in that direction.* Uncertainly, he stepped several paces toward it down the trail. The breeze stirred the leaves again, and the beam briefly exposed itself a second time.

Seized now with curiosity, John pressed forward yet some more. He needed to ascertain the source of that light. *Is there someone camping in the woods? Perhaps Skip heard them and that's who he's run off after.* He persevered forward on the path, following the elusive glow, which persisted to shine intermittently and always to disappear. He was certain now. There was no possibility that his eyes were playing tricks on him. The light was unquestionably real.

As he traveled still farther, he apprehended something odd about the source of the light, as it appeared to him no closer than when he'd first spied it. *It's moving! Heading away from me. Maybe someone has grabbed poor Skip and they're taking him!* He doubled his pace. A half mile later, he reached the end of the path at Hobart's pasture.

His chest was heaving for breath as he tripped forward through the edge of the dense thicket and burst out into the tall grass. At last he could see the source of the light plainly, and it wasn't at *all* what he'd imagined. He sighed with relief, for the glow was just the moon, a slender crescent, barely hovering amidst the treetops far off across the vast field. *How it had fooled him!* Now he understood why he hadn't been able to catch up to it.

The sense of imminent danger drained rapidly away from him, and he took a deep draught of the brisk, night air. Tilting his head upward to the vast space above the moon, he scanned the heavens, which shone with countless stars, all illuminating the pasture with their celestial glow. *How unusual to see so many stars in the summertime*, he thought. The storm certainly had cleared the air.

Searching for familiar constellations, his eyes meandered across the firmament. John had learned some of the star patterns from his Uncle Jack, studying especially those that lay along the ecliptic, the path on which the moon and planets move across the sky. But the canopy above him was so filled with the competing brilliance of countless lesser stars that this presented him with a challenge to distinguish the main groupings.

He strolled farther out into the field to get his bearings and to view the sky that lay behind him toward the west—that is, the early evening portion of the heavens that were more familiar, now making ready to set. And seeing the constellations above the western forest, he recognized a distinctive sign. It was Scorpio above the treetops, situated as if above his family's house, which lay beyond in that direction. *Look at that*, he thought to himself. "The scorpion" seemed poised as if ready to strike its venomous stinger at some unknowing prey there. But apprehending now this clue (Scorpio as situated), he was able at last to reckon the time to be near three hours past midnight.

Knowing the lateness of the hour, the boy's adrenaline abruptly faded and exhaustion filled his limbs. He decided he should look for Skip in the morning. *Besides*, he thought, *the dog will come back on his own, as he always has.* John needed to bed down, get some sleep. He would be starting his morning chores all too soon.

Working his way back through the tall grasses, he paused before the dark entrance that led back into the forest.

A rustling sound alerted his ears.

Startled by the noise, he wondered if it had come from the thicket before him. Or was it from behind him in the grass? He turned back toward the field and gazed all around. He softly called, "Is that you, Skip?" No response. He looked all around again and waited. Nothing.

Deliberately he faced back toward the woods. They seemed now to be engulfed in an inky blackness. Fear was rising in his bones. He took a deep breath and shook himself, trying to steady his nerves. He reassured himself. *I came this way once already. It was fine. There was nothing there.* Gathering his resolve, he stepped forward through the grass and entered a half-dozen paces back into the woods.

A twig distinctly snapped—in the path immediately behind him.

He froze in his tracks. His heart was racing. *Is it Skip?* he wondered. *Or a bear?* In that same instant, a terrible odor passed his nostrils. *It's musty. No, it smells like something dead.* He listened intently but heard nothing more.

Daring himself to move, he turned slowly back toward the starlit opening, with his gaze fixed downward at the path. He hoped to find Skip there; instead, what he saw stunned him. His eyes panned ever upward to make sense of his vision. Standing before him was the black outline of a huge man, more than a head taller than himself, poised with arms outstretched *and reaching forward to grab him!*

P. GIFFORD LONGLEY

Flight was his immediate instinct, but before he could turn to make his escape, the dark arms ensnared and restrained him, pulled him, and pressed his face tightly against a naked chest.

John reacted instantly. With all his strength he twisted his body, flailed his arms and kicked his legs, battling to free himself from the grasp. He managed to land a good punch—an elbow to his assailant's face—and for a second the grip loosened and he turned to get away. But there were others suddenly there who grabbed him and threw him hard to the ground, thrusting him downward onto his back, knocking out his breath.

Confusion ensued. Shadowy figures rudely flipped him over onto his stomach. They held him down with their substantial weight. They violently shoved his face into the earth. They twisted his wriggling arms behind him and pummeled his back and legs with their fists until he was rendered senseless. Unable to resist their torture any longer, he stopped struggling and drifted toward unconsciousness.

Searching for protection from his attackers, longing for safety, for innocence, John's mind flew far away from the agony and confusion of the moment, straight to a time of dearest comfort.

His mind settled on a favorite scene from when he was four years old and youngest amongst his siblings. The family was seated at the table for the evening meal. Mother, Will, Lydia, Betty, and Jemima were all there. But Father wasn't yet home. Then he heard him just outside, his solid, familiar footsteps as they creaked across the back porch and drew nigh to the door. Anticipation filled the room, and smiles came to all their faces.

John exclaimed, "Daddy!" as he dropped from his chair and ran to greet Father, who was pushing the door open and stepping through.

So tall and handsome, he cheerfully greeted them with his booming, "Hello!"

The big man dwarfed his little boy, who rushed over and clung to his legs.

John looked up at him and their eyes met.

Father smiled broadly back down, an expression fashioned entirely for his benefit. "John, you're so *strong*! Now, just a moment. Let me remove my coat and hat." Grinning at the greeting, Father continued in an animated voice, "Here, *I shall hang my hat upon the hook*." But instead of placing it on the wall where it belonged, he dropped the hat onto the youngster's head. Its adult size fully engulfed it as the brim came to rest on his shoulders.

The little one had now become a silly source of entertainment, being buried in a hat far too large. Father and the others giggled with simple delight.

But pleased by the sudden attention, John took hold of the brim and raised it up to peek from beneath, glancing out at his happy audience. Seeing their joy, he proudly addressed them, "Look! *I'm* Father!"

The big man bent over and lifted his son, holding him close in his powerful arms. He gently asked him face-to-face, "Now would you hang that up for me, please?"

Very glad to help, John stretched his stubby arms out toward the hook, depositing the hat in its rightful place there. Then twisting back toward his daddy, he flung his arms around his neck and embraced his trusted provider with a tight grip and fervent grunt.

Father whispered in his ear, "I love you, John," as he kissed his neck and caressed his cheek with his scratchy beard.

John had felt so safe then in Father's loving grasp, so secure from any harm.

Then drawn by the strong hand that gripped his hair, John drifted back to awareness of his torture. His head was pulled up now, and his neck twisted. From the corner of one eye he spied the glint of a polished blade—a knife that seemed to be poised and ready to slit his throat. *Is this how I am to die?* he wondered.

P. GIFFORD LONGLEY

But before he felt the fatal cut, a second hand reached in and rammed his face, his nose, his mouth down hard again into the soil, mashing his lips into his teeth with the force of the impact.

A moment later, he was rolled over. A palm firmly clamped his mouth shut as he vainly gasped for air. The metallic taste of blood oozed from his lips and filled his mouth. For the first time in his young life, he knew how fear tasted.

John lay motionless in the grip of his captors, awaiting the end and aching for breath, yet curiously straining to distinguish the dark forms of his tormentors. He wondered how many there were. Three or four?

Then he heard the utterance of a deep, ugly voice—a sound he would never forget. The fetid breath was blown out just inches above his face. "You stay quiet ... you live."

The words were English, but the accent revealed the speaker to be an Indian, whose large body was hovering there just above him. He smelled again the musty stench. He gagged. He reckoned it to be the odor of blood, the rotting scalps that were tied to the Indian's belt—his recent victims. In his dread, he made no sound.

Then laying there quietly with his heart pounding, he felt his hands being bound in front of him. The cord cut tightly into his wrists. And just as quickly as he'd been beaten down and subdued, John was roughly yanked upward to his feet, being lifted by the black figures that surrounded him. Moments later they jerked him and then dragged him off by the rope, away from the trail and into the gloom of the forest.

Many questions raced through John's mind as he stumbled along through the darkness. *Will my captors let me live? Where are they taking me? Will Father be regretful and angry that he'd let me sleep alone in the woods? Am I ever going to see Father or Mother again?* But then— then the most terrifying thought occurred to him: *Will my family be attacked next?* He felt his heart sink to the pit of his stomach.

There was no way he could warn them.

DEADLY RUSE

Friday, July 27, 1694

Lydia was unsure how long she'd been shivering on top of her bedcovers. The dawning bird songs had floated into the edge of her pre-conscious thoughts for quite some time, the gentle cooing of the mourning doves in the brisk air. As she drifted awake, she at last reached for her blanket and pulled it over herself to welcome its warmth. With her eyes blinking open, she gazed up through the gloom toward the sloped ceiling, the underside of the log rafters and grass thatch that formed the roof of her house. Her bolster being just below the open window, she rolled her head back and peered upward, out through the aperture to survey the sky, finding there the stars as they faded against the brightening backdrop. The sun would soon be up.

How different the clear, fresh air felt compared to that of the evening before—a welcome ending to a dreadful, hazy, humid week. The glorious dawn foretold the best day of the season.

Lydia closed her eyes to enjoy it. She rolled to her side, snuggling in her blanket, trying to relax, hoping to settle back into her slumber. But sleep would not come. After a few minutes more, though worn out and unrested, she resolved to get up, this owing to her burden of responsibility, the firstborn among her parents' eight children. The twenty-one-year-old knew the morning chores were nearing, and if she drifted back off, oversleeping was likely. She sat up and rubbed her eyes. *How unseasonable*, she thought. There was dawning such an extraordinary summer day, yet there could be no shirking the necessary obligations of life, the ordinary tedium that would make this day like all the others.

There were two double beds there on the floor of the loft, situated up beneath the high gabled ridge and located over the single bedroom below. She shared her mattress with the eldest of her sisters, Betty, age sixteen. The other bed belonged to the oldest of the boys, Will, nineteen, and John, twelve. Betty to her left and Will to her right, both were peacefully at rest beneath their covers. They shouldn't be disturbed just yet or robbed of a few more minutes' slumber. *Her* benefit had been such close proximity to the open window all night, the bit of fresh air. They too now deserved some favor of their own, so she remained silent and would let them sleep a little longer.

She stared across at John's empty cushion. She wondered how her little brother had fared in his first night camping in his "fortress" in the woods. He'd been so excited to stay there. She trusted he was relishing the time by himself. *Most assuredly his night wasn't ordinary.*

Several cows lowed outside. Lydia took comfort in the soothing sounds of the cattle beneath her window, still drinking in the refreshing coolness. Initially she hadn't recognized anything peculiar with the farm sounds, these being so familiar, as her lingering drowsiness yet clouded her reasoning. But then she was struck. *That's unusual. It sounds like the cattle are in the side yard … in the corn.* She rolled to her knees and pulled herself forward to the window, and with her fingers, she tucked her long, dark hair behind her ears; then stretched her chin up to the sill to investigate.

The tiny opening faced to the south, and with the sky glowing orange to the left, she could plainly see straight down the long rows of corn that paralleled Hollis Road. The cows mooed again.

There they are—several lumbering along in the pale light, breaking the stalks as they went. *This is a problem that can't wait.*

The young woman rose from her bed, climbed down from the loft, stepped softly to her parents' bedroom door, and knocked. After a minute, detecting no response, she knocked yet again, louder, finally hearing a muffled reply within. It was Father's voice.

His feet shuffled toward the door. The latch raised, and it squeaked open a few inches. In the dim light, Lydia inspected Father's face now peering out and down at her, unshaven, his hair sticking up, and his eyes mere slits. He waited blankly to hear her voice her concern.

She whispered, "Father, the cattle are in the corn."

His expression held blank initially, as if he hadn't heard her. Then his head tilted down. He sighed through his inconvenienced lips, rolling his eyes in frustration. He stood still another moment. At last he stared at her calmly and nodded in agreement. She'd done right to wake him.

Leaving the door ajar, he scuffed back out of sight. Mother was overheard mumbling something, and the two had a brief private exchange. They were trying to avoid waking the baby, asleep in the same room.

Through the open bedroom window the cows were heard once more.

Father soon appeared at the door fully dressed and stepped out into the main room. Mindful of his three children dozing just there on their cots, he bent forward and whispered, "Would you kindly wake Will and send him out?" Then he tiptoed over to the back door, donned his boots and hat, and stepped outside. As he exited, Lydia thought she overheard him mutter a complaint—that John had "once again" improperly secured that troubling corral gate.

The young woman returned up the ladder to the loft. Her brother and sister were already seated in their beds, rubbing their eyes awake. In a low voice, she explained the situation to both and gave Father's instruction to Will. The young man rose up without hesitation and began fumbling with his clothes.

As he did so, Lydia thought she heard something outside—a thud.

Believing the sound was near her window, she climbed forward onto her bed to take a look for the source. The sun was close to cresting the horizon as she observed the cows yet amidst the rows, but Father was nowhere in sight. She wondered about the noise. *Has he fallen?* She glanced at her siblings. Neither Will nor Betty seemed to have heard the sound. She listened intently again but detected nothing more. Several doves cooed—normal morning sounds. She reasoned, *Father would have yelled for certain had he needed help.* So she made no mention of it to the others. *Perhaps my ears were mistaken?*

She watched Will as he hurried to get outside, the tall, strong, young man—a handsome image of Father. Everyone understood Father's impatience. He slid with reckless speed down the ladder, strode over across the floor, pulled his boots on, hustled out the door, and closed it behind him. His footsteps were heard passing along the planks of the back porch, and then there was quiet.

Lydia laid her head back down on her bolster, noting Betty to do the same, as they relaxed in the fresh morning air. Both dearly wanted to delay the imminent milking and the other routine chores. *This hasn't been exactly a "routine" day thus far, what with the cattle getting out*, she thought. But soon everything would be back to normal, and then they should each be immersed in their labor. She was intent to rest a few minutes longer, and then, *then* she would get straight up to help.

Will screamed, shattering the peace. Outside, there arose a tremendous commotion, the sounds of *struggle!*

Adrenaline surged through Lydia's veins as she snapped her body over and drew herself again to the window. She was fully alert now. *What is happening? What's besetting Will?*

Her view into the corn revealed nothing. The vantage point was all wrong. The chimney blocked the immediate left. Will was apparently behind the house and out of view. She steadied herself and looked at Betty. They listened carefully together. There were other sounds—voices, grunts, punches. *Will is in a fight!*

P. GIFFORD LONGLEY

Downstairs, the bedroom door burst open. The sisters flew to the railing to look over. They watched Mother as she darted toward the rear window. And there, at the opening, Mother could clearly see the fracas; and from there, she yelled frantically to inform the house what it was.

"*Indians!*"

Outside, Will's cries rose to a crescendo and then, just as suddenly as they'd begun, went dreadfully silent.

Mother remained a moment at the window. She'd seen it all happen, transfixed by something unthinkable. Wide-eyed, mouth gaping, she raised her hands to her heart and groaned. Her whole body bent forward, her breath pressed out, as if crushed by a loaded wagon. Blood fled from her face.

Lydia struggled to believe what was unfolding. What she'd overheard was confusing, and what she'd seen with her own eyes wasn't actually anything. She wondered if she wasn't yet asleep. *Is this a terrible dream?* But the vision in her eyes of mother's reaction and the echoes of the screams that had filled her ears seized her imagination. She remembered the recent past in town: other Indian attacks on the village, how Uncle James had been killed by the savages just two years prior. And as she considered the possible dreadful reality of this emerging moment, terrible questions quickly followed. *Has Will been murdered? And where... where is Father?*

The stillness that ensued lasted only a second.

Hair-raising shrieks filled the air surrounding their house. These echoed across the fields, filtered in through the open windows, and rebounded from the walls and rafters. Like mighty weapons, the yells tore into the souls of the next round of victims, purposed to cripple them. All of the children were awake now—Jemima, Joseph, Natty, and the baby—each upset at the sight of mother's anguish and the frightful howling. The little ones screeched in their innocent terror as their senses became filled by the emerging nightmare.

Mother hearkened immediately to the cries of her children. Her instincts took over as she flew into action to try to save them. She instructed Jemima to gather the boys and take them to the bedroom while she closed the shutter over the window and latched it, reached across and barred the door, and then retrieved the gun from the mantel. But the youngsters, they hadn't responded; instead they remained huddled on their cots, as if paralyzed and oblivious to her commands. On seeing this, Lydia could no longer remain a bystander to their disobedience. She began to climb back down to help to shelter them.

"Jemima!" Mother snapped now more forcefully to her fourteen-year-old daughter. "Take your brothers, *now!* Close and bar the door behind you, and latch the shutters!" Then she quickly motioned for all to be quiet.

Compelled at last by Mother's urgency, the children closed their mouths and complied. Jemima and eight-year-old Joseph took Natty by both hands, the little one sniffing back his tears as they went together into the bedroom. The door was shut, and the bar was heard dropping into place.

The shouts in the yard subsided, and a terrible lull overshadowed the tiny house. Everyone inside, stunned by the unseen threat, waited for what would happen next. Lydia remained poised on the ladder, listening.

Footsteps on the porch approached the entrance. Lydia tensed. Her heart raced. Mother gathered herself, raised the gunstock to her shoulder, and aimed the long, heavy barrel toward the barred door, trying to steady the unwieldy weapon, just as she'd seen Father do before. She turned her head toward the loft and focused on her daughters, her eyes anxious for them. She whispered firmly to the two.

"*Hide!*"

Lydia clambered back up and flung herself headlong to the floor at the foot of her bed. Betty did the same. The young women considered where to hide, but there was no place there in the loft, as the beds sat directly on the floor. There was no space to crawl beneath them, and ducking 'neath the covers—such would only be too obvious. The situation seemed hopeless. They would just have to stay low, back from the railing, and pray that the Indians wouldn't examine the loft. That is, if they were to gain entry to the house.

The battering of the door soon followed.

Mother prayed out loud, *"Dear, sweet Jesus, please watch over my children!"*

A few firm kicks splintered the jamb apart, and the door burst open. It swung hard and rebounded off the wall as the downstairs flooded with a red-orange beam from the just-risen sun.

Several Indians could be heard entering the room as the wide pine planks creaked beneath their deliberate footsteps. At that moment, Lydia dare not raise her head to try and see how many there were. She glanced across at Betty, who was also keeping low.

Mother tried her best to warn the intruders, "I shall surely kill one of you!" Her voice quaked with desperation.

Everyone knew Mother's musket had but the one shot, so Lydia prayed that the fear of a single death might cause the murderers to reconsider and leave.

But the intruders did not reply or speak. Instead, their footsteps were heard continuing, advancing farther into the room, undeterred by the fragile threat.

Lydia glanced at her sister. She was quivering with her eyes tightly shut. She knew the pretty teen had always been such a gentle person, often taken advantage of, entirely too feminine. How she had depended on grace, and how unable she seemed to be to fight for herself. But Lydia was determined to keep her own head clear, determined not to panic or freeze. And then she prayed for deliverance.

The downstairs abruptly filled with frightful shrieks.

Lydia's body trembled. *They yell to scare their victims into submission.* The realization did nothing to calm her nerves.

Mother's gun instantly reacted to their assault, exploding as white smoke filled the room. But no one was heard to fall as a result. The shot had apparently missed its mark.

Without hesitation, the Indians rushed at Mother. She was heard resisting for a few seconds, cried out, and then was pounded into silence, groaning and whimpering as her body fell hard onto the wood. Her struggle had been so futile—and so brief.

The four children in the bedroom below screamed in alarm, but their cries would not last long.

The Indians made fast entry to the bedroom as they battered the door with their kicks. It gave way far too easily. They rushed the helpless little ones that were hiding there and muted each of their cries with a ghastly *thud*. Jemima, Joseph, little Natty—each became tranquil. Even the baby, precious Zachariah, was hushed by them.

Frozen in place, Lydia stared at Betty; the younger one's eyes were still squinted shut, and her whole body was quaking. *Is this really happening? How can they brutally beat Mother and the children... even the baby? What did any of these innocents do to deserve such... such bashing?*

With the last whimper gone, the ferocity of the downstairs simply departed, being replaced by apparent motivation to complete the next task, an earnest sense of *busyness*. Talking was heard, though Lydia couldn't make out what was being said. Nevertheless, the tones were apparent: boastful speech between comrades, even laughter. Soon, footsteps on the porch told her that others were entering the house. More proud conversation followed. The language was unfamiliar.

Then the pillaging began.

Objects were heard being taken down from the shelves, some strewn on the floor, furniture moved and overturned, cabinets opened and slammed shut, items collected and thrown into piles. Lydia again studied her sister. Betty remained still. Then after some time, the Indians stepped out onto the porch, and the house grew quiet. A group of them remained just outside in the yard, where they were heard speaking amongst themselves.

The young women gazed at each other and raised their heads, sensing, *hoping* that they might yet escape. Betty daringly rose up and dragged herself to the edge of the loft. She peeked down through the balustrade into the room below and then immediately pushed back. Her face grew white as she grabbed her mouth and stomach and lurched forward. Lydia crawled over to see for herself.

P. GIFFORD LONGLEY

There on the floor lay Mother, face down, wallowing in her own blood. Her arms were raised above her head, as she remained motionless, with her long, pretty, golden hair flowing down the back of her nightdress. She appeared to be dead.

Betty became inconsolable.

Lydia crawled to her sister's side and took the teenager in her arms. Seated, she hugged her and whispered in her ear, desperately, "Please, be quiet!" But her sobbing wouldn't stop.

Footsteps were heard again on the porch. Someone was returning.

The older sister grabbed her sibling and hurled them both forward onto the floor between the beds. Her heart pounded. She dared not breathe.

The intruder stepped back into the house, seemingly as yet unaware of their presence in the loft. But Betty had fallen in an awkward position with her leg twisted and her foot caught in the folds of Lydia's nightdress. The younger one would simply have to remain still and endure her discomfort until the intruder left.

They both listened as the Indian moved Mother's body about below them—grunting, fumbling, speaking all the while to himself with tones of *enjoyment.* The very thought of Mother being touched by the savage, this made Lydia feel sick to her stomach. She raised her head just enough to examine Betty, who was grimacing from something, holding her breath and turning redder in the face by the second. Lydia then spotted the cause: her contorted leg. Carefully she pulled her dress up to try and free it, but the fabric slid loose all at once. Betty's foot flopped out onto the wood.

The downstairs hushed.

Footsteps were heard deliberately approaching the ladder; then the wooden rungs groaned under the intruder's weight. The young women could only hope that somehow the ascent of their assailant would be interrupted or stopped. Lydia focused her attention toward the ladder. She watched helplessly as the top of a head gradually raised itself up and into view with the fearful, black eyes following after.

They'd been discovered.

With a burst of energy the Indian clambered up and stood erect on the floor of the loft. Lydia clutched Betty and cowered at the sight.

He was a dark man, older, middle-aged, yet very muscular, menacing, perhaps six-foot tall, bare chest, loincloth at his waist, tasseled leggings, and moccasins on his feet. In his right hand he held his tomahawk, still red with blood. Tied to his belt were several scalps yet dripping with crimson. Around his neck he wore a string of slate pieces and a small sheath that dangled farther down, holding his scalping knife. Mud adorned his shoulders and neck, some of which had emulsified and was running down his chest, a chest heaving and glistening with sweat. His long, stringy, black hair, decorated with shells, framed a frightful face—a horrific, painted pagan image scowling down, scarred by a silver ornament that pierced his nose.

The intruder glared at the girls, now sitting up between the beds, pushed as far back as they could, leaning against the outside wall. Lydia held her sister in her arms and stroked her blonde hair, burying Betty's face in her breast for protection. Betty had begun to shake and sob uncontrollably again.

With his muscles tensed, the warrior bent and skulked toward the girls, gritting his olive teeth in a sickening, drooling grin. He brandished his tomahawk in his right hand and paused at the young women's feet, hissing out his fetid breath.

Lydia braced herself for the end and prayed to God that it would be swift and without pain. She thought of Mother's courage in facing these assailants, the *ruthless* savages. She too would be brave.

"Go ahead!" she snapped, yelling before he drew any closer. "Go ahead and kill us now! I'm not afraid to die!"

The Indian stopped his advance. His face tilted back and his eyes widened with surprise at her boldness. He straightened and stared carefully at Lydia, sizing her up. He eased his grip on his tomahawk and lowering his right hand. He leaned forward again and gently extended his left, palm up, as he calmly spoke to her in his deep voice, "You come with me; *you stay quiet*, you live."

P. GIFFORD LONGLEY

The sisters sat holding each other, being unable to make sense of the mercy they'd just been offered, for it was too strange to be believed considering what had just happened.

The savage straightened, turned, and yelled something over the edge of the loft, and several of his companions came directly into the house. After exchanging a few more words with them, these others came over to the foot of the ladder. Their assailant then stepped across and rummaged through the items that lay at the foot of their bed. He found several pieces of their clothing, tossed them to Lydia, and motioned for them to put them on.

The girls rose dumbfounded but quickly dressed, setting aside any modesty as they were spurred by his continuing visible threats. Then they climbed down to the main room. Two of the Indians there grabbed them roughly by their arms to drag them to the outside. And as Lydia stumbled toward the exit, she hesitated, then bravely turned toward Mother's bloodied body there on the floor. It had been stripped naked, and the top part of her scalp was now missing. It didn't look much like Mother anymore.

Betty also stared at the corpse. Her sobbing had stopped. She seemed not to be repulsed by the ravaged sight of Mother. Maybe she hadn't looked? Lydia sensed right then that something inside her sister had changed. Betty's eyes looked dead. Though wide open, they saw nothing.

The two young women were rudely dragged past the open bedroom door. Lydia dared not glance into the silent chamber as they were taken outside. From the porch, the sisters witnessed Will's mangled remains lying nearby in the grass. His face had been split open and was unrecognizable. Lydia groaned at the sickening sight, turning away.

Will indeed was gone; she'd confirmed it. But there was yet another who may have somehow survived. She raised her eyes, her body shaking, hoping. She looked all around for him, first in the grass nearby and then over toward the barn. Nothing. But turning toward the edge of the cornfield, she finally spotted him. Father. His bare feet protruded from the end of a row...unmoving. *Now the massacre is complete. Only Betty and I have survived. No, wait*—she caught herself—*Thank God! John is not here.*

The girls stood waiting for the raiders to gather their plunder, items stolen from the house and barn and several pieces of flesh that they'd butchered from a cow. Lydia studied the motions of her captors. There were five of them, and the *wretched beast* from the loft—the tallest and biggest—this one seemed to be in charge.

The leader went back into the house and came out with an assortment of shoes. He motioned for the girls to don theirs, which they did. Lydia helped her sister. He instructed the other four Indians to gather up the booty into burdens. Then the leader stepped to the side, picked up his robe—a brilliant, red cloth cape—and fastened it to his right shoulder. He stood for a moment, pridefully adjusting his garments to his satisfaction, and then strode confidently over to the young women. He grabbed their wrists and tightly bound them with long, leather ropes. He examined his two hostages and spoke to them in a matter-of-fact tone, "We go now."

The big Indian set off, hurriedly jerking and pulling the girls behind him by their ropes as they stumbled northward through the pasture. The others followed, hustling their bundles of booty on their backs.

After a half-hour's march through fields and woods, the band neared the River Squannacook, which formed the wild, western boundary of the Groton settlement. As they came within sight of the banks, the five Indians began to scream and holler. Ahead, other natives were seen through the trees, standing near their many canoes along the shore. Excitement swept through the camp, and all of the natives joined together in the shouting. Lydia tried to number the Indians, but they kept moving about. She could only guess there were several dozen.

Studying the many faces as they approached the camp, she spotted other captives among the group. There was the young John Shepley, and several of the Parker children, and then her jaw dropped—for she saw him. *There was her little brother!*

"John!" Lydia exclaimed.

But the young captive dare not speak in response to her cry, though his eyes grew wide at seeing them—surprise and dread—to see his sisters alive, yet held captive. He remained quiet with his fellow prisoners, bruised and battered. He would not make himself an object of attention for further punishment.

The big Indian, who had been pulling the young women, turned and glared at the dark-haired one, aiming his white-hot anger at her.

Lydia now realized, too late realized, she'd spoken out of control. She returned to her captor a worried gaze and closed fast her lips, waiting for her punishment.

But this was the leader's moment of glory, and he would not be distracted by anything. Thus he did not retaliate, to Lydia's great surprise. Instead, he raised his bloody tomahawk and joined with the others in the great shouts of victory. Then, dragging the sisters toward the other captives, the leader stopped and unexpectedly released their ropes to the ground.

Lydia wondered, *Is he taunting us? Or are we really free to visit with the other prisoners?*

He fixed his stare at the two, and before he turned to go, he closed to within inches of their faces. With his eyes filled with rage—as if deliberately revealing images of what his eyes had seen, endless flailing, smashing, crushing, bashing—like one crazy, he *screamed* at the top of his voice. When the girls flinched back as if to faint, startled perfectly as he'd intended, he *laughed* at them, proud of his acting. Then he turned away light-footed to go and celebrate with his fellow warriors.

With the big Indian gone, Lydia ran to her brother and hugged him tightly in her arms. The two cried together without speaking.

John lifted his eyes toward Betty, who was yet standing where she'd been abandoned. He ran to greet his other sister and gently hugged her and kissed her neck. But she stood limp, expressionless, with her arms dangling.

"Betty, *it's me*...John. I am *so* glad to see you...and you're not hurt."

But Betty could not respond, crippled by the terror.

Departure

Friday, July 27, 1694

The moment that John had seen Betty and Lydia entering the camp he knew his worst fears had been realized. His home had indeed been a target, and his family had been attacked. Still, he clung to the hope that there yet would be some good news about Father, Mother, Jemima, and his four brothers. But looking at Betty, her unresponsive, somber gaze, this made him insecure.

Lydia's demeanor was strange as well. And though she seemed firmly in control of herself, she was *different* somehow, as though less an older sister and more a mother, evidenced by the manner in which she attended to Betty. Yet there was no offense of inappropriate authority in her mothering; rather, he was endeared by the love and care he saw in her. Still he wondered, *What has happened to them and the rest of my family?*

He dared to ask.

The oldest drew in her breath. Her eyes welled with tears. She hesitated and then stared at him, unable to form words.

Can the news be so bad? John thought. After all, the two of them didn't appear to be injured or bruised as he was. *Could there have been a struggle? Could some have been hurt? Surely Father, a member of the militia, is right now mustering with the other men to come to our rescue.*

Lydia's tears flowed as John's concern was piqued.

"Tell me!" he insisted at last.

"Oh, John!" Lydia clutched her arms across her chest and dropped her eyes. "You would just not believe—"

"What? Believe what?"

Lydia brushed the tears from her face and breathed in deep. Her body swayed and her eyes roamed the scene, refusing to look John in the eye. But at last she steadied herself, faced him, and blurted, "They're *gone*, John. They're *all dead.*"

"What?" the boy whispered, dumbfounded. The color vanished from his face.

Lydia wrestled with herself then at last became calm as she faced her brother. Standing at the same height, for he was rather tall for his age, she gently took hold of both his shoulders. Her moist, brown eyes gazed at his with tenderness as she sniffed back her tears and regained her self-control.

At last she spoke softly and gently, "Only Betty and I have survived."

The simple, grave news at last struck him. He turned his back to his sister. His heart raced. He dropped to his knees, feeling faint. *How can it be true?* He turned and glanced across at Betty, eyewitness to what had happened, seated on the ground, rocking back and forth, her face between her knees, disconnected from her surroundings and situation. He watched as Lydia crouched down and drew Betty tenderly into her arms.

Now John could see with his mind that what he'd heard with his ears was indeed the terrible truth. Stoically, he crawled over to join them and there embraced them both.

Still, despite the shock of the news, and owing to their immediate and present danger, John urgently demanded to know more. Lydia, too, wondered how her brother had been captured. They briefly shared their stories. Through this interchange John tuned himself to the cunning mind of his captors, apprehending how they'd executed their plan of attack—how they'd first selected those most challenging to their mission, drawn them out unawares, then struck them down with deadly force. He looked around and examined the camp, seeing the many bundles of goods—these that had been taken as well as the other prisoners. He realized then why they'd come. The enemy's mission there had been to steal, and *they* were hostages taken to be sold. *They were chattel.*

John pondered the source of the Indian's deadly success—the secrecy—and postulated, "I suppose then that not a single other person in town yet knows we've been taken."

Lydia reacted, "Why, yes. How *could* they know? It all happened so fast."

From the moment of his capture, John's hope of rescue or clever escape had never waned. The militia could help them. But how could they if they yet remained unaware of the attacks? *There must be some means to deliver the news to them*, he thought.

"So you hadn't done the chores yet?" John inquired.

"No. Except for Father and Will, we were all still in our beds when they came."

"And the sheep are yet in the barn?" he probed.

"Yes, *of course.*" Lydia seemed annoyed by an unnecessary question.

John nodded and turned toward the other prisoners. Walking discreetly over to them, he inquired who might know a contact nearby, someone unharmed who could bring help. Shepley, age eighteen, convinced by the circumstance of his own capture along the road, was certain that members of his family would be available to assist—that is, if they could just be alerted. This information pleased John since the Shepleys were his closest neighbors, about a half-mile nearer to town. Their house was visible from the Longley property set up high on the side of the hill.

The boy rejoined his sister and quietly explained his developing plan.

But the older sibling sternly objected without hesitation. "*No.* It's too dangerous. They will see right through it. They shall kill you for even suggesting it. And then they shall kill us."

"But we can't just let them spirit us away without *attempting* to do something," John appealed. "Do you see those two dozen canoes over there?" He turned and pointed with his eyes. "Those are two-man canoes, and by my count, half of the Indians are yet off somewhere taking more hostages and goods. They will no doubt return soon, with half the town just getting out of their beds. And we shall be leaving before the militia has even had a chance to know that the intruders are about. *Now* is our only time for rescue… before we are whisked away downriver and far away from help."

Impressed, Lydia conceded, "I see that you have been thinking about this; yet, as the oldest, I must say… that we… *we* have to make the right decisions to protect what's left of our family."

"Father would approve of this," John argued. "You *know* that I'm right."

Lydia studied her brother's eyes, eyes filled with strength and reason. She couldn't bring herself to say "yes," but she didn't say "no" either.

Then the situation forced the answer.

The big Indian, who'd been studiously and suspiciously watching the prisoners conferencing, walked briskly over to them, bringing with him a band of warriors. He approached Lydia directly, she being eldest of the prisoners and suspicious of her leadership. He menaced his club at her with a frightening stare. "Anyone try to escape get *knock* on the head!" He pounded the heavy wooden tom hog into his palm.

She noted the sharp spike on its end.

Seizing the moment, John fearlessly stepped forward. "We were not planning to escape. I was just sharing with the others here my concern over learning that my father's sheep are yet in the barn. And since there is no one to feed and care for them, they will starve." His voice settled as he continued with courage. "They have been such good animals, so it would be unfortunate if they were not set free to forage for themselves in the fields."

The Indian leader gazed down at John, attracted by his handsome blue eyes and blonde hair, notably impressed by the brave plea.

Yet, the man of obvious leadership was not about to be fooled. "Suppose I let you go … free your sheep. You will not run away, will you?"

"No, sir." John strengthened his appeal, "My sister here has told me that my father is now dead. And I swear to you by my dead father that I will free his sheep and come straightway back here. And you shall do the soul of my dead father a great honor if you will allow me to obey him and to do this last bit of service to him, to save the lives of his sheep."

The big Indian wavered as he looked at Lydia, then back at John. "What your name, son?"

"John Longley."

The leader silently studied John's honest face as he considered the request. He thought a moment and responded in his deep voice, "You may go … free your father's sheep, but you come back right away." His eyes flamed as he turned and grabbed Lydia by the back of her head, pulling her hair, and continued in a blast of foul breath, "Or I *kill* this, your sister, and *cut* her hair off." The savage peered down at his belt, at his scalps. He stroked the long, golden, wavy hair he now understood belonged to John's mother.

"Yes, sir." John shivered as he examined the scalp. He swallowed hard, raised his eyes, and looked straight at the big Indian, unwavering. "I promise."

Satisfied by John's commitment, the Indian leader quickly changed his focus onto some other matter more pressing. He walked away from the prisoners and motioned to two other natives, these being of some apparent import, as they wore impressive robes like his. He motioned them to join him in a private discussion.

After a few minutes, the sagamore turned and addressed all of the warriors in the camp in their native tongue. In the midst of his instructions, he mentioned the name "John Aw-geh-ree" and motioned directly at John, and all eyes turned toward the prisoners. Continuing, his words riled the group up into a froth, and several of them shouted their excitement. Then after he'd concluded his speech, the big Indian, joined by his two robed accomplices and two others, ran off up the trail, headed again in the direction of the village, equipped with fresh purpose in their strides.

Those that were left guarding the prisoners relaxed and moved a few paces away.

Finally alone, Lydia furiously chastised her brother, "I can't *conceive* you would do this, to put us so at risk! Indeed, you are brave for trying to save us—." She placed her hand on her mouth and stared down on the ground. After a moment she sighed, lifted her eyes at his, reached across, and gently touched his cheek with her palm, "But you've convinced them now. And so you must be swift on your mission and come straightway back here. Do not tarry *anywhere!*" She placed both hands on his shoulders and locked eyes with him. "And John, *please* ... don't ... *don't* go in the house."

"I promise, and I'll hurry."

John hugged Lydia and bent down to Betty, who was still seated quietly on the ground. He kissed the top of her head. Then nodding at Shepley to confirm the plan, John turned and jogged up the trail away from the camp, heading in the direction of the Shepley farm.

The boy ran swiftly through the tall grasses in the hillside pasture. The Shepley house was near to him now, but he wisely made no call for help. There might be natives about he reasoned, and besides, he was out of breath and could hardly yell if he'd wanted to.

John entered the first building he came to, the barn, passing through the open door and panting for air. He made fast inspection of its interior, but the barn proved empty. He quickly refocused his attention over toward the house, just across the lawn.

From his position in the shadows, John scanned the grounds for danger while still collecting his breath. The place appeared undisturbed and serene, but the door to the house was bothersome. It'd been left ajar.

Two crows swooped down into the tall grass just in front of the porch. He watched as they fought with each other over something. One at last chased away the other and then began to pick among the grasses. John wandered over cautiously to get a better look at what was lying there.

Human corpses were not a bit loathsome for John to gaze upon, as he'd seen them before at funerals (sadly, death was not uncommon in his time). The sight of blood and guts was neither strange to him, nor did it cause him to be squeamish, as he'd killed and gutted animals before, even butchered hogs and fowl. Yet, even though he believed he had a strong stomach, he'd never seen a sight so ghastly as this. Still he purposed to view it "clinically," intending to be emotionally detached, searching only for facts.

It was Mr. Shepley for certain, as his bald head was instantly recognizable. The victim lay on his back. His neck and bowels had been ripped open, and he had wallowed in his own blood; a significant amount of it had collected and congealed in the grass. His outstretched arms and legs were also bloodied, having oozed from the many hack marks that tore his clothing.

John wondered if the cuts had been delivered while Mr. Shepley was yet alive and struggling with his assailants, or if they had been administered in a rage after his gut had been slit and he'd expired. But in examining the victim's face, seeing the horror in the open eyes and gaping mouth, this confirmed to him what poor Mr. Shepley's last few moments on the earth had been like—his arms had been beaten, held down, whilst he'd been eviscerated. John could only imagine what any onlooker might have thought upon witnessing such torture.

The crow hadn't been frightened by his approach, having stayed there brazenly and voraciously picking at the feast of blood and flesh. John shooed it away and watched as it flew off over the peaceful pasture, hurling its protesting caws, which echoed in the silence.

John relaxed his purpose right then as he knew this corpse wouldn't be there in such a horrid state if there had yet been anyone around to help. Nonetheless, he was committed to the task. He decided he'd better look through the house next. He backed away from the body, turned, and climbed up onto the porch.

Without entering, he gaped squeamishly in through the open door. The main room was a wreck with furniture tossed about and overturned and goods strewn across the floor. But, thankfully, no bodies were in sight. He was instantly relieved. He entered quietly into the shadows of the main room, and, stepping gingerly over the chaos, he approached the bedroom door. With trepidation, he pushed it open and reluctantly peered within.

The bed was a pile of death. Unrecognizable bodies had been left there in a heap, stripped naked, covered with streams of congealed blood. Flies were already swarming on the flesh and refuse, the excrement that they'd released when they'd expired. This sight was too horrible to gaze upon for more than a few seconds, and the smell was repulsive. He clamped his hand over his nose and mouth and hurriedly looked for faces, but all he saw were heads, bereft of their scalps, and hands and feet of varying sizes, together arranged in the cruelest positions.

He turned and bolted from the house back onto the porch, bent over, hands on his knees, gasping for fresh air. The remains must have been Mrs. Shepley and their other children, he concluded. None could possibly be alive.

His heart sank as he knew his hope of rescue had fully departed. Now all that was left for him to do was to continue through the motions on the rest of his mission. That is, to go to his home … and this for perhaps the last time.

The boy sprinted down the hill and onto the road, arriving in just a few minutes at the end of his drive. There he paused to regain his breath and to behold the familiar sight of his property, to give it a careful look.

Never having assigned much importance to this view before, he felt the sudden need to do so, to paint its present precious appearance permanently into his memory.

Beneath his feet, the rutted, grassy drive went forward and divided the property in two—running up between the house and pastures on his left and the cornfield on his right—and leading straight beyond all the way to the barn at the back. Skip would always greet him there when he returned home from work. But the drive was empty now. Skip was nowhere in sight.

To the right, the long rows of corn stood tall, still maturing toward the harvest, with the silks barely showing. To his left, his house stood proudly near the road. It was a simple structure, modest in size—one story, the walls made of heavy, hand-hewn pine logs, long darkened by the weather. The steep thatch roof faced directly at the road, anchored by fieldstone chimneys that stood tall at the left and right gabled ends. Across the façade, from left to right, was the front door, which entered into the kitchen and main room, and two other small openings, windows, which Father had imported from England, each fitted with leaded glass. The window on the right was to Mother and Father's bedroom; the outside shutter was left open, but the inside shutter was curiously closed.

The house cast a long shadow, which extended all the way to where his feet stood at the end of the drive, as the early morning sun was rising up behind it, ascending into a deep blue and cloudless sky. The scene revealed no signs at all of the violence that had supposedly happened there, and the landscape seemed at once serenely picturesque, belying the truth.

He stepped forward up the drive and walked past the side of the house. As he went, he glimpsed to his left the loft window, perched high in the gable, next to the chimney, overlooking the corn. He'd slept up there a thousand times. He stopped a moment and continued to stare up at the window. But, suddenly mindful of his sister's instruction concerning the house, he suppressed his curiosity to inspect it, as he felt a sudden cramping in his gut over what he would find inside. He purposefully turned and redirected his eyes forward toward his promised goal, no longer looking to the left as he resumed his march and passed by the rear porch. His mission was to let out the sheep and to quickly return to the camp. Besides, there was no time to enter in or to go elsewhere to summon help.

But as he walked farther down the drive, his vision was drawn to his right. There he spotted two bare feet sticking out from the corn. He knew right away who it was that lay there.

"Father!" he gasped.

The young man ran toward the body but then slowed with caution, as his gut further tightened. He deliberately angled his head away and glanced toward the body, using only the corner of one eye.

There was Father all right, lying face down on the ground, still clothed, but with his hat lying near his head. There was little blood—surprisingly. He eased, turned, and looked directly, approached deliberately, and knelt beside the body, still hesitating and now tasting the acid sickness rising in the back of his throat. He squinted his eyes shut, held his breath, and tensed his stomach to fight it. When he finally opened his eyes again, he saw no gore, rather the face of a man at peace, as if sleeping. At once relieved, he let out a sigh and the color returned to his face.

John's curiosity immediately took over. He wondered how Father had died and looked more closely for details.

The injury that had taken Father's life wasn't immediately visible, being on the side of his head that rested upon the ground. The blood was there. He was glad he'd not had a better view of the wound. Father's countenance strangely showed no pain. He must have been killed instantly by a single mighty blow.

He looked at the hat lying beside his head, right where it fell, knocked off by the stroke. He reached forward, retrieved it, and straightened to his knees, yet fixated by father's peacefulness. His silvered, sandy brown hair was still there—*Thankfully*, John thought to himself—lying softly on his shoulders, apparently spared by urgency. *How handsome Father was.* He'd just turned forty-two.

He leaned forward, lifted his hand, hesitated, then touched Father's cheek. The unexpected coolness was immediately disturbing. He quickly pulled his hand away.

At last overcome by the sight, he bent and hugged the body, resting his full weight on it as he anguished. He imagined a conversation, the advice that he would seek in this desperate situation. But the persistence of silence only left him unfulfilled.

Quietly the boy clung to the frame, leaning his face against his shoulder and squeezing the arms that would not respond to his presence, as if refusing to enfold him. After a few minutes he pushed him-

P. GIFFORD LONGLEY

self back to his feet, dissatisfied. The shock from touching Father's lifeless body ruled his limbs, causing him to shake and feel woozy.

After a moment in a stupor, he realized that he was still grasping the empty hat in his hand. He lifted and studied the black, felted item, holding onto the wide brim. It was a fine accessory. *Well suited to Father's good taste*, he thought.

Coming to his senses, he wished he could give the man he loved a decent burial. But there was no time. Instead, he bent to lay the hat down as a "proper" covering for Father's face. But in clutching the precious garment, he hesitated to leave go of it. The smooth, silky lining had for him a sense of Father within it. He couldn't possibly leave it there.

Standing erect, he turned the hat over and stared into the lining, thought a moment, and then lifted it up and dropped it onto the top of his head. But it fell right down over his forehead, being stopped there by his ears as they stuck out. The hat was still too large.

Finally, clearing his thoughts, he remembered his mission. But before he stepped away, he spoke his good-bye. "Father, I must go now, and I shall see you no more here upon this earth. I do not know what shall happen to me, but I want you to know...I shall never forget you!"

He turned again toward the barn and resumed his task. He ran to the entrance of the stone and wooden structure and swung open the heavy door. The warm, pungent aroma of the livestock greeted him—the natural part of farm life. The sheep instantly reacted to their shepherd's arrival, bleating to him. Instinctively he spoke back and caressed several of them with his hand. This routine refreshed his spirit. He stepped waist high through the soft sheep, pulling and then turning and pushing them toward the opening and to the outside. As they left the barn, he stepped forward several paces to watch them waddle ahead out into the pasture, happily bleating as they went.

John set his final gaze toward the house. *The morning is extraordinary*, he thought, the finest day of any summer he'd ever seen. And there, across the brilliant, green lawn sat the house, the innocent structure, bathed in golden sunlight, with its open door calling, telling him that just inside was his family, unseen prisoners of the shadowy interior, left there for dead. *How twisted*, he thought, *that my kidnappers would permit me to set free these animals, these sheep, yet show no mercy on a mother and her children, her little lambs.*

Beckoned by the open door, John wished that he might cross over and enter one last time to say good-bye to them. But he could not forsake his promise to Lydia. He understood it best to remember each and every one of them as they had been … *alive.*

Turning to his left, he watched and listened as a breeze rose up from the south and rushed toward him through the rows of corn, gently bending and twisting the tassels. Then arriving where he stood, it glanced across his cheeks. He spun around to the north and watched it continue amidst the tender, green grasses of the pasture, seeming to follow after the last of the sheep as they bounded over the crest of the field and out of sight. Farther ahead he stared at the tops of the trees now swaying toward the river that he knew lay beyond them, showing him the path he must now take.

Then he departed into the pasture, sprinting down through the tall grasses, flying back toward the Indian camp and his sisters, speeding on his promise, giving no thought to his own escape—racing back to them with Father's hat held firmly in his grasp.

John reentered the camp, now bustling with activity. Since he'd left, the number of Indians had swelled and more prisoners had been brought in. He searched the many and spotted the familiar form of his oldest sister. He pushed his way through the prisoners and quickly joined her. Betty was still seated there on the ground.

Lydia's eyes filled instantly with relief when she saw him. The two embraced.

She took note of Father's hat in his hand. "I see you were at the farm." Grabbing the garment, she raised it to her face and breathed

P. GIFFORD LONGLEY

in the memory of Father, longing for his presence to soothe her wounded spirit.

"Yes," John said, still out of breath, "and I let the sheep out just as I promised."

Lydia looked again at the hat as worry filled her expression. "You obviously saw Father."

John nodded. "But I did not enter the house; neither did I see Will."

Lydia squeezed her brother, so glad that he'd honored his word. And as the two embraced, she felt Betty's hands reach up and seize hold of Father's hat. Then looking down, she saw that her little sister had lovingly pulled it to her bosom and was holding it tight. Lydia reached down and stroked Betty's hair, glad for the simple comfort that the hat now brought her. Turning again to John, she measured his face for some blessing of hope. "Did you see anyone else?"

"No. No one."

Shepley, having seen John's return, tried to press his way forward through the growing crowd to inquire of him, but he was restrained and pulled back by a warrior. The Indians had begun to separate the prisoners, and they were binding their wrists again.

John turned and watched Shepley being dragged farther away from him. Their eyes met, and Shepley's face pleaded for good news. But John could not mask his sad expression. He shook his head deliberately from side to side, delivering the bad report.

Shepley crumpled, gripped by his grief, yet his own sense of self-preservation caused him meekly to cooperate with his captors. They led him away in tears.

Curious of the urgent movements in the camp, John turned to Lydia. "What's happening?"

"They seem to be making ready to leave. Dozens more Indians returned while you were gone. They've been loading the canoes."

"Have you seen their leader?"

"No. I...I don't believe he has returned. Neither have the men that attended with him."

Additional guards approached the prisoners, bringing with them ropes to secure their hands, intending to lead them toward the canoes being loaded at the river's edge. The three siblings were quickly separated, pulled apart by their captors. John watched Betty, now wearing the hat, being dragged over toward the water's edge, where two natives helped her into a canoe and made ready to shove off.

Still curious, John looked all about the camp, but he couldn't see the sagamore, the leader, anywhere. How could they all leave without him? Surely some pre-appointed time had elapsed—the length of the shadows on the ground? Somehow they had determined to evacuate, and to do so now.

But in that anxious moment, a call was heard from up the trail. It was the voice of the big Indian as he ran down and toward the camp. The natives stopped in their positions, pleased at their leader's return but worried for him. Presently he rushed into view, breathless, gasping out several important words.

Though John couldn't understand the message, he observed the sadness and shock that formed on the faces of the warriors, those who stood there beside him, for what they were hearing was bad news. John turned to examine the leader. The sagamore was alone, without any of the men that had been with him. His hands and wrists were red with blood. As he continued to speak, he spread open his robe for all to see. It had been riddled with bullet holes, though he himself appeared unhurt.

When the sagamore had finished his report to them, he turned his gaze across the many faces in the camp, eyeing them all one by one. Finally he fixed his eyes on John and froze.

The boy's heart raced. He'd been singled out, but for what? Did the sagamore hold him responsible for being fired upon?

But on finding John's face in the crowd, the leader did nothing further. He merely nodded at the boy, an apparent acknowledgment of the boy's presence back in the camp, faintly curling a smile to show his appreciation of the captive's bravery and honesty.

The leader reset his focus to his apparent urgency. He yelled out commands, and several of his men began to push their canoes

into the river, hastily leaving downstream. The prisoners, number-
ing about a dozen, were placed individually in the middle of the
small boats—birch bark kayaks about fifteen feet in length—each
with one warrior paddling at the front and another at the rear. John
watched as the vessels bearing Betty and Lydia departed.

The canoes without prisoners—about half of the entourage—
had been piled with food and bundles of plunder. The big Indian
walked briskly along the banks, examining the contents of each boat
as it left, taking fast account of his haul. John's canoe was at the
rear, the last to be inspected. John was already resting in the vessel upon his knees when he approached. Two warriors stood fore
and aft, restraining it, knee-deep in the torrent and making ready to
shove it off.

The sagamore walked straight to the aft of the last canoe and
traded places with the steersman. He waited as the other canoes left.
Finally, he joined with his comrade as they pushed away from the
shore and hopped in, beginning their paddling.

The river, which had been recharged by the storm the night before,
raged rapidly. John felt the boat bob along in the swift, muddy current. He held on tightly to the cross frame to his front. Then turning back, he watched over his right shoulder as they floated swiftly
downriver, around a bend, and out of sight of their camp.

They'd departed Groton, and John wondered if he would ever see
the town again.

MISSING

The Afternoon of Friday, July 27, 1694

Jack scrounged amongst the stones that formed the crude wall behind the cornfield. He cleared several of the smaller rocks away and at last saw the one he wanted beneath, half sunken into the soft earth. *This will do*, he thought. It was a good shape, large and flat, though very heavy; he estimated more than three hundredweight. Still, they should be able to raise it onto the wagon with the three of them working together. It would be strenuous, he knew, but no one ever said this was going to be easy.

He lifted his eyes and gazed back down the drive, far over across the grass to the right of the house where the others were just finishing. Only the tops of their heads were visible from down in the hole as they threw the last few shovelfuls of soil up onto the pile. He would go and help them finish.

As Jack returned toward the others, he slowed his walk to take a better look around the property. He grappled with the questions that were coming to him, hoping to find the right one to ask. The day had started out so beautifully with the welcome departure of the summer furnace—swept away by the storm the night before. But the delightful, fresh morning had quickly been greeted with uneasiness when his nephew, John, hadn't shown up for work. That was so unlike him. Then, as the afternoon turned, the two riders arrived, militiamen, bearing with them the terrible news. And now there he was at his brother's farm confirming with his own eyes ... *the unthinkable*. Burdened by the pain of loss, he beheld the golden sun yet shedding its life to the lush, green meadow, and now descending toward the perfect, cloudless, brilliant horizon. At last he could only think of the one legitimate question to ask: *Why?*

Jack approached the edge of the hole as Thomas and James were just tossing their shovels up and to the side. He reached in and gave James a hand climbing out.

James stood up and dusted his hands off and then motioned for Jack, whose shock was still showing heavy on his face. He should follow him and assist with the next necessary task.

Silently, the two walked back toward the house to where the bodies lay in the grass, each shrouded in linen. One at a time, they carried the different sized corpses to the pit and handed them down to Thomas, who gently arranged them there. Jack bore the last one by himself—the little bundle, Zachariah. He lowered it down and asked, "Lay him with his mother ... would you?"

Thomas completed the somber yet thoughtful task, then straightened. He stared a moment at the pile, hushed and un-stirring. The blood stains had soaked through in a few places as morbid reminders. He turned and climbed out.

The three gazed down into the large grave, disquieted by the dreadful sight of it, each of them close-mouthed.

Jack once more counted the seven. How terrible it was to say good-bye to them, there and then, with just these three witnesses— no other family or friends being present. Then after brief reflection, he was glad no one else was there, for the bodies had been mangled. No one else should be made to see what they'd beheld. And no, nature would not wait. This was the proper thing to do, to inter them now.

James turned to Jack and broke the silence. "I'm certain we shall have a proper memorial for them after your mother comes, and

P. GIFFORD LONGLEY

the others. But, John, is there something you would care to speak now ... about your brother and his family?"

Jack stirred from his stupor and looked up at the two men, members of the town militia: James Nutting, age forty-one, his brother-in-law, married to his sister Lydia; and Thomas Tarbell, age twenty-seven, his nephew, eldest son of his late sister Hannah. Jack's family had always called him by his given name, John, and he never bothered to correct them. His closest friends, including his long-time business partner Joseph Farr from Lynn, these only ever knew him as Jack, and he took fondly to that name.

"Yes, I must. I ... I shall say something." Jack removed his hat and bowed his gray head.

Grasping for the words, Jack's mind drifted to his memories of his little brother, William, Junior.

The others doffed their hats as Jack stared downward and began to speak in a soft, strained voice. "William was a kind man and someone always willing—no, *looking* for the opportunity to serve others. He cared for people and gave ... gave when he didn't have to. I experienced it myself ... " His voice faltered. "He reached out to me when, as the oldest, *I* should have been the one reaching out to him. He loved his family, served his town, and, being in the militia, helped to defend it ... with his own life."

Then Jack briefly remembered the others: Deliverance, so lovely; and then, able only to utter their names, the children: William the Third, Jemima, Joseph, Nathaniel, and Zachariah. "I will miss these dear ones all very much." Jack clenched his jaw tightly. His fingers abused the rim of his hat, turning it over and over as he stared unseeing into the pit, unable to form the words.

James and Thomas stood attentive and patiently absorbed the sobering moment. The only sound they heard was that of a warm breeze sweeping through the tall grass that surrounded them.

At last Jack cleared his throat and, summoning his strength, he raised his hands and gazed up into the perfect sky. "And now almighty Lord, Ye Maker and Guardian of all things, we bury these bodies here in the earth, but commit to Ye their spirits. Amen."

"Amen," the others responded.

The three quietly put their hats back upon their heads and set about to complete the task. They covered the bodies with the earth and set the large stone on top of the grave mound, laying it flat to the surface. They stood back and studied the spot, situated just a few rods northwest of William and Deliverance's empty house. It was a lovely site in the shade of an apple tree with its wide branches overburdened with un-ripened fruit.

Thomas turned to Jack. "We've done everything we can do here today. The sun is setting, and we should be leaving… for safety's sake. There *is* more to be done, to put the house in order. And we can commence with such tomorrow."

"Yes," Jack responded painfully. "Tomorrow."

In agreement, the three men together retrieved their horses from the corral and set off in different directions for the evening. But Jack's spirit was deeply troubled as he rode toward the safety and comfort of his own home. His heart was suddenly seized by the question, *And what about the missing?*

MEMORIAL

Saturday, August 4, 1694

After a lengthy day at his brother's property assisting Thomas with the inventory for the estate, Jack returned to his house in the south of town. The sun was almost setting when he steered his horse from the Lancaster Highway and onto his drive. Upon nearing the house, he noted a new carriage ahead, parked at the front of the barn. They had visitors.

As he rode past the porch, the front door swung open and out stepped a woman in her mid-thirties with sunny, blonde hair; attired in a fine, blue linen dress; beautiful; and very pregnant. He recognized his youngest sister right away.

"Sarah!" he exclaimed. Pulling back on the reins, he came to an immediate stop, dismounted, and jumped onto the porch. The two fervently hugged, twisting slowly in a happy embrace.

"John! ... *So good* to see you!"

Jack straightened, leaned back, and clasped his sister's arms, holding her there to get a better look at her. He hadn't seen her since Christmas, and these reunions seemed so seldom any more, considering the thirty-five-mile trip from Charlestown to Groton—a hard push for one day on horseback and two days in a carriage, what with the difficult roads and stream crossings. And the fearful nature of the times had made travel even less likely. But this was no social visit, and there was nothing that could have kept her from braving the journey. So he took great comfort in having her there, holding her, feeling the strength of a bond that only comes from family, and in such great need of support after what had happened.

Fearing it too painful to speak about the real purpose to her visit, he smiled broadly and engaged in safe distraction. "You look just as good as you always do, little sister. I did receive your letter in the spring. But now I can see with mine own eyes that you *are* indeed expecting again."

Happy to elude the mournful topic, Sarah willingly participated in the pleasantries. "Yes, next month," she said as she placed both hands high on the curve of her stomach, emphasizing her condition.

Jack sized her up purposefully and grinned as he gently placed his hand upon her paunch. "I have to tell you this, Sarah; this one looks like it's going to be a girl." The long-wanted daughter to go with her five sons.

Then turning more serious, he asked, "Did you bring the entire family?"

"Yes. They're all inside."

"Splendid! The old place could suffer some little ones to run about it again," Jack said, ever mindful that his own children were all grown, married, and moved away.

Sarah continued sedately, "Mother is here." She turned and pointed toward the door. "We were all about to have supper."

He glanced over his shoulder at his horse, then acknowledged, "I'll be right with you."

"I'll tell them you're home."

Jack walked his stallion to the barn, and when he returned a few minutes later, Mother had come out and was standing on the porch, waiting for him. As he drew closer, he examined her posture; her seventy-four-year-old frame tilted noticeably forward. She seemed shorter than he remembered, her back and shoulders rounded. She leaned against the wooden post, as if needing it to steady herself.

He reached the bottom step, paused, and looked up. The two said nothing, just gazed at each other knowingly as he deliberately climbed the stairs up and onto the porch. Both knew the impetus to this meeting, the reason she'd come back to Groton.

He stepped directly to her, gazing at her, the twice-widowed, yet ever-present strength of the family. Mother's hair, which had long since turned silver, in that moment was glistening angelic, bathed in the golden light of the late day sun. She tilted her face up at his, and he studied her light blue eyes, welling with tears. She lifted her arms toward him. He took hold of both her hands and gently pulled her sweet, frail body to himself. He bent over her and lovingly wrapped his arms around her shoulders as she melted there in his gentle strength. The two cried together a while. Neither said a word.

With the side of her face still resting against his heart, she spoke, "A mother should never outlive her children ... and grandchildren."

Holding her, he whispered, "I am so glad to see you here."

She squeezed him. "I do not know what I should do without you. I *thank God* that you are here."

Mother pushed back, looked up, and admired him. She was trembling, as had been her way the last few years; even her voice was affected. She raised her cool and delicate hands and softly cupped his face with them, and then stretched up on her tiptoes and gave him a little kiss on the lips. Ever the optimist, and still in command of her faculties, she smiled and continued in a resolute tone, "We are going to get Lydia, Betty, and John back. I just know it. I've been praying for them every day."

He immediately looked away, but then spoke to reassure her, "And I have been working with Thomas and the militia. We are doing all that we can to find them." He hesitated and then turned toward the door, hoping to quickly go inside to join with the others. He always felt an odd sense of guilt when Mother spoke of her faith. He wanted to escape.

But Mother clung to his arm and held him back from leaving her so quickly. Taking him by the shoulders, she turned his body, stared straight into his eyes, and asked, "And, if necessary, are you prepared to do *more than that* to save your brother's family?"

He drew in his breath, closed his eyes, and pondered Mother's question, trying to imagine a quick way to dismiss it. *Was* there something more he could do? She had no idea really what he'd been through—and neither did she need to know the awful details. But even aside from the gruesome images fixed in his brain, this had been a terribly frustrating week. For each day had passed without news of any sort about William's children—the captives—leaving him with a feeling of utter helplessness. There seemed to be no place to look, no place to begin. Nothing he could do.

Realizing he couldn't avoid her, Jack opened his eyes and promised, "I shall indeed do everything that I can." He smiled and nodded as the two stepped into the house.

Nevertheless her question—*Was there more he could do?*—had effectively been lodged in his brain, and he couldn't clear it from his thoughts.

Sunday, August 5, 1694

From the size of the crowd, it appeared as though all of Groton had turned out for the afternoon memorial service to honor the dead, remember the injured, and to pray for the missing. Townsfolk, visitors, and extended families collectively filled the meetinghouse to capacity, with scores more spilling out of the open doors and onto the lawn. Captain James Parker, Sr., whose own sons' families were among those who suffered under the attack, read the roll call of the victims:

> Those killed:
> William Longley
> Deliverance Longley
> William Longley, III
> Jemima Longley
> Joseph Longley
> Nathaniel Longley

Zachariah Longley
Nehemiah Hobart
Elizabeth Rouse
Sarah Rouse
John Shepley, Sr.
Susannah Shepley
James Shepley
Hepsibah Shepley
Elias Shepley
Thomas Shepley
James Parker, Jr.
Mary Parker
Zachariah Parker

Those Injured:
Enoch Lawrence
William Lakin

Those Missing:
Lydia Longley
Betty Longley
John Longley
Thomasin Rouse
Gershom Hobart, Jr.
Abigail Lawrence
Susanna Lawrence
John Shepley, Jr.
Lydia Lakin
Mary Parker
Samuel Parker
Phinehas Parker

Reverend Gershom Hobart, who had one son killed and another taken, somehow had enough presence of mind and spirit to give a moving message and to lead the townsfolk in prayer. Everyone joined together in singing psalms, words of encouragement, the mighty hand of God prevailing amidst the trouble.

After the service, the people filed out to return to their homes, many still in shock over the losses, for it was a human toll that was worse than any ever suffered by the town, including the attacks of a half-generation earlier during King Philip's War.

But the fond memories, the spirit of togetherness, and the confidence in Providence, these gave to many a tiny first step of healing.

Monday, August 6, 1694

In order to inform the citizens of their plans to find the hostages, the Town Selectmen and the leaders of the militia conducted a special meeting with representatives from each of the families—those with loved ones that were missing. Thirty-some-odd people assembled in the meetinghouse. Jack was among those present, seated at the back of the audience. None of the leaders spoke to each other as they filed in, seeming very businesslike. They arranged themselves in chairs at the front, facing directly at the families. Among the militia were James and Thomas, Jack's relatives.

The audience remained hushed, with each man and woman respectful of the others present, and at the same time nervously alert and expectant, like children in their first day of school. Jack sat there and waited, forcing optimism. He feared this session would be like so many other town meetings—listening to self-important people babble, without anything getting accomplished.

Selectman Lieutenant Jonas Prescott presently rose to address them. He loosened his collar and read from his notes, "I am pleased that we have the opportunity to meet with you today concerning your family members that have recently been taken captive by the Indians. We hope to inform you here as to what we have learned about their captors and to discuss what measures we are undertaking to secure information concerning them and their whereabouts.

"You surely must know by now, we were unable to capture alive any of the Indians that participated in the attacks. Thus we have not yet had the benefit of direct testimony regarding the *wretches* who planned and conducted this grievous assault upon our town.

"We were able to kill four of the savages during their raid. And with advice from several of our friend Indians among the Nipmuc, we have been able to identify, by means of their dress, hair, and paint, that these savages were Abenaki. Two of the dead appeared to be princes, sagamores. And though these leaders could not be specifically identified, their belts were recognized as being indigenous with the natives that occupy the western part of the Province of Maine."

Prescott stopped and paged through his notes, stiffly concluding he'd read them all. A quiet murmur swept through the audience as he turned to Captain James Parker. He extended his hand for him to continue with the presentation, and then sat down.

Parker, despite being heavily burdened by his own personal losses, with three grandchildren taken, understood the importance of his presence there to address the families. His position in the town as a faithful, servant leader for decades, always brought him out to help resolve difficulties, especially those most trying, like this. He rose, gathered his breath and looked at the audience a moment. Feeling encouraged by the sympathy he felt in all the eyes before him, he addressed them. He had no notes.

"You know that our fellow English have been at war with France these past six years… and during this time, there have been few attempts by our government to enter the native's lands, to go to Maine. You may remember the failures… Governor Phips in 1690, and again in 1692. For we have seen that Maine is a very dangerous place for any Englishman, it being filled with savages who serve eagerly the king of France. Therefore, it appears that until such time as our great mother country across the ocean is able to prevail, we shall have to resolve the matters of our hostages ourselves, by means of diplomacy, and… therefore, to rely on men skilled at negotiation and fearless of traveling between our two cultures.

"And as for our hostages," he grew noticeably redder in the face, and louder, "I can't help but note that our colony… our village… has been exposed to this dreadful practice of taking captives ever since the first war, and that, sadly, such kidnapping is neither foreign, nor is it misunderstood to many of us, especially me." He swallowed hard. "Now, I suppose that more than a few of you have read Mary Rowlandson's book, her *Narrative of Captivity and Restoration,* and understand from her brave account that the Indians are only motivated by one thing: *money.*"

Parker regained his unflappable strength. "You can expect, once we make contact with the savages that took them, that we should be able to purchase their freedom for a price. Toward that end, we have already appealed to the general court for relief…because I know several of you would be consumed by the cost.

"But, alas…I am afraid they shall not be able to help us until such time as we have unequivocal demands. And at this juncture, we have not received any, let alone decidedly identified their captors or point of origin…"

Enoch Lawrence rose up abruptly from the audience and raised his left hand. His right arm and head were bandaged.

Parker allowed the interruption and invited him to speak.

"James, *how* are we to learn where they've been taken?"

Parker didn't hesitate. "I've written letters—appeals, as it were— to several towns nearby along the frontier, including Dunstable, Tyngsboro, and Chelmsford. I've asked for any information that they may have—perhaps through Indians they might know nearby, or traders that may have learned of the attack. Some of you may also have heard that Oyster River Plantation was assaulted a week prior to Groton; and we are still trying to learn if there be a connection between the massacre there, and what happened here, in our village. And if there proves to be a connection, we'll have an opportunity to combine our resources.

"But you must understand that communications are trying at this time. I am indeed troubled to report that a great many people have learned about what happened here and at Oyster River, and as a result they remain in the confines of their garrisons, fearful of another assault, at any moment. So we are relying, at least presently, upon brave couriers as we await their news.

"And there is one other matter," Parker continued. "I asked the general court to keep us informed of military action and any intercepted messages. They indicate they are listening for such and intend to share what they know when the intelligence becomes available.

P. GIFFORD LONGLEY

We do remain hopeful, therefore, hopeful that we shall learn something in the next few weeks. *But I hesitate to be so direct*—yet I must––I tell you all...that I cannot put a time limit or a precise estimate on when we shall better know exactly what to do next."

Frustrated at the lack of information, Jack rose to his feet and raised his hand.

Parker bade him speak.

"Is there anything that *I* can do?" Jack asked.

Parker's eyes dropped. He hesitated, then turned and looked at the other leaders, seated to either side. Each wore blank expressions. A few stared at the floor. He faced forward and collected his thoughts. He was their spokesman, so he responded with what he reasoned they all were thinking. "We have several of the militia out as couriers delivering messages and are hopeful to receive responses. It is dangerous work, as I am sure you must know. And we shall leave this work to our brave soldiers." He paused, turned, and looked up at the cross behind him, mounted on the wall (for the meeting hall served also as the church). He turned back to Jack. "But, there *is* one thing that you can do...and that each of you can do."

All eyes focused on the captain, the audience now at full attention.

"*Pray*," he suggested, "and do not give up hope."

A murmur passed through the audience. Some took immediate comfort—they smiled and nodded their heads. But many were disappointed that nothing seemed to be in the offing, nothing substantive, no mention of counter raid or attack by the militia, for there was no lack of hatred of the Indians on account of what had happened. Yet there was present a surprising spirit of restraint, as the audience kept silent.

Jack was among those frustrated by the inaction of the leaders. And despite the militia's obvious intent to exclude him, he *still* found himself wondering if there wasn't something more that he could do.

SEPARATED

Saturday, July 28, 1694

The native band's flight from Groton had been urgent, vigorously paddling their canoes down the storm-freshened Squannacook and passing through several steep drops marked by dangerous rapids. Thankfully, those navigating the vessels were expertly skilled, and not one had overturned as the swift water brought them to the wide Merrimack in under an hour. From there, the going had not been so easy, as they turned north against the current of this larger body. Then, for the rest of Friday and all of this day, they had been paddling hard upriver, portaging a half-dozen times past the whitewater and fighting the indefatigable flow. Now, as the purple sunset showed the onset of evening, they were arriving at the Indian village of Pennacook, exhausted.

Pennacook lay on the western bank of the Merrimack, near the mouth of a rivulet that descended from the low hills in the southwest. There at the confluence of these two rivers was a level plain of fertile, alluvial soil in which the natives had planted their summer crops of corn, beans, and squash. The canoes turned past these fields and headed up the smaller tributary, passing through darkening curves and disappearing out of sight of the Merrimack.

After several hundred yards, they spied their landing point, situated on the left bank, a sandy strip encompassed by the dusky forest. There were many canoes already there, pulled up onto the shore, an indication of the Indian enclave presently concealed from their sight.

As they approached the beach, Lydia watched the Indian leader, her captor and master, as he paddled hard to speed his vessel to the front of the line, with John still kneeling in its midst. This leader, whom the Indians called Taxous, was the first to step ashore, greeted there by several from the village. Soon the rest of their canoes landed, and the scene became a bustle. The disembarked warriors' spirits were high, relieved to rest their weary selves. This was their safe haven, there amongst their allies.

From their landing point, a trail led up into the dense woods, and the whole band began to move in that direction, leaving most of their goods behind in the boats. The captives were taken with them, each dragged along rudely by their wrist ropes, up the path through the thickets and into the trees, rising some fifty feet in elevation onto a wooded plateau. The gloomy trail continued a hundred yards farther on through a stand of tall pines, their black trunks devoid of branches, spread out across the needled carpet. Ahead they marched toward a gap in a wall of underbrush, an open door through which the fading, purple day pierced the thickets; the dense underbrush thriving at the edge of the forest, beside the un-shadowed brink of the canopy. Then passing through this hedge, the trail gave way to the clearing—a glade marked by human development, filled with dozens of dome-shaped structures overlaid with large sheets of birch bark. Smoke hovered above this break and ascended higher than the surrounding firs, rising from the native's campfires. This was a home to the Pennacook, a part of the Abenaki Nation, where a hundred of the migratory Indians lived in the spring and summer.

As the band marched forward from the woods, the Indian captors cried out, announcing their arrival with shouts of joy and victory. The villagers who were out and about paused in their doings to behold the sudden spectacle. These were joined by the rest who

P. GIFFORD LONGLEY

climbed out from their dwellings, with broad smiles of anticipation fixed on their faces. This was an event!

As Lydia and the other captives were roughly dragged down the avenues between the lodges toward the center of the camp, she felt their cold stares. They examined her from head to foot. How could she be human to them? And how much to them was she worth?

At the center of the hamlet was an open area of some apparent jurisdictional purpose, encompassing a fire ring. Several ample logs were blazing there, shedding their glow into the gathering darkness while lifting woody smoke high into the air. Taxous gathered the leaders of his band close to the ring, joined by several of the Pennacook. The rest of the troop, including the prisoners, remained at the perimeter, invited to sit.

The leaders stood as dark silhouettes against the flames, speaking amongst themselves. Their weary posture indicated their desire to conclude the day with rest. After a few minutes, the council ended and the band began to disperse to the lodges. Lydia watched John and Betty each taken away separately by their guards. At the last, Taxous approached, grabbed her rope, and led her off, following after one of the Pennacooks.

Taken to the door of a nearby dwelling, Lydia accompanied the sagamore as he bent low and stepped inside. She wondered what she would find there.

The one-room home was about fifteen feet in diameter with standing room only near the center, where there was a fire pit dug into the earth, ablaze with several logs. The glow of the flames revealed the presence of four Indians: an elderly man and woman, who rose to meet them. Two other females sat back in the shadows. Taxous bowed and greeted his hosts before he turned to Lydia and ordered her to sit.

The old man, their host, was apparently a leader of the Pennacook. She recognized him as one of those who had first met Taxous at the water's edge and then again at the center of the camp only minutes before. He bent his tall frame forward and leaned a kind face toward Lydia, thus permitting his long, silvered hair, which was ornamented with shells, to dangle down before his still muscular chest—he being proudly naked but for his breechclout and ornamented apron. Beside him the eyes of the old woman sparkled in the wavering light. She seemed to be the proprietor's wife, being of similar age with thinning white hair and heavily wrinkled, yet she was attractively arrayed in a lovely, hand-stitched dress.

The two other women, shy and aloof, were much younger. Lydia supposed them to be daughters, yet they surely were mature enough to have been married. Perhaps they were other wives? Such stories of polygamy among the Indians abounded. And after the greeting, those standing sat down around the fire, with Taxous at his prisoner's side.

From across the blaze, the Pennacook sagamore continued to stare at Lydia. At last he addressed her as he pointed toward himself and spoke deliberately, "*Wo-na-lan-cet.*" Then he leaned forward and silently awaited her response.

Taxous turned to the English woman and explained, "This Wonalancet. What your name?"

In the two full days of her captivity, this was the first discourse—other than a threat—that Lydia had experienced with the Indians. So she hadn't expected to be asked to speak. And as she hadn't had a thing to drink in that time, her throat was too dry to form any words. She tried to clear it and responded in a rasp, "Lyd-ee-ah," whilst pointing politely at herself and trying to restrain a choke. The irritation from the pungent smoke caused her eyes to burn.

Wonalancet acknowledged her response as he repeated her name back and maintained eye contact, hoping to see her approval of his pronunciation. The host then turned and instructed the old woman, who, without hesitation, picked up a skin containing liquid, poured some of it into a bowl, reached across, and gently handed it to the English girl. She motioned for her to drink as she spoke in Abenaki, "*Ka dos mo wo gan.*"

Lydia glanced at the dark contents and hesitated. Suspiciously, she raised it to her mouth while scrutinizing the woman, who maintained her steady and gracious demeanor. A sip of the cool solu-

P. GIFFORD LONGLEY

tion revealed it was merely fresh water in a dark bowl. She hesitated no further to empty the vessel before handing it back, nodding her appreciation.

Taxous entered into conversation with Wonalancet in their native tongue. After several minutes, Taxous was heard mentioning "Lydia" as he turned and faced her. Abruptly the discussion ended. The two men rose to their feet, nodded, and shook hands. Then her captor bent down, grabbed Lydia's binding, and motioned for her to rise.

Expecting they now would be leaving, Lydia watched as Taxous deliberately handed the end of the rope to Wonalancet, said his last words to the old sagamore, and maneuvered toward the door to leave. He ducked for the opening, but just before stepping away, he turned back to Lydia and commanded her, "You stay here now." Then he passed to the outside and was gone without any further explanation.

The prisoner stared out the door a moment then turned toward the other natives. She stood uncomfortably before the old man, unable to look him in the eye, instead staring at the fire. She was dumbfounded, being left there with these strangers. She wondered, *Will he be back in a few minutes? Am I to sleep here for the night? Will he be returning in the morning?* There was no way for her to ask the people anything. They spoke no English. She continued to stare out the opening, feeling uneasy and desperately alone.

Observing Lydia's insecurity, the old woman promptly rose to her feet and gestured to get Lydia's attention, introducing herself, "*Wag-u-a-la.*"

Lydia turned, swallowed hard, and focused her attention onto the woman's face. She repeated the name back, forcing a smile.

Waguala then briefly discoursed with Wonalancet, received a nod of consent from the man, and stepped close to the prisoner, taking the end of the rope from his hand. The shriveled little woman gently drew Lydia's bound hands straight out. And then, with peaceful eyes, she delicately untied the knot and cast the binding aside while politely motioning for her to sit.

As Lydia lowered herself down onto the mat, her limbs began to shake beyond her ability to control them, revealing her growing hunger. Waguala perceived the young woman's condition and, from the scraps that had been left over from their evening repast, offered the prisoner "*ska wakw*" (cooked, fresh meat), "*pa gon*" (nuts), and "*ab on*" (a modest cake cooked from corn).

Lydia seized each item as it was handed to her and returned a glance of appreciation and then consumed it ravenously, without any consideration to her mealtime etiquette. She hadn't eaten anything in two days.

After the meal, the prisoner was offered a place to stretch out on the floor and given a skin for a blanket and bolster. Refreshed from her supper and the unexpected kindness, she reclined and tried to relax. The four Pennacook then spoke at ease amongst themselves. But since there was nothing she could say to them, Lydia lay back and felt quite detached.

She stared awkwardly up at the ceiling. The flickering firelight revealed the details of the framing: bent maple saplings that were evenly spaced and cross-lashed at their intersections. These were so delicate when considered individually, yet strong when bound together as such. *How different this abode is from home,* she thought, this new structure that encompassed her above and around. And in that moment, a stiff breeze swelled and pressed down hard on the lodge, transferring its force into the frame, which strained and creaked as the twisted little members worked in unison to hold fast and to stand firm against it. She recognized that any one branch, though it be set free from its bindings and permitted to return to its natural shape, could not so resist such a gust by itself.

And that downdraft, which had also pierced the aperture in the dome and momentarily brightened the fire, had also caused the dwelling to be filled with woody fumes and uncomfortable warmth. Lydia rolled onto her side, away from the strangers and the flames, to avoid choking. She faced the bark wall and tried to be complacent. As she lay there, with her eyes watering, she apprehended the benefit of the smoke, for the mosquitoes that'd ravaged her for two days at last were gone. Then closing her eyes, she silently gave thanks for her circumstance and unexpectedly dozed straight off to sleep.

Sunday, July 29, 1694

Sunday in the Indian village had brought unanticipated peace to Lydia, as she had been bettered by the nourishment and a good night's rest. And though the young English woman had to endure being watched closely with suspicion by Waguala all the day, she relished being taken down to the river to wash and being permitted to attend to her personal needs. Most of the day had been spent by the natives in preparation for a feast that was to be held that evening. The old Indian woman patiently coached her with light chores to assist with the food: grinding the corn to make meal, shelling nuts, and digging and cleaning turnips.

Throughout her comings and goings, Lydia hadn't seen any sign of John or Betty, and this had caused her to worry. Yet mindful of her situation and fearful that the kindness she momentarily enjoyed could easily be withdrawn, she remained purposefully attentive and obedient to the instructions of the old woman—to the extent she understood them.

When the afternoon turned late, the men of the camp fetched branches and logs to build a great pyre at the fire pit. Others brought the meat that had been butchered in Groton and gave it to the women to cook. The preparations for the event were nearing their end.

When the sun had fallen behind the trees and drawn low to the horizon, the whole assembly gathered at the center of the village. The men had washed themselves, put on their finest clothing, trimmed their hair, and donned fresh ochre paint. The women also had decorated themselves with jewelry, powdered their faces and hair, and painted their lips with red berries in anticipation of a grand occasion.

The festivities commenced with speeches from Wonalancet and Taxous, and then the songs began. The drums beat out the rhythm as the people joined in the dance, forming together in a large circle.

First came the spirit leaders, then the elders, followed in order by the men, the women, and the children as all of the natives entered in the celebration. And when the sun at last had set, the bonfire was lit as the women brought out the food.

During the festivities, the prisoners, who had been mustered to the edge of the scene, were kept bound and guarded there by a dozen armed warriors. Lydia was pleased to be reunited again with her siblings, and they stayed close by each other. And after the natives had eaten, there was even food left over so that each prisoner was provided a bit. Lydia and John both ate all that was offered them, but Betty, who remained silent the entire time and still hadn't spoken since her capture, refused to eat, despite their urgent pleas. Lydia had a growing concern for her sister.

After the feast, as the flames of the bonfire subsided, the natives dispersed to their lodges. Lydia was once again separated from her siblings and returned to the lodge of Wonalancet and Waguala for another night.

Monday, July 30, 1694

In the early morning, the camp grew alive with activity, and Lydia soon surmised that Taxous and his band were leaving to continue north. And as the camp began to file out of their dwellings and move back down the trail toward the canoes, Waguala came to Lydia and motioned for her to follow along with the others, holding fast onto the young woman's arm as she went. As they marched along with the crowd, Lydia observed several of the other prisoners with their hands tied, yet hers had remained free. This surprised her. Waguala seemed to her to be unusually lenient.

Ahead at the water's edge, several canoes were already being pushed into the stream and were leaving. Near the foot of the path Lydia spotted Betty up ahead as she entered a boat, still wearing Father's hat. Her sister's canoe quickly departed, and she didn't have the chance to wave or speak to her, nor did she even see her face.

At the trail's end, Waguala pulled Lydia off to the side of the strand and out of the way of those first leaving. The old woman stood by, holding Lydia's arm, and they quietly observed together as the rest of the band came down the trail behind them, entered their canoes, and paddled away.

Amidst the bustle, Lydia searched for John's face among the others, but could not see him anywhere. Finally, the last of the group descended the trail, and John was with them, bound and led by Taxous. Lydia readied herself to be taken to her boat, but which one would be hers? There were only a few canoes remaining, and she couldn't see either of the men that had taken her the first two days. She grew worried. *Were they planning to leave her?*

Her fears were soon confirmed as the others all departed, leaving just the one canoe, John, and the last two warriors. She saw it clearly now. *She'd been sold!*

Lydia turned to Waguala with tears forming in her eyes but made no attempt to speak. Nevertheless, the old woman understood and released hold of her arm. She motioned consent for her to approach the water's edge, graciously allowing her to say good-bye.

There Taxous helped his partner push the final canoe down the embankment. They left John standing alone on the strand, fixed between the two remaining women and the two departing men. He himself was wondering why his sister hadn't yet left.

Lydia ran to her brother and flung her arms around him. She kissed his neck. "Oh, John," she cried. "They're keeping me here!"

The boy stood silent and limp.

Lydia pleaded with him, "John, now *you* shall have to watch over your sister by yourself. I *pray* that you both will be safe ... and that we shall soon be joined back together." She pulled him closer and bemoaned, "You're all I have!"

The last canoe was already in the current, restrained there by one of the Indians. Taxous approached the two prisoners and grabbed the end of John's rope from the sand. The sagamore waited a second and then impatiently gave it a tug to jar them apart; this while clenching his fist and threatening Lydia with it.

Fearful of the consequences, she briefly let go. But as John started to turn and plod away, she reached forward and grabbed him for one final hug and cried, "Good-bye, John. I love you. I shall *always* love you!"

John kept silent, resolutely fighting back his tears. He tilted his head forward and leaned it on his sister's shoulder. It was all he could dare himself to do.

Taxous snarled at Lydia, twisting a scowl of angry eyes and presuming that such a display was sufficient to repel her. He seemed anxious to press on with his business.

But she remained undaunted by this last frightful threat. Instead, she glared back at her captor, unafraid of who he was, the *murderer* of her family. *You can hurt my body*, she thought, *but you cannot rule my soul!*

Taxous glowered, ready to strike, but hesitated. He lowered his fist and loosened his clench, curling his lips ever so briefly in respect for her courage. Had she not been studying his countenance, she never would have seen it. He quickly resumed his purpose and brusquely ripped John away from her, knowing she couldn't stop him. He dragged him off, splashing through the shallow water toward their canoe. There the three climbed in and pushed off downstream without further adieu.

With the old squaw, Waguala, joining her at her side, Lydia stood fixed on the shore as the savages furiously paddled away, all the while with John staring back over his shoulder, deliberately straight-faced. She stole her final precious glimpses of him until at last he was gone round the bend and out of sight.

Thus, the oldest sister had been separated from her only remaining family. Alone she stood, not knowing if she would ever see Betty or John again. And as she turned to face her new captor, Lydia came to the full realization of her circumstance: she would have to be strong to survive.

P. GIFFORD LONGLEY

STARVING

Monday, July 30, 1694

It had all happened too fast. One moment he and Lydia had been together as fellow survivors of a tragedy, traveling through the pain together, there to comfort and look out for each other on this perilous journey into the unknown. And then they had been separated. He never saw it coming.

For certain, he was the "man" of the family now, but he had depended on his oldest sister, on her wisdom, experience, intelligence, *her courage*, and care. But Lydia had just been left behind; her voice to him had been silenced. What was he to do now? No one there knew him all that well, except for Betty. But there was something deeply wrong with his other sister. She was so melancholy. She would follow their captor's commands, do what was asked of her compliantly, yet she spoke to no one. He couldn't carry on a conversation with her or ask her opinion on anything. Besides, even before, before this happened, Betty had always been such a fragile person, delicate like a flower and not at all suited to endure such harshness.

No, there wasn't anyone left that he could turn to for strength anymore. And like the canoe he now sat in, he was powered along by forces he could not control, being taken to a destination he did not choose or know.

Once they'd turned the corner and resumed their northward direction heading up the Merrimack, John kept his face forward, not daring to look back at Taxous, who sat paddling right behind him in the stern of the canoe. John wanted to hang his head and cry, but he could feel those eyes behind him, boring into the back of his head, most assuredly watching him for signs of weakness. Perhaps if he focused on something else he could avoid showing emotion. Sitting very still, his mind flew away, searching, as he grew oblivious to the scenery they passed. He turned off all his senses and became numb. Grasping out for guidance, something to anchor himself to, instead he felt the full weight of his isolation descend on him like great pieces of iron heaped upon his chest, crushing out his life.

In his loneliness and weakness, he could but focus on one thing—breathing—and as he struggled to draw in each restoring breath, his reason slowly revived. What would Lydia do if she were there? She would be strong in everything that she could *control*, and though that wasn't much, it included not creating trouble or calling attention to himself before his tormentors. Yes, she would agree with that. He knew he must regain his composure and that time would be his fortunate ally. He would be restored in a while if he was just left alone. He could always cry later.

John kept his head erect and his eyes forward, stoically, fully appreciating that his oppressors had plenty to occupy themselves with other than him—namely, the hard work of paddling northward against the flow.

The upper Merrimack turned out to be easier to navigate than the lower sections. The line of canoes followed its course as it rounded the bends turning left, then right, then left again, snaking through a level plain, free of rapids, making steady progress. The penetrating sun quickly took the chill off the morning, glaring from the thousand tiny mirrors of the moving water and baking the sweaty backs of the men as they labored forward toward their goal. So they pushed hard against the current for many hours with the sun rising above them toward its zenith in the humid sky.

In the early afternoon, the band came to a fork, where they departed the main branch and entered into a smaller tributary that diverted them toward the northeast. There the canoes veered ashore onto a gravelly spit to give the men a rest. The eleven prisoners were pulled from their vessels and assembled together on the bank. Several guards took turns watching them as the other natives ate their trail provisions and cooled off in a deep, still pool. The prisoners, five boys and six girls, could only watch as the Indians refreshed themselves. No food was offered to the captives; neither were they given a chance to bathe or to tend to personal needs.

It wasn't long before both Lawrence sisters became seized by a sense of injustice over the unbalanced treatment and then lost control of their tongues. They'd forgotten their new station in the master-slave relationship, where they were, in fact, entitled to nothing. Abigail, age fourteen, was the most vocal. Frustrated, she rudely snapped at the guards, "We have needs too, you know!"

One of the warriors reacted without hesitation to her nasty tone. Snarling, he raised his tom hog. Shepley, now the oldest prisoner, bravely positioned himself between the two. In as gentle a tone as he could muster, he appealed to the Indian, "Sir, I believe she needs to relieve herself, as some of us also must do."

The guard paused, apparently understanding both his English and sincerity. He lowered his weapon. The request had indeed been legitimate, so one at a time he untied their hands and permitted the prisoners to take care of their needs, squatting in the tall grasses and washing at the water's edge. No privacy was afforded. The native watched their every move. But the opportunity to rest and refresh overcame all modesty.

By the time the last one had taken their turn, they were rounded up and returned to their vessels as the natives made ready to continue their trek. John noted that not one of the hostages had been offered any provision to eat.

Their new watercourse remained easy to traverse as it turned east and then northeast through a level forest, with tall elms growing right to the edges of both banks. The cool shade was welcome, but the mosquitoes that infested the stagnant pools became a menace. At times, the trees would pull back in favor of expanses of reeds and the sun would drive away the insects, but it would scorch their exposed skin. John wondered which was worse: the oppressive heat or the pests. As the afternoon grew late, tall, puffy clouds began to mount, portending of an evening thunderstorm.

The river advanced from the woodland at last and into the open, where it divided a swamp, with the main channel barely distinguished amidst the summer grasses and reeds. Spotted turtles and frogs sunned themselves on snags and rocks, and these were startled into the murky water as they passed. The sun was drawing low when the seemingly endless marsh at last gave way and the stream grew steadily wider. They'd found the source of the river: a mountain lake, which spread out some several hundred feet wide to greet them.

Out across the open water, their progress was aided by a welcome southwesterly that rose at their backs. Pressing onward, they diverted through a narrow neck and up a canal and then into another lake, larger than the first. And so they continued through the chains of small lakes and connecting channels until at last they entered the main body, Lake Winnipesaukee, which extended in impressive fashion several miles across to the northeast and to the right toward the far horizon in the south.

There were many islands there, several of good size, and with a sense of urgency brought on by the stiffening breeze and ominous black clouds gathering behind them, the band put in at the first one that they came to.

The island was a steep hump that rose abruptly from the water, overgrown with trees and scrub that extended down to a narrow, grassy shore where they landed. There was no sign of a boat landing or any clearing, suggesting the isle was uninhabited. The prisoners were assembled together amidst the green tussocks, with several guards posted to watch them.

P. GIFFORD LONGLEY

Soon the winds intensified, and thunder began to roll. The natives realized their good fortune in being able to ride the storm out on the island on account of their respect for the wind and fear of the lightning on the open water. And since it was dusk, John presumed they would stay and rest for the night. The Indians hurried to pull their canoes up from the waves and to flip them over to make a covering for their provisions.

The rains came straightway, hard and fast, falling in great sheets that were hurled at them by furious gusts. In a matter of minutes, John and the other prisoners were soaked to the bone. At first the wet seemed like a welcome shower of refreshment, this after the heat of the day. But as the rains continued, the temperature plummeted and a chill set in. By the time the deluge had blown over, the hostages were all shivering in the damp, hungry and exhausted.

The possibility of a campfire was ruined by the rains, which had drenched all the kindling on the island. So there would be no cooked dinner or opportunity to dry out and find warmth. The growing darkness also meant there was no chance to forage and that their evening meal would have to be the trail provisions.

The Indians retrieved their rations and sat down to consume them: dried beans, grains, roots, and dried meat—all in modest portions, at best; these for the laborers alone. Nothing was offered to the prisoners.

Once again Abigail Lawrence grumbled and then became belligerent with one of the guards as he openly savored his piece of meat in front of her, as if taunting her. This went on for several minutes, to the increasing laughter of the others with him.

"Is there no food for us?" She flailed her arm toward the others beside her, none of whom dared to speak or join in her complaints.

Surprisingly not put off by her tone, the Indian conferred privately with his fellows, and when one of them left to walk over toward the supplies, he blurted at Abigail, "We get you food. Then you quiet!"

The guard returned carrying a small bundle or pouch. In the gloom, it was difficult to discern exactly what it was. Entering then amongst the prisoners, he handed something to each of them.

John received his portion with anticipation. It felt like a piece of meat, but of what sort he didn't know. It was about six inches long and a little more than an inch in diameter. Betty hadn't extended her hand, but John made certain to also take a piece for her.

The Indian came lastly to Abigail. She strained to see what he was giving her. With the portion finally in her desperate hand, she examined it up close. But upon discovering the claws at one end, she exclaimed her disgust, "Dog feet!" and threw her meal to the ground.

The native smirked at Abigail and scolded her. "Dog feet good. Don't throw away. Enjoy!" He and the other guards laughed. And when she dropped her head down between her knees, sobbing, they roared even louder.

John quietly examined the two segments that he held, feeling the claws and pads, then raising them to his nose to smell. They seemed good, not gamey. He hadn't eaten dog before, but he'd heard that it was regarded by the Indians—though they probably enjoyed better cuts than the feet. He gnawed a bit on one end. It was salty but tasty. Turning to Betty, huddled close to his side and shivering, he placed her portion before her eyes. "Here, take it; it's pretty good."

Betty said nothing and made no move to accept it.

Her persistent lethargy was becoming a source of great disappointment to him. Nevertheless, he tried to console her. "Well, you don't have to take it now. I'll save it for later." He reached down and tucked it in his pocket. He knew she would need to eat something.

John finished his meat, gnawing it all the way to the bone, chewing and swallowing the sinews. He sucked on the shin for a while, drawing out the last bit of marrow. He'd never been so hungry.

The prisoners stayed huddled together on into the evening. None said anything as their stomachs grumbled. John missed Lydia. He would have been talking to her were she there. She would have been trying to help their sister, even sleeping at her side, just like at home. He wondered if Betty had even noticed Lydia's absence. He remembered the events of the morning and spoke to her. "I saw Lydia at the camp ... before we left."

Betty raised her head and looked at him.

"She said I should help you now, since she would no longer be here with us."

His sister kept silent. He wasn't sure if she'd understood, yet John sensed a connection. Then being exhausted from the hunger, and he was sure Betty felt the same way, he suggested, "We should lie down and rest."

Betty removed her hat and lay over onto her side. She faced away from him and leaned her head on a wide hassock while clutching the garment to her chest. John lay down beside her, rolled to his side, and placed his arm over hers. They shivered together for a few minutes and then began to warm each other. It wasn't long before he fell asleep.

Tuesday, July 31, 1694

The next morning was marked by a wispy fog that clung to the surface of the lake. They rose early to resume their journey, setting off without nourishment. They steered across the wide water toward the northeastern shore with their goal barely visible through the mist. Aided by a southwesterly breeze, the band navigated between the islands and arrived on the opposite shore in under an hour, just as the fog was lifting. Ahead of them, to the north, a mountain rose up high above the forest and dominated their view. White granite outcroppings broke through the tree-covered hillsides and cast their long, morning shadows down onto the forest.

Their water route had apparently ended. The Indians pulled the canoes up above the bank. There the bundles were taken from the vessels and stacked beside a path that had been beaten through the grass and which led up into the forest. The prisoners were assembled there and addressed by Taxous as he pointed to the pile and gave his stern instruction, "We march today. You carry these."

The Indians helped to load the bundles onto the backs of each of the prisoners. John's burden, about thirty-to-forty weight, was lashed tightly to his shoulders and waist. Each prisoner was given a similar pack. The girls all carried as much as the boys.

With the packs secured, the troop set off. Two Indians carried each canoe inverted upon their backs. And since there were no additional warriors free to guard the hostages, these were separated along the line: canoe, then prisoner, canoe, prisoner, and so on.

Leaving from the lake, the troop marched east into the woods along the well-used trail. Everywhere in sight of their path, great mature oaks made for a thick canopy of shade—these stunting the undergrowth, serving to keep the forest floor clear, and making visibility good in all directions ... and inconspicuous escape impossible. The band continued its march along the trail for several hours without rest as the sun burned away the last of the fog and mounted higher into the cloudless sky. They were fortunate to be keeping in the cool of the shadows.

The monotony of the path at last gave way to a clearing at the base of the mountain cliffs, which afforded dramatic views to the rocks above. There the trail crossed up and over an expanse of boulders, a mighty avalanche that had tumbled down and made for treacherous footing over the toppled crags. At the far side of this rocky racecourse, the Indians finally halted, with each staying in formation. They set their boats down on the grassy slope, a meadow that descended from the base of the cliffs astride the highway and extended downward toward the woods below. They would rest.

The prisoners were permitted to remove their packs. John doffed his—a scratchy, brown blanket tightly bound over its lumpy contents. Something hard inside it had been rubbing his lower back with each and every step. He raised his shirt to examine his hip. The spot was red and raw, and a blister had formed and burst, but it wasn't bleeding. He would have to reorient the pack when they resumed their hike.

Being at the end of the line, John studied the other prisoners that were ahead. The next one forward was Abigail Lawrence, who had quickly removed her pack and was already lying prone in the grass, motionless. Next was Shepley.

He wondered where Betty was.

Looking far ahead, near to the front of the line, he spied her, seated with her arms rested on her knees, gazing to the right, staring down the slope into the center of the sunny meadow. Her face was shaded by the wide brim of Father's hat, so he couldn't read her expression. Her posture showed no strain from the march. John was relieved.

As the troop rested, many of the Indians descended through the meadow and found blackberries growing in abundance. The natives enjoyed the juicy pickings and returned, sharing handfuls of the crop with those that had been left guarding the hostages. John and the other captives sat patiently and watched, hoping to partake in the harvest. Eventually a few of the berries were passed their way, but not near enough to fully satisfy. Nonetheless, the juice was welcome to his thirsty mouth. Then, all too soon, the break ended as Taxous announced that it was time to resume. Their packs were strapped back on, and the group set off.

The trail went on for hours into the late afternoon. Judging from the pace they'd kept all day, John reckoned they'd traveled more than a dozen miles. Still, the burden had begun to wear another sore in his flesh; the narrow strap cut his left shoulder each time he swung his arm. Thus, pressing onward through the pain, each and every step became more and more of a challenge. But rather than be defeated by the torture of it, he turned his focus ahead and onto the others marching before him.

The two Indians to his front were well in control as they carried their canoe. They were conditioned and practiced, easily finding a comfortable position for the sturdy, yet light, vessel. Beyond them, Abigail trudged along, fidgeting with her pack. Obviously the load was rubbing her the wrong way. Her feet dragged through the grass and leaves. Several times she stumbled over rocks and twigs that lay in the path, yet somehow she managed to keep her balance. He noticed over time, however, that a gap had opened and was widening to her front. She wasn't keeping up with the pace.

As the path wore on through countless agonizing paces, word filtered up the trail for all to stop and rest again. John welcomed the pause, and he quickly removed his pack and laid it down with a thud. It occurred to him that it might be too hard to get back up; thus, the trunk of a tree became his brace. He leaned there against it with his knees wobbling. Tired, sore, and famished, he fixed his hope on the thought that, with the late hour, they would soon be stopping for the night.

But after the rest, all too brief, the announcement came to resume. John bent and retrieved his pack and searched momentarily for yet a better position to carry it to save his mounting sores. As he fumbled, a ruckus arose that drew his attention immediately toward his front.

Abigail, still seated on the ground, was arguing vehemently with one of the warriors. The young woman whined, "I need to rest a bit longer. I have sores on both shoulders and my back! My feet ache ... I'm thirsty, *and I'm starving.*"

As the warrior continued to negotiate with her, John heard footsteps approaching swiftly from the trail behind. Taxous blew right past him, holding his tom hog firmly in his angry right fist.

Abigail continued to carp as he ferociously drew up behind her. So fervent was she in her disagreement that she hadn't even heard him approach. She did not see him as he quickly planted both his feet and, with a mighty swing, knocked her on the back of her head with the heavy mallet.

It sounded a solid *thwack* as it struck the bone.

The girl fell straight forward to the ground, quiet. She lay completely still a few seconds. Then she rolled herself over and moaned loudly as she flailed her arms in agony.

The powerful savage raised the weapon high above his head then plunged it straight into her face. Her shrill cries were silenced and struggling limbs stilled. Not satisfied, Taxous's face continued to twist with rage as with several more quick and angry swinging thuds he made certain he would *hear!—her!—no!—more!*

Everyone within sight of the assault stood motionless for a moment. Taxous calmed himself as he curtly wiped the fury from his face—so easily, just as if he was removing a garment. He bent and picked up Abigail's pack, stepped forward briskly, and dropped it at the feet of Shepley. Then he went back to his position at the end of the line, with all eyes fixed on his every move.

The show of force had been both efficient and effective, like that of a wealthy proprietor unflinchingly disposing of land that would not produce, as though ready to cut his losses and focus instead on the remaining fertile ground—and all the while *loving* his work.

As Taxous hoisted his end of the canoe, the others silently lifted and reloaded their burdens and then set off again up the track, each with a little extra bounce in their step. There was no time to mourn or say good-bye to the girl, as just another impediment to their progress had been removed. John trod forward and glanced at the lifeless body of Abigail as he passed it. What a brutish sight—to be left there oozing among the leaves, waiting for nature to return it to the earth. He wondered if Abigail's sister, Susanna, had been looking back and had seen the violence. He hoped she'd been spared the vision of the sudden, *cruel* departure. It would forever be marked in his memory.

The day was nearing its end when they descended the last portion of the trail and stepped out of the woods, out into a meadow of lacey, white wildflowers, situated on the western bank of another peaceful mountain lake. Oh, the contrast of vision he'd seen that day. The beauty and brutality!

Ahead, the smoke of many campfires rising signified their destination for the night: the Indian village of Ossipee.

Thursday, August 2, 1694

The day prior had been a welcome respite for Taxous's band as they stayed in Ossipee and basked in a second victory feast with more of their Abenaki allies, and there restocked provisions to make ready for this next leg of their journey. John had seen Betty several times during the day, and he noted that word of the death of Abigail hadn't seemed to have impacted her. But he was never sure if she listened when he spoke to her. He saw no emotion on her face. Yet she yielded to everything the Indians asked of her and, thus, created no trouble. He wondered if Betty was faring better under the stress of this endless trek—better than he. Yet, she did look tired and weak.

In the morning, they learned that another prisoner had been left behind in Ossipee, John presumed as payment for their provisions. It was Susanna Lawrence, and her disposal had the added benefit of solving the problem of not having to deal with her emotional collapse in the wake of her sister's execution. She would no longer be a drag on their forward progress.

Now entering its seventh day, their trip resumed over water, a welcome break to the marching, as this would give John's pack wounds time to heal.

The flotilla set out across the two-mile lake and arrived at its eastern shore under a bright, clear sky. From there, the procession entered the upper Saco River, which flowed eastward toward the ocean. John marveled at the sights as they passed: the crystal-clear water, the purple-tufted grasses, the yellow ox-eye daisies, the eroded granite outcroppings, the thirsty coyotes, the black-orange butterflies, and the soaring egrets. How unfortunate he felt to behold such beauty, to behold it with no one else to enjoy it with.

The trip down the Saco stayed uneventful, as the paddlers were aided by the current. They covered many miles before the early afternoon when they put ashore on the north bank. From there, they made another overland portage, this one just five miles, which brought them to the shore of the broad Sebago Lake. They arrived several hours before sunset.

The Indians stopped there and set up camp for the night, lighting their fires and taking time to fish and forage for roots. They speared several bass. The meal was cooked and enjoyed by the Indians. A few scraps were shared with the prisoners.

Friday, August 3, 1694

Hunger had been dominating John's thoughts the past several days. At first on this journey, it hadn't been an issue, since he "fed" off the shock of his cruel circumstances; he'd felt little desire to eat then.

P. GIFFORD LONGLEY

But by the time Lydia was left behind, the pangs in his stomach persistently tortured his body, and there was no relief.

The two Indian villages that they'd passed through had been the only venues for fresh food for the natives, all of whom had eaten heartily there. But the natives had shared only meager morsels with the prisoners each time. On the other days, the trail provisions had been the warrior's rugged fare—roots (called "ground nuts") and dried meat that had been boiled and salted—but these had been too precious to be shared with the hostages. There had been several days when nothing at all had been offered them. Today, apparently, would be one more.

John was glad he'd yet saved the dog's foot. He offered it to Betty when they first awoke, before the camp made ready to resume. But she refused it. They both sat and looked out across the open water toward the rising sun. A second time he extended the morsel to give it to her—this time with insistence.

Betty gently pushed it away, raised her eyes, and spoke softly, "I want you to have it." She smiled at him, felt for the hat at her side, and put it on, pulling the edge of the brim down to cover her face.

Surprised by her brief lucidity, John didn't quite know how to react. She'd seemed so peaceful and normal just then. *Maybe she is going to be coming out of her doldrums*, he thought, and he was glad. He examined the tidbit. It had been in his pocket several days and was very shriveled. It wasn't appetizing at all. The black claws reminded him of Skip's. Yet he was so hungry he could faint.

At last, he raised it to his mouth and chewed tentatively on the foot. But then, at the first taste of it, he devoured it without any sense of satisfaction. Immediately he became haunted by the guilt that he hadn't been more persistent—persistent that his sister consume it.

Soon the Indians broke camp in earnest, and together they set out across Lake Sebago, a wide, round body, five miles diameter. At the far side, they entered a neck between two immense islands and arrived at the outflow of the lake, a steep cataract that cascaded into the Presumpscot River, flowing toward the east. There they portaged down the trail that ran alongside the whitewater and set their canoes into a pool at the base. For the next five miles downriver, they encountered more falls, each of which they bypassed on foot before finally descending to the steadily navigable portion of the course. From there, they wound in a general east-southeast direction for many miles, toward the ocean.

At last, the tributary made one final turn directly east, and the Atlantic came into view, five miles distant. There they turned their canoes north, up a muddy rivulet, paralleling the coast. The waters of this course became steadily shallower, and in just a few miles their vessels began to scrape bottom. Spying a highway along the right bank beside their watercourse, the Indians pulled the canoes up onto dry ground.

They must portage once again.

A sense of urgency that John hadn't seen since the day they first left Groton came over Taxous. He apparently desired to get some miles up the trail before making camp. The loads were hastily placed on the backs of the prisoners. Since just nine remained, each carried a bit more than previously. The added work and quickened pace became grueling.

It remained overcast all afternoon, and as they labored along incessantly, it was difficult to sense what time it was, for the sky wore a thick, gray cover that blotted out the sun's position. They trudged to the point of exhaustion until the light gave way and the trail grew dim. Now needful that they quit, unable to march in the dark, they finally made camp, stopping beside their wooded highway where they laid their burdens down. The prisoners were briskly assembled into a tight group, and their wrists were bound for the first time in many days.

John read wariness on the faces of their guards as he collapsed to the ground next to Shepley. He whispered to his fellow, "Why did they bind our hands?"

Shepley tried to be discreet. "I heard one of them bastards mention 'Fort Loyal,' so I assume we're near the fort."

A guard snapped a glance in their direction, and they quickly grew quiet.

Shepley continued in a hush a moment later. "They must be afraid we'll escape."

John, so dazed with exhaustion, didn't know how to react.

Shepley posed, "We may not get any closer to an English settlement than we are right now. We could make a run for it during the night. What'cha think?"

The thought of escape brought a sense of excitement that John hadn't felt in days. It jolted his stomach, which punished him again. Yes, almost anything other than just continuing on this endless voyage of starvation would have been a good idea. But could they really make it, he and Shepley? *No ... What about Betty?* He couldn't leave without her. Could the three of them make it?

He studied his sister seated to his left. Her head was tilted forward, with her face concealed beneath the hat. Her delicate hands, *so frail*, rested on her knees, reminding him of her weakness, her lack of nourishment. He hadn't seen her eat anything in more than a week. Surely she was as hungry as he was, if not more so. How far could she run before she collapsed? And then, what would happen if they were caught? Surely, they too ... they would get a knock on the head. John gave his considered reply. "I don't know."

"The way I see it," Shepley bemoaned, "there ain't a whole lot to lose."

Darkness soon came over the camp, and the prisoners lay down on the leafy ground. John couldn't help but mull Shepley's proposal as starvation and exhaustion overcame him. Nevertheless he couldn't stop himself from falling asleep.

The arrival of a light rainfall awoke John in the middle of the night. He tilted his head and squinted in the gloom to try and make out the others around him. To his right, Shepley was sleeping soundly. If he was going to make his attempt, perhaps it would be later. To his left, Betty lay quietly on her back. He couldn't tell if she was asleep. He raised his head up and looked down past his feet. There he spied a guard, standing close and staring back at him. John rolled onto his side toward Betty, and placed his face on her shoulder. She reached her bound hands up together and felt for his face, gently stroking his cheek with her fingers. They shivered together in the damp as John fell back asleep.

Saturday, August 4, 1694

The rain had stopped and started many times during the night. When John finally woke in the morning, he was still huddled with Betty. He felt cold and exhausted. Rolling over, he spotted Shepley seated, his head sagging toward the ground in disappointment. His escape simply hadn't materialized. And now it was time for all of them to move north, deeper into enemy territory, farther from the hope of rescue.

The dreary day degraded from there into a blur of discomfort.

As soon as it was light enough to clearly see the trail, they continued their portage. Some groundnuts and water were offered the prisoners. John consumed his meager portion, but hardly felt satisfied. Betty again took nothing. They were to labor together along the gloomy trail, shivering in the cool, steady rain, weak from lack of nourishment and exhausted from their harsh condition. At least their bindings were removed from their hands again.

After about five miles, the rain stopped and the sky grew brighter. It was a good sign to them since they had just come upon a brook that was deep enough to end the crippling portage. They would continue in the canoes once more.

Downstream they paddled for several miles as John lurched forward in his seat and fell unconscious. Ahead, the stream discharged into a larger watercourse, and there they turned against the incessant current, paddling ever farther north through many slow-moving twists and turns. And as the hour grew late, they finally arrived at a slender mountain lake, marking the end of their day's effort. To continue any farther to the north, they would have to portage once more, in the morning.

The band disembarked and made their camp on the shore under the gray overcast, which hadn't departed the entire day. The gentle rain resumed—heavy drops that would not cease. John was chilled to the bone, and his feet were drenched, blistered, squishing in his shoes with each step; he reckoned they probably were white, shriveled, and bleeding. He wished for a warm fire to dry them out. There would be none tonight.

John drew close to Betty again as evening descended. They sat huddled together in the wet grass. Father's hat kept Betty's head dry as big drips fell from the brim.

In the diminishing light, Betty turned to John, raised the brim, and gazed longingly into his eyes. She smiled at ease and spoke after a long quiet in her weakened voice, "I love you, John."

John felt awkward hearing such sweet words from his sister. *Siblings aren't supposed to speak to each other in those terms*, he thought. But he knew what Betty had been through—what they both had been through—and how much they needed each other right now. What other people might have thought didn't matter at that moment. With a gentle smile of encouragement, he responded, "And I...I love you too." He peered several moments at her, being not in the least embarrassed to do so. She was coming out of her melancholy. He could see it.

"Would you tell Lydia that I love her?" she asked.

John nodded to reassure her that he would. But it struck him as an odd question. Maybe Betty hadn't realized that Lydia was no longer there. *She* would have as much chance to speak to their sister as he would—that is, someday, when they all are free.

The young woman shivered in the damp. Her eyes were sinking. John wondered if they spoke of sadness, or just exhaustion. He examined her skin, which was normally so white and delicate. A rash was apparent under her chin and on her neck. He gently took hold of her hands. They...they were shaking. He gingerly turned them over. There was redness on the wrists. *Is it more of the rash*, he wondered, *or just soreness from having been tied the night before? How terribly ill she appears.*

"Are you all right?" he asked with mounting concern.

"I'm tired, John. Very tired … and cold."

"Then, we should rest and keep each other warm."

They both lay down. Betty was on her side, facing away. John rolled over close and placed his arm around his sister. She was shivering hard, almost convulsing. He hugged her more firmly and rubbed her wet arm quickly, hoping that the friction would create some warmth. But she felt too fragile, and he didn't want to bruise her by being too vigorous, so he became gentle. Soon he felt her grow calm and still. They seemed to be warming each other.

Exhausted from the dreadful day, he soon fell into an uneasy slumber.

Sunday, August 5, 1694

In the morning, John peeled open his unrested eyes. He'd rolled onto his back at some point as he slept and now found himself gazing straight up into a brightening sky. The rain had stopped during the night, and the air was much warmer, though he still suffered a chill from his damp clothes. He sat up in the wet grass and turned to his left. Betty was beside him on her side. She lay facing away, eyes closed and very still. *I shouldn't disturb her*, he reasoned. *She needs the rest.*

The camp was roused by the coming light. People got up and made ready to depart. Like the others, John tended to his needs and washed at the lake's edge. He placed his face down to the edge of the still water and studied his reflection, his darkening eyes. He took a long drink. So hungry, he filled his stomach with the liquid, hoping that it would take away the hunger pangs. He was certain there would be no breakfast again. How quickly he was ready.

Taxous soon gave the instruction they were to leave, explaining the good news that this would be the final portage of their journey and that this one was not to be difficult. But John had no idea where they were going, or where they were, for that matter.

The canoes were lifted into position up to the start of the trail, and the prisoners were ordered to don their packs. John bent to pick

P. GIFFORD LONGLEY

his up from the pile as all the others did the same. He looked for Betty but didn't see her standing there among them. He surveyed the camp, up the trail and back down to the water's edge. She was nowhere in sight. Worried, he faced around toward the grassy area where they'd been sleeping. There she was, yet lying on the ground.

The moment he spotted her, Taxous was already approaching the young woman, approaching to see why she hadn't joined with the others. John immediately left his pack and trailed down after the sagamore, nervous, *dreading* that she might be punished.

Taxous stepped close to Betty, bent over, and spoke firmly to her, "We go now. *No more sleep!*"

But Betty didn't respond. She lay there motionless.

Taxous reached down and grabbed her by the shoulder. Pulling her toward himself, he rolled her onto her back. Her arm flopped loose onto the ground. She didn't otherwise stir, lying precisely where he'd moved her.

Just a short distance away from where she lay John stopped in his tracks, anxiously watching the interchange.

Taxous crouched low and gave his order to her a second time. Still there was no response. He reached out and touched her face. Quickly he withdrew his hand from her, wearing a look of surprise. He pushed himself to his feet and turned his face toward John.

The stunned young man kept silent.

Again the sagamore turned back to the body. He bent low and retrieved something from the grass beside her. It was Father's hat.

Taxous straightened and directed his gaze at John again. He studied the boy, watching as anguish filled the young man's face, obviously fearful of the worst. The sagamore stood there a moment, examining the hat and its fine construction. Then without further hesitation, he spoke. "She's dead." He purposefully lifted the hat and placed it on the top of his own head. He took several steps toward John, and as he was much taller, he glared straight down at the boy. "Come, we go now."

John lurched forward as if to pass by the Indian, desiring to confirm the report, refusing to accept it. *No. She's not dead! She's just sleeping.*

But the strong hand of Taxous clutched the boy's shoulder to restrain him as he commanded more forcefully, "Come!"

John tensed his muscles in resistance, refusing to comply, leaning and pressing forward, urgent to pass by, with his welling eyes fixed steadily on Betty's lifeless form. Then feeling the strengthening grip of his tormentor now crushing his shoulder like a vice—like it was choking out his very life—he at last yielded, eased, straightened, and turned; then followed with obedience, stepping closely and quietly in the footsteps of Taxous, his master.

And as John walked up the trail toward the north, led by forces he couldn't control, his whole life flashed through his memory. For every *place*, every *thing*, and every *one* he'd ever known and loved had been swept away—completely; and through it all, he'd never had a chance to say any proper good-bye.

P. GIFFORD LONGLEY

PART TWO:

A New People

PROLOGUE

May, 1694

All eyes were fixed on Taxous as he finished his speech. He turned his back to the council, looking anxiously ahead, gazing expectantly down the empty avenue. He waited, wondering. *What's taking them so long?*

Distracted, he glanced down at the buttons on his new shirt, solid silver, glinting in the sunlight. He smoothed the cotton ruffles on his chest, hypnotized by his pride, the memory of having received the handsome new clothes, the gift from French Governor Villebon, who'd adopted him as brother. He remembered his promise to him, *I go to assemble a large war party, but I will not stop there. I will make up another immediately after and induce Madockawando to join with me… or, I will render him contemptible to all the young Indians!*

The crowd behind him buzzed with interest.

Taxous looked up. They were coming now, marching down the avenue between the lodges, carrying the gifts. He turned back around, smiling broadly as the entire assembly rose to their feet.

His men carried the presents and laid them out for all to see. One by one they kept coming, setting them down at the feet of Taxous. There were barrels of powder, shot, and French guns—the goods necessary for the attacks. The sagamore counted the items as they arrived, each adding to his welling confidence, confidence in his plan. It was actually happening.

But too soon they brought out the last of it. Taxous stared worriedly at his men. *Something is wrong.*

Passahomegett took several steps toward him, holding both palms up, shaking his head. The two leaned toward each other in confidence.

"Where's the rest?" Taxous whispered to his cousin.

"That's all there is."

Taxous struggled to avoid drawing attention to himself, clamping his lips together to choke the angry outcry building in his throat. His chest heaved with the effort. He glared silently at Passahomegett in disbelief.

His cousin shrugged his shoulders and whispered one word. *"Villieu."*

Taxous spun and spotted the Frenchmen conferencing with Bomaseen. And as he kept staring, the Frenchman turned and faced him.

Villieu flushed and swallowed hard. But a sinister grin of impudence slowly bloomed on his face. Villieu was a thief, a greedy trader who'd lusted after the goods for his own business. But he was a thief that had supported Taxous's plan, helping to put it into action. If Taxous were to say anything now against the Frenchman, that would only harm his purpose, for the natives needed little to be dissuaded. They were already suspicious of their allies. No. Taxous wouldn't be able to do anything about the theft. He needed the weasel.

Wenobson stepped forward to be heard as the others sat. "These gifts are long overdue!" He glared at Villieu, pointing. "We have traded many years with the French, and many years we have come up short! If I and my people go to war, it will not be because I have been won over, bought with 'gifts,' by a foreigner." He puffed his chest out and pounded on it with his fist. "If I go to war, it will be because it is best for my people."

Many in the audience wagged their heads, nodding in agreement.

Taxous looked out at the skeptical faces in the crowd. They were a loose coalition at best, each sagamore acting on his own. It was going to be near impossible to unite them. He sensed he was pushing too hard, too fast. They needed time. And as it was already late in the day, and they were weary from the many long discussions, he adjourned the council to resume it the next afternoon. That would give him the morning to meet privately with several. He was very effective one-on-one.

But the next day Madockawando arrived. Craftily, the grand sagamore seized upon the grumbling and disagreement, intent on thwarting the war. He addressed his fellow sagamores, "My brothers. Last summer we met with the English at Pemaquid. We all remember why we were there."

As Madockawando spoke, Taxous bristled at his failure to keep his brother out of the council. Madockawando had, after all, been able to keep *him* out of the Pemaquid peace treaty. Why hadn't he been able to turn the tables—turn the tables with his plan to violate that peace agreement, the impetus to this council?

Madockawando studied the faces of the crowd, young and old. He appealed to the older sagamores, hoping the others might also be swayed. "For years we have been at war with the English. They have disrupted our lives, our trade. No longer can we safely enter our hunting grounds..."

Taxous stewed as he listened. He hated the English and was famous for it. That's why Father Louis-Pierre Thury, a Jesuit missionary, had come to find *him*—right after the Pemaquid peace disaster. Surely, had Taxous been there, there never would have been peace with the English. Now he, *Taxous*, must restore the people to the right path. This was his perfect opportunity to show the people his rightful place as a leader. A sneer lifted one corner of Taxous's mouth as he endured his brother's words.

"...and we know that the English have promised to trade with us at rates far better than the French—French who promised us gifts for this war...and then stole part of them!" Madockawando turned and glared at his brother. *"For that is what Villieu has done!"*

Whispers swept through the audience, sweeping the sneer off of Taxous's face. He stared back at Madockawando, aghast. The clever old man had always had his sources. Sources he used at precisely the right time.

Madockawando turned back to face the crowd. He held his hands up to quiet them. "We must hold to the peace and abide by the laws. *They are not such a burden to us.* And if we do ... if we can just hold the peace longer ... then our brothers will be returned to us."

Many in the crowd rose and applauded. They feared for their brothers held as collateral, imprisoned in Boston: Edgeremett and his brother Ahassombamett; Wenongahewitt, a cousin to Taxous and Madockawando; and Bagatawawongon, alias Sheepscoat John. If they violated the treaty, these men would surely be hanged.

Madockawando's sympathetic plea had been targeted squarely at Taxous's plans. A great stalemate ensued, lasting five days. The older men supported Madockawando's words of peace, tired of war and greedy for English goods. The young warriors supported Taxous, shunning English goods and greedy instead for their blood.

Villieu sat and listened to the ongoing disagreement, perched on the edge of failure, frustrated, and ready to depart. The French captain had been put "in charge" by Governor Villebon—the hopeless task of shepherding the Abenaki, turning them in unison back to the French. Surely if this council failed, then the English could freely range Acadia, unhindered to attack their fragile positions in Naxouat (Nashwaak) and Quebec. He needed this war, and had gone way out on a limb promising success. He was already at odds with Villebon. Failure would ruin him.

Villieu carefully used his time between group sessions. He met privately with as many of the Indians as he could, hoping to sway them with persuasive words, or to compel them by any other means. He longed for some bit of intelligence to use against the peace mongers, some tale that would restore his advantage. Even as he prodded and cajoled he kept his ears open for any bit of information he could twist. He never guessed he would find out something about old Madockawando that would require no twisting, just the plain telling of facts.

The council resumed. Madockawando sat by as the disagreement persisted. If the matter could not be resolved this day, then everyone would leave. The treaty would stand. The old sagamore's shrewdness would have won.

Taxous, conspicuously missing from the council's conclusion, burst on the scene with Villieu right behind him. He came forward, parting the crowd, pumping his powerful arms as he strode, clenching his fists. At the front he raised his hands to get their attention. They sat, stilled by his urgency. "My brothers, we have not been told the whole story."

He turned and scowled at his brother. "Madockawando has not told of his recent meeting at Pemaquid . . . a secret meeting on board ship . . . with the English Governor . . . and none of us were invited!"

Madockawando rose to his feet, shaking his head and raising his hand, for the crowd had begun to stir with conversation. "I have nothing to hide. Governor Phips and I spoke merely of commerce and peaceful trade, for we are already bound by treaty."

"But that treaty doesn't give away our lands!"

Several gasped. The audience leaned forward.

Taxous's face reddened in anger. He gritted his olive teeth as he glared at the crowd. "And that treaty does not give one sagamore the right to promise our land to the English swine, and then to confirm it by burying his hatchet in the ocean . . . where no descendant can find it!"

The assembly erupted. Promising to sell tribal land without their knowledge was a gross insult! Taxous glowered with confidence. He had the crowd right where he wanted them.

After a moment he held his hands up to restore order. He quieted his voice so that they would listen more carefully. "And we must call into question what motivates this *tired* old sagamore. Is he interested in what is good for the people . . . or merely driven by what is good for himself?"

CAPTIVE

Soon after, order was restored and the council reached agreement with Taxous's plan. The details fell quickly into place. They would attack the English plantation of Oyster River, a rich target with light defenses, sitting in close proximity to Maine, making for a fast escape.

On June 7, Taxous, Madockawando, Villieu, and Father Thury, together with the main group of warriors, set off up the Penobscot River, north to Passadumkeag to make their final preparations. Along the way, the band portaged past the whitewater that lay just beneath their destination.

When Villieu set his vessel back into the river above the hazard, it overturned in the swift current. Villieu was pulled downstream and into the cataract. The Frenchman clutched his canoe but dashed against a boulder, striking his head, knocked unconscious.

His lifeless body floated downriver through the turbulence, his broken form tossed against boulders, plunged into whirlpools. Each time he buoyed up, spinning this way and that, churned as so much debris thrust downward by the foam. And all the while the waves took him, the others ran along the shore, watching helplessly. Beneath the rapids the men retrieved the captain, barely alive and senseless. They carried him the rest of the way to Passadumkeag. For five days Villieu clung to life, his body racked with fever.

Madockawando seized the opportunity and assembled the sagamores to speak with them. His first appeal was to the superstitious. "This injury to their Captain Villieu, this is a sign to us from *God* to abandon this attack ... to keep the peace.

"I tell you there is no glory in war, my brothers, this glory that Taxous speaks of. For today, while the French are able to sleep safely in their forts, far away in Quebec and Nashwaak, *we* are the ones, here and now—*the people of our villages*—who are exposed to the English guns."

He reminded them of the disaster at Wells, another attack planned by Taxous, and the utter disruption to their lives ever since the conflict had begun. Yet it had not been a war that he, Madockawando, had at first rejected. Pentagoet, his summer home, had been attacked, his village destroyed, along with the fort under the command of his son-in-law, French Baron Jean-Vincent de St. Castin. Thus he had not been unsympathetic to war with the English. But it had gone on too long and at too high a cost.

He concluded by reminding them, "If we will yet hold this peace a little longer, then we shall have our four brothers restored to us."

Many were persuaded by the leader's careful arguments.

But on June 14, Villieu awoke from his stupor. The Frenchman's remarkable recovery quickly stole substance from the old sagamore's position. Spurred by Taxous, many began to doubt him. Differences of opinion formed a generational rift amongst the leaders. The young sagamores sided with Taxous, including Madockawando's own son, in favor of war. But the old man, Madockawando, and thirty elders remained convinced of peace.

Taxous and Villieu called for a new council to resolve the differences, to draw the entire fighting force back together. But unanimity proved impossible.

At the council's conclusion, a feast was held with dancing and singing, served with the favorite meal of roasted dog. During the festivities, Madockawando and his thirty sat to the side, frowning, watching, refusing to participate.

Spurred by Taxous, several of the boisterous, young warriors taunted their elders, tossing dog bones at them and hurling insults, calling them, "weak cowards."

Villieu grew desperate over the schism. He was out of time. He met privately with Taxous to discuss the problem.

Villieu pleaded, "How can we fight with half an army?" The Frenchman feared the political impact of striking with anything less than the overwhelming support from the entire Abenaki Nation—especially without the highly respected *Grand Sagamore* of the people, Madockawando. There could be no half victory for him.

Taxous stared distrustfully at the Frenchman. He was so close now to marginalizing Madockawando, pushing him aside and out of the way. "We have many warriors who thirst for English blood. And after we have spilt a little, then more Abenaki will come to our side. They will know the rightful path to take. I will show it to them."

"And what will you show them if you fail? They remember Wells."

Taxous turned his eyes away, shivering at the thought. Twice he had promised victory over that settlement, and twice he had failed to deliver, each time departing Wells empty handed. In the second assault they didn't kill a single Englishman, except for a boy he tortured to death, threatening the swine to come out of their garrison and fight like men in the field. But they refused, instead firing upon the natives from their protected positions, wounding many of his Kennebec brothers. That last failure had caused many to question his leadership.

Villieu placed his hand on the sagamore's shoulder and spoke softly. "And if we do go ... with the full might of the *united* Abenaki people ... they will all remember whose plan it was that brought them victory, *for they would all have seen it with their own eyes.*"

Taxous turned his head back. He wanted to shake Villieu's hand off his shoulder, uncomfortable at being touched by him. He measured his face, his lying eyes. But this time they spoke only the truth. A failure of the raid would only show the whole nation that Madockawando had been right. He swallowed hard and spoke. "What do you propose?"

"Neither you nor I can reason with the old sagamore. But there is someone else here who can ... someone who can convince even a shaman."

"Thury?"

Villieu nodded.

Taxous wrestled with himself. *I need neither Madockawando nor his thirty!*

Villieu self-consciously pulled his hand away. "There are some things we must do, if we are to succeed."

Taxous stared down at the ground and exhaled dispassionately. "Then those things must be done." He glanced at the Frenchman, turned and strode quickly away.

P. GIFFORD LONGLEY

Later that day Father Thury approached Madockawando in private. He appealed confidently to the old sagamore, "This resurrection of the Captain is a sign that God is behind us."

Madockawando stared at the missionary. He understood all too well how Taxous had used the Frenchman. Or, had the Frenchman used his brother? Either way, they'd become coconspirators, thirsting for the blood of the English, stopping at nothing to forward their misguided aims, aims that cared little about the life and ways of the Abenaki, their unwitting tools for personal gain.

And Thury had shamelessly used others as well to further his plans. He'd solicited two other missionaries, brothers Jacques and Vincent Bigot, because those men possessed "good reasons" to support the war: the dogma of the Catholic Church. Those religious leaders had traveled throughout the territory, assuring the Abenaki that the gods were on their side—the gods of France—suggesting to the natives that it was their "holy responsibility" to rid the earth of heretics, the English Protestants. They quoted their Bible, lifting passages depicting the people of God as under divine decree to "enter the land of those that follow after false gods, to utterly destroy the heathen, including women and children, to burn the crops and kill the livestock." Thus they'd called the Abenaki to execute the righteous judgment of God, becoming his strong hand, his hand wielding the tomahawk. These had been their words, their perverted dogma, words that supported his brother's plan. That was all that had mattered to Taxous.

But Madockawando was not to be swayed by those words: *Villieu's recovery interpreted as "a resurrection ... a sign from God."* He folded his arms, unconvinced. Though he himself was a shaman, sympathetic to the influence of Providence, he believed neither Thury nor the Bigots. He knew the truth when he heard it. And this wasn't the truth.

The twinkle that had been in Thury's eye when the meeting began faded as he studied the wise old sagamore. He saw that he'd met his match. He would have to take a different approach. He leaned forward confidentially. "There's going to be a war, with or without you. But I tell you this … All the people here, even these rambunctious young men who taunt you now … these are looking to you for leadership. If you will lead this war, they will follow you, as they have for many years. *You* are the leader of this great nation. No one else."

The old sagamore stared wide-eyed at the missionary, shattered. Thury was right, yet in his perverted reasoning, his manipulation, he hadn't understood why Madockawando would have to succumb. True, if Madockawando did lead the war, then he would preserve his own prestige, his power. But it was not pride that moved him, lust for personal glory. *He was a man not much like his brother!* Madocka-wando instead focused on his true motivation: as long as he was in power, his misguided brother wouldn't be. *That* is what would be best for the people, even if this attack cost the lives of the four Abenaki held in Boston. A delay of peace was better than the whole nation's destruction under the guidance of a fool.

Madockawando seethed at the Father, trapped by circumstances over which he had no control. The Abenaki *were* going to war with or without him. A shiver ran down his spine, as he gritted his teeth. "I will join your war."

When the other sagamores heard of Madockawando's "change of heart," they stayed one more day in Passadumkeag to celebrate. They would honor the Grand Sagamore with their respect.

Two weeks later, Taxous's and Madockawando's group joined with Bomaseen's & Warumbee's Kennebecs at the Amir Kangan Rapids along the Presumpscot River, swelling their numbers to two hundred and thirty. They set off from there, following a lengthy inland route, traveling by canoe up and down rivers and streams, portaging past white water, and crossing lakes. The last leg was a three-day march, purposed to surprise the plantation from the west. They arrived at Oyster River, surrounding it just past midnight. It was July 18.

Taxous's plan was launched with deadly success. The Indian troops attacked and killed nearly everyone they saw, men, women, and children. Before sunrise and on into the morning they fought, setting buildings ablaze, destroying crops, and slaughtering live-stock. By afternoon, the killing and pillaging became more difficult as the remaining settlers entrenched themselves in their fortified garrisons. From these protected positions, the English could easily fire upon the Indians as they approached. Finally recognizing that pressing the attacks further would prove too costly, and with little more to gain, the Indians called off the assault.

The count of casualties among the English included more than a hundred scalps and twenty-seven prisoners—taken to be sold as slaves or held for ransom. The natives had been more fortunate, as their dead numbered six, with a mere dozen injured. Father Thury led a mass to thank God for the victory. They held it in the church, the only building in the village they spared from fire.

Three days later, the band arrived at the native village of Pennacook, weary from the fight and march, yet proud in victory. They rested several days before setting off to the north. Madockawando, Thury, Villieu, and the others were going home.

But Taxous, flush with success, appealed to his cousins, Passahomegett and Nodamaguogan, to join him in pressing the war farther south. They assembled fifty warriors thirsty for more scalps and plunder.

They would fall on Groton.

FRUITS OF WAR

Wednesday, August 9, 1694

The raid was nearly over. It had been thirteen days since leaving Groton in the canoes, traversing north and east over land and water. Many of the men would be returning to their homes today. Taxous and his warriors hadn't seen their families or villages for three months since they'd left for Nashwaak to appear before Joseph Robineau de Villebon, the French Governor of Acadia, where Taxous was recognized as the rightful leader of this great raid. At last, all of Taxous's plans were working themselves out to his satisfaction, and soon, when he was back among his people, he would be feeling their admiration. Admiration he was certain he deserved for the glory he had brought to the Kennebec and Penobscot.

He had accomplished his first step toward correcting a lifetime of trouble—trouble created by Madockawando, his illegitimate "brother"—trouble that had to be fixed. He remembered yet again, for he could not put it from his mind, the single event that had seized control of his young life and ruined it, sending it careening down the wrong path.

It had been late autumn in 1670, and Assiminasqua, the Grand Sagamore of the Penobscot Indians, lay dying in his lodge. He had summoned his two sons, Madockawando and Taxous, to attend at his bedside that he might bless them both.

The brothers came quickly to their father's village, Norridgewock, arriving in the chill of early evening. Several women sat outside the Grand Sagamore's lodge, weeping, sensing the end was near. The old man had been in and out of consciousness for several days.

Madockawando and Taxous lifted the door flap and entered the lodge, a longhouse. The smoky interior was dimly lit by the campfire in the center pit and stale with the stench of sickness. A village woman sat there tending the flames, striving to keep the air uncomfortably warm, as the old man seemed to be suffering from the raw temperature. The brothers acknowledged her presence as they removed their capes and set them to the side.

Quietly they stepped past the fire toward their father, who lay at the rear of the vault on a bed of animal skins. The old man was covered with blankets, sleeping, but not restfully. He was a shocking sight to them—not what they remembered—and one they weren't prepared for.

Assiminasqua, a man of great strength and stature in his days as a leader, had become frail and gaunt, with his thin matt of hair having gone completely white. His once-strong eyes had receded into dark sockets. One arm was exposed from beneath the blankets. It was *so* withered, emblematic of his great weight loss. The restless ancient shivered and shook as though cold, yet beaded with sweat, his breathing labored and uneven.

The brothers anxiously knelt, one to each side, shoulders slumped, eyes downward, tongues silent.

Madockawando looked at Father, turned across toward Taxous, then hesitated. Summoning his courage he placed his hand upon the old man's shoulder and was the first to speak. "Father...Father, we've come...I'm here now, with Taxous."

Taxous joined in, whispering, "Yes, Father. We're here for you."

P. GIFFORD LONGLEY

The sleeper stirred. His breathing steadied, and a smile formed on his lips. The hoary man angled his head to the side and squinted at Madockawando, then slowly turned his eyes toward Taxous. He extended his shaking arm and took hold of his younger son's hand. He addressed them in a feeble voice. "I was having a vision."

Taxous asked, "Can you tell us, Father? About it ... the vision?"

Too parched to speak, the elder vainly attempted to moisten his lips with his tongue. The brothers gingerly raised his feeble frame, helped him to a drink, then gently laid him back down.

Regaining his breath, Father described his vision. "I imagined a great bird, an eagle, soaring in the heavens, and I called to it and asked it to tell me its name. It told me, 'Psonen,' and then it flew away. And as it flew far off toward Mount Katahdin, a *great* storm started, and it was snowing very hard and would not stop for a long time. Then I found myself standing in very deep snow—so deep that I could not move my arms or legs. And I was very cold. So I closed my eyes and fell asleep. But I ... then I heard someone call for me, and I woke up. And you were here."

Taxous responded, "Yes, it was us calling. And we are here now to see you."

Assiminasqua became more alert and tilted his head, squinting his eyes. He looked about the lodge to reorient himself. "But it is not snowing *in here* ... and I am so *stinking* hot!" He thrust his blankets to his side, exposing his skeletal chest, and sighed. "There. Now, that is *much* better." Raising his head, he spied the woman by the fire, wrinkled his brow, and crabbed at her through toothless gums, "Woman! Could you cool that fire down and get some air in here? I think I will *die* if I cannot get some air!"

The woman immediately arose and tied the front door flap open, then walked across the lodge and did the same for the back. A cool evening breeze crossed through and freshened the interior.

The elder faced Madockawando and rejoined his feeble tone. "I would like to sit up, but I am afraid I will need some help, my son." Madockawando gently lifted the frail body as Taxous made a prop of blankets. They laid Father back down, and he relaxed with improved comfort.

"I have something for you both," Father muttered as he reached in among his many blankets and finally pulled up a long deerskin bag. His fingers trembled as he struggled to untie its top, to no avail. Turning to Taxous, he asked for help. The young man untangled the cord for him and then sat back on his haunches, holding his shoulders straight and keeping his eyes focused to see what was in store for him.

The old sagamore stretched his hand down inside the bag and fumbled amongst the hidden contents, clutching at last what he wanted. He strained as he pulled forth a long ceremonial belt, ornately woven of wampum beads. Both men immediately recognized the sacred tribal belt of the Kennebec.

Assiminasqua began, "Because I go away and soon will sleep with my fathers, I want to pass along these things. You are both men of strength and will be the guardians of my people, of our great nation created by our god, Gluskabe."

Madockawando and Taxous continued to kneel silently at attention.

Father cleared his throat and turned his quivering head to face his younger son. "Taxous, you are flesh of my flesh and blood of my blood, and I give to you, my son, this belt of the Kennebec people, my people from my birth. I give this to *you* as a testimony to the Kennebec that you are their rightful sagamore. I trust and hope that you will grow in wisdom of *mind* that matches your great strength of body, so that you may lead my people." He paused to clear his throat, took a deep breath, and furled his brow. "But as I give this to you, you must understand that I am afraid that the wolf, Malsum … that he is lurking near to you to *tempt you* with his beauty and cunning." Father smiled again, stretched his arm out, and firmly squeezed the young man's hand. "And you must learn to think and act with a kind heart, and not so much with your pride."

Taxous respectfully took the belt and carefully draped it across his knees. He silently admired its beautiful patterns. Now it was his.

P. GIFFORD LONGLEY

Assiminasqua paused to regain his breath. He reached back into the bag and pulled out a second belt. He turned toward his adopted son and continued his rehearsed lines. "Madockawando, you are the son of my youth and have always been a delight to my eyes. After I found you as a boy, I raised you as though you were my own flesh and blood. You went with me to many places, and I saw you grow into a great warrior of my people—very strong, but also very wise. Because you have become a part of my family by adoption, I cannot forget you, my son, and I give to you this belt of my adopted people, the mighty Penobscot Nation. I give this to *you* as testimony to the Penobscot that you are their rightful sagamore." Smiling proudly, his head quaking as a sparkle came to his eye, he reached over and squeezed Madockawando's arm. "I trust that you will continue to lead them in all the ways of wisdom you have already shown."

Madockawando took the belt and laid it across his knees without looking at it. Tears, a sign of his weakness, were welling in his eyes. His shoulders slumped with sadness as he kept his focus on the old man's face.

Assiminasqua labored to reach once more down inside the bag. Groping in its bottom, he found the object he wanted. Taxous bit his lip nervously. His eyes widened as Father drew forth the ornate pouch made of black fabric stitched with colorful wampum beads— the pouch of a shaman, the great spiritual tribal leader.

The tired relic heaved a sigh, then lifted his gaze back toward his adopted son and continued with the rest of his speech. "Madocka-wando, my son, you have shown to me your insight into a great many things, and I do believe that you understand the ways of our people, as well as those of the white man. But you have always thought about the important things of our people first. Many years ago, the great Gluskabe went away when the English and French came among us, and many of us grew sick and died. And now I fear that more of these white people are coming here every day, such that they stand as a great threat to our nation. So I give to you these things and declare that these shall be a testimony that *you* shall be a shaman and the *Grand Sagamore* to all of the Kennebec and Penobscot Nation."

Madockawando took the pouch, opened it, and pulled out the shaman's rattle to examine it. He lifted his gaze across to Taxous as his own brow wrinkled with surprise. Turning to the old man, he insisted, "But Father, this is *too* much. I do not deserve—"

Assiminasqua placed his tremulous hand on Madockawando's and interrupted him. "I have given this to you because I knew you would say 'it is too much.' I tell you that any man that grabs at the right to rule and is not humble, as you are now, cannot lead these great peoples."

Silence fell over the lodge as the old man took several dissatisfying breaths, exhausted from the interchange. He sagged back into his blankets, dropped his chin, and closed his eyes. Madockawando leaned forward, kissed his elder on his forehead, and whispered, "I love you."

Taxous glanced across at Madockawando with anguished eyes. *He does not deserve such an honor! How could a foreigner, a Maliseet, be Grand Sagamore and shaman of my father's people... and not his own flesh and blood?* But seizing control of his emotions, Taxous also bent and kissed the old man, forcing out wooden words, "Thank you, Father. I hope I will not disappoint you."

Assiminasqua's breathing became increasingly labored and shallow. In a few moments, he breathed his last. A sudden stiff breeze swept through the open door and snuffed out the tiny flame that flickered in the fire pit. A second later it reignited. Assiminasqua was dead.

The next morning, the village awoke to find a thin dusting of snow on the earth scoured about by a bitter wind. High in the sky above, a majestic eagle soared toward Mount Katahdin and to an uncertain future.

Taxous had heard all the blessings from Assiminasqua that day, not just those for Madockawando. His time would come to be properly recognized; he would show them he was worthy. *For there is no pride in truth and fact—only in real accomplishment.*

P. GIFFORD LONGLEY

So now, Taxous and his band were just a few miles from home—mere miles until that wrong, at last, would be set right.

And if there was to be any regret to the whole invasion, now—thirteen days since Groton—it would be the loss of his two Kennebec cousins. *But those men had been brave, and they shall be remembered as such.* He would see to it that they were properly honored. Yet, despite these losses, he anticipated the adulation from his people. *They will recognize my essential role in planning, leading, and executing the raid—all of it.* And there were the spoils, the stolen goods—and the hostages. The ten to twenty pounds a head would indeed make him a wealthy man.

Now rounding the last bend in the Kennebec River, before seeing Norridgewock and his Kennebec people, Taxous sat tall in his canoe, recounting the hostages, recounting the bundles of booty, and rehearsing over and over again what he would say to his people and how it should be said.

Going North

October 1694

Lydia understood that the key to surviving her captivity was, first and foremost, in maintaining a healthy mind-set. Granted, she was now at the bottom of her new society—a slave, entitled to nothing—and thoroughly devoid of control over her circumstances, a stark contrast to her prior station as a member of the upper-middle class. Yet, even in her new low estate, there *were* things only she could control—namely, her *attitude* and her *hope*, which would work together to hold her up.

Her attitude, despite her mean circumstances, would influence how she was to be treated each day. A positive one would soften the hearts of her captors, or so she intended, through the testing of her parents' teaching to "do unto" the Indians as she would have them "do unto" her.

Her other buttress—hope—was the root that she would draw upon for nourishment to face each and every day. *Hope* that she would be treated with kindness, *hope* that she might somehow be ransomed, and *hope* that she would see her brother and sister again. She dared not lose her hope in her future and her purpose, fearing the inevitable fall into depression that would quickly drag her life to a dreadful and irrelevant end. She just had to survive, somehow, until she was redeemed. Then she could go back to her home.

Since the departure of July, when Lydia had been sold to the Pennacook sagamore, a uniform daily routine had emerged for her in the tiny native village. Within a surprisingly short period of time, she had lost all sense of which day of the week it was, as each seemed so much like the rest. There were chores to do every morning, afternoon, and evening, and she was required to serve, otherwise she would not be fed—or be subjected to worse treatment, even violence. Taking no chances, she guarded herself against bitterness and cooperated without hesitation, occasionally even forcing a smile.

Her work had not been so difficult or unfamiliar, being tasked with helping to prepare the food for her master's family together with laboring in the fields to harvest the beans and squash. She could do those chores easily enough, as they were much like working the farm at home. It was the comforts that she dearly missed: English food, her bed, time to read, being able to change her clothes, to privately wash and keep herself clean without fear of being exposed, and, particularly, to do any of these whenever she desired. But beyond the tasks and "things" of life, most of all she yearned for the opportunity to socialize and to care for someone. Alas, none of the natives desired to visit with her or cared what she thought; and there were none she could fully understand even if they had. Surrounded by so many people, all of them strangers, she'd never felt so alone.

Realizing the harm that came from her isolation, Lydia made every effort to quickly learn the native tongue. Whenever her captors would speak, she paid careful attention. Yet in her position, she could only listen, bite her tongue, and mostly act to avoid drawing attention to herself or testing their patience. This made for few chances to ask the sorts of questions that would improve her learning. Yet on occasion, Waguala would give her new tasks, and such moments of interaction proved to be the safest to inquire and to understand better, taking full advantage of the old woman's extraordinary patience. It was through this interplay that Lydia had been able to reveal her aptitude for sewing. Soon after she was put to work

P. GIFFORD LONGLEY

repairing and making shirts and dresses for Wonalancet's daughter, Magoua, and her family.

The sagamore's daughter was at first friendly with Lydia, having proudly introduced her five children, who needed to be outfitted; they ranged in age from toddler to adolescent. The young ages of the children made it apparent that Magoua was still a comparatively young woman herself, though the squaw's face suggested she was as much as twenty years older than she appeared, considering how the harsh outdoors had prematurely aged her skin, leathering her cheeks. And though a woman's smile would normally enhance one's face, Magoua's had the opposite effect. Her teeth were a hideous brown from her habit of chewing tobacco and sucking her pipe. Yet Lydia refused to act put off by the woman's appearance, as she found a little extra meaning each day in spending time with the squaw and her family. This gave her a sense of belonging.

But that which had begun as a positive relationship for Lydia soured after Magoua received her needed clothing. The squaw quickly determined she was finished with the English slave and wanted nothing more to do with her—to put her away, as it were, to rid herself of a new problem that was emerging in her household. For her husband, Skok, who often stared at Lydia, had become captivated by her appearance—her tender white skin and intriguing figure, as he imagined it somewhere beneath her modest skirt.

To Lydia, just being near Skok felt awkward and uncomfortable. He never did look her in the eye. She would often turn and spy his gaze intensely focused on her feminine form. And then, when he saw her face, he would nervously redirect his eyes. His sweaty, shifty looks set her ill at ease and eventually became the substance that drove Magoua, who well understood her man, to action. The squaw's jealousy became a cancer, which caused her to speak falsely about the English slave to others in the village, accusing her of seduction. This turned Wonalancet and Waguala against her, making it impossible for Lydia to form even one friendship and driving the slave into a worsening isolation. But her problems would not end there with just a stare or simple allegation.

One morning Lydia went to the river to wash privately. It was her time of the month, and she simply had to tend to her personal needs. She found a spot amongst the reeds that seemed to her to be secluded and there removed her outer dress. She reached down and tore a strip of fabric from the fringe of her chemise to use as a washcloth and then raised the hem to her knees and stepped ankle deep out into the water. There she bent and used the rag to clean herself as discreetly as she could. But the awkward bathing was ineffectual as she still felt unclean. At last her modesty yielded to her circumstance. She looked all around, and seeing no one, raised her skirt above her waist and stepped farther out into the stream to dip herself. But in that brief moment of exposure, she heard a sudden stirring behind her on the bank. She was certain someone had seen her.

Instinctively, she let go of the skirt to cover herself, letting it fall into the stream. She spun her head and looked back toward the shore, staring at the tall grasses on the riverbank, trying to locate the peeping eyes. The greenery stirred again and she called out, "Who's there?"

Just two rods distant, a man's head rose up sheepishly from amidst the grasses. He stood to his feet. It was Skok. He remained there, silent, staring, breathing heavily. And despite the cool morning air, he was glistening with sweat. He reached forward and parted the growth and stepped downward toward the water's edge, cutting in half the distance that had separated them. Then with one hand, he reached up and menacingly clutched at his knife sheath, dangling from his neck. With the other hand he motioned anxiously, demanding that she come to him.

Lydia stayed still and wondered. *What shall I do? If I cry out, who will help me? If I try to run, I will surely be caught and punished or become a source of sport… and probably be beaten and put to death. If I resist him, the big man will surely overpower me. He shall torture me, have his way, then slice and stab me.*

She measured his face. His eyes were focused on her bodice again. His chest heaved with excitement. But then he deliberately lifted his eyes and fixed them on her troubled face, not turning away as he had before. He was intent this time, and she could sense it. Yet she refused to move.

Skok grew impatient, and his face began to curl athirst. He reached both hands up and drew his knife slowly from its sheath, licking and biting his lips, feigning his intent to use his weapon, threatening her. The sharp edge of the blade glinted in the sparkling wet reflections. Again he motioned for her to approach, this time more forcefully.

Lydia had to think fast. She agonized. *This snake will rob me of my innocence. The one and only thing I yet retain.* She knew she must move, but her legs seemed stuck to the river bottom, her bare feet set, sunken amidst the smooth and slimy pebbles.

Again she measured the eyes of her assailant—black eyes that revealed his commitment to ravishing her, absent of desire to know who she was or to care for her, filled only with frustrated physical desire. She studied his bare chest and imagined its full weight lying on top of her and the evil heart within it, pulsing and pounding. Then she panned her eyes downward past his waist to his legs, seeing his powerful thighs tensed and strong, ready to chase forward after her if she did not comply.

She sensed his anxious rage building higher and higher as he awaited her, making himself ready to crush the delicate flower of her hope. He raised his knife and purposefully twisted and turned it in his tense fingertips. There seemed to be no escape. She could delay no longer.

Her body moved, but not by her own control. Slowly one foot raised and then dropped forward in front of her, first one step, then the next. Her yielding caused her heart to race. She was giving herself to the beast and couldn't believe it. She began to quiver and shake, to lose feeling in her hands and feet, trembling and tingling; they were no longer hers. Her head was spinning, her stomach plunging. *Dear Jesus, save me!*

As she drew up close to him by the bank and near faint with dread, she felt an uncontrollable release—wet warmth flowing down her legs. She stopped and tilted her eyes downward past the bottom of her skirt, staring at her ankles. She watched as her flow descended and dripped into the gentle current, the distinctive color of blood. She gasped in horrific embarrassment and quickly looked up wide-eyed at the violator.

He'd seen it too. His face turned suddenly pale and peaked. Skok stared into Lydia's eyes as he lowered his weapon.

She made no further move and did not speak. She just stared resolutely into his sickening face, unflinching, yet waiting to be taken by him.

But the gaze into her innocence proved too much for Skok. He spun away and took several quick steps, climbing back up the bank. He stopped and turned round, thinking that he might not leave. Just as before, he couldn't look Lydia in the eyes. At last, he spoke downward to the ground in his broken English, "I not go away." Then he strode up the bank and left her at peace.

Lydia stood alone, flush and quaking. She breathed deep and shook herself and then stared back down at her feet as they were washed in the crimson current. She knew she'd been saved by the blood.

As she pondered her momentary escape, she suddenly loathed her beauty—the source of Skok's interest. She realized she could never be alone again. She must become like a common, ugly beetle, blending with the dung. And she must draw ever closer to her source of vexation, the jealous Magoua, setting aside any animosity she had for the squaw, whose relentless and watchful eyes would keep her snake of a man from fulfilling his secret desire. She must retreat within herself and patiently await her redeemer.

September had brought new activities, with the focus on bringing in the corn crop. The women, children, and old men all labored together in the harvest, as this essential task would serve to feed the tribe for the next year. The corn was removed from the dried stalks and laid out on grass mats for drying. Some of the kernels were then sheared from the cob and put into sacks, ready for the winter. And since the Indians had no cribs or barns like their English counterparts, the balance of the crop was secreted into pits that they dug into the earth to protect the grain from animals, and to preserve the seed for planting in the next year. Acre upon acre was thus harvested in earnest to forestall the damage that would surely have come with the autumn rains and frost. And as the September days grew shorter, the last great task in this, their summer home, was nearly complete.

At the end of the harvest, the men of the village set up in the center of their camp an arbor made of pine branches. Beneath the arbor, they placed a drum, and the spirit leader and elders sat in this small shelter and beat out songs for several days to celebrate the yield. At night, there was singing, dancing, and feasting.

Lydia became a silent witness to these festivities, unable to understand it all, save for a few scattered words, yet cognizant of the apparent spiritual significance this ceremony held for her captors. And though she kept to the fringes, always hovering within sight of Magoua and beyond the sweaty clutches of Skok, she, like the rest, became a benefactor of the good will from the harvest, enjoying the all-too-brief bounty.

The coming of the first frost brought change for the Pennacook and meant the end of their southern season. October was the time to gather their goods and to head north to their winter home.

The task of moving the village involved everyone, young and old, male and female, hunter, warrior, worker, and slave. Their summer lodges would be left to stand through the cold season, but whatever goods they contained must either be taken with them or secretly buried. Their means to transport all these goods, food supplies, and people would be their canoes, and their highway would be the river. So with the celebrations over and the stashing and packing complete, three dozen canoes, some nearly twenty-foot long, were at last fully laden and readied for the migration.

On the morning of their departure, Lydia found herself seated in a canoe with Waguala and two young warriors who paddled fore and aft. They pushed off from the shore amidst the flotilla and drifted

CAPTIVE

downstream a short ways to the confluence with the Merrimac, where they turned north, upriver.

The three-hundred-mile trip to the winter home of the Pennacook took a month, fighting against the current, portaging rapids, and ascending into the foothills of the mountains under bleak skies as the first snows began to fall. At the midpoint of their migration came their most exhausting trek, as they carried their supplies and vessels through the mountain passes until they found, on the far side, a northward flowing stream.

Their return to traveling by canoe came none too soon for Lydia. She'd been feeling weakened from lack of food and from carrying her heavy burden, and her feet were wet and cold from the snow. It seemed there were never enough provisions to go around, and she was only offered leftovers, the meanest portions. By this time she was losing her desire to eat, as she daily contested with a bug that was giving her fits, gnawing at her stomach. At least there was always a crowd around her, which eased her trepidation at the persistent presence of Skok. She hardly slept amidst the constant dread of him.

With their vessels launched back into the water, the balance of their journey became easy for her, floating with the watercourse ever northward, down from the frozen mountains, traversing the lakes across the vast, untamed flatlands, and finally discharging into a wide estuary several miles below their destination: the French and Indian village of St. Marie.

November 1694

Situated on a large island at the confluence of the St. Lawrence and Ottawa Rivers, Ville St. Marie was far more developed than Lydia had expected. The Indian settlement was positioned at the base of the tallest hill on the island, Mount Royal, which rose up a mile inland from the western bank of the St. Lawrence River. Several hundred natives made this their home, but most surprising to Lydia

P. GIFFORD LONGLEY

was the sight of European-style dwellings in the larger community that yet lay beyond the teepees and the lodges.

More than a thousand French settlers had made this their home and place of trade. And though the smoke rising from the chimneys of the stone and frame dwellings reminded her of New England, Lydia was hardly at ease. This was, after all, enemy territory, as her mother country, England, had been at war with France for six years.

The Pennacook shared their winter home there in Ville St. Marie with the Cowasuck, another Abenaki tribe, and the village bustled with their combined activity, with many natives seeing old acquaintances and entering into friendly conversation. Though this created a sense of excitement, Lydia benefited not in the least, being as yet isolated from their discourse as a social scourge. To make matters worse for the young woman, the gnawing in her gut had developed into a serious illness, robbing her strength and giving her chills. There was no doubt she'd lost many pounds and was feeling now but little strength to stand firm, to brace her delicate frame, so easily shaken and tossed by the stiff and bitter November winds.

Her first night's sleep back in her master's lodge, and being safe from the stares of Skok, was clearly welcome, but it did not yield the remedy she'd hoped for. From evening until dawn, she tossed and turned, sought and failed to find a comfortable position to rest. Her throat was sore, and her stomach disagreeably churned all the while, and this kept her awake. The morning brought no improvement, and too quickly the ever-present demands of her chores were there to greet her. Fearful of punishment, she forced herself to persist with her labor.

By early afternoon, Lydia was summoned to return to the lodge, but for what she didn't know. Feeling faint, she fashioned a fantasy, desperately longing for rest, to simply be permitted to curl up on her bedding to sleep, perhaps under the watchful eyes of Waguala. Yet deep down she couldn't imagine that such kindness would ever be extended to her.

Upon entry to the lodge, she found Wonalancet speaking there with a stranger, with both men seated by the fire. And from their language, which she couldn't comprehend, and his appearance, she surmised that the visitor was a Frenchman.

"*Mademoiselle*," the stranger spoke in a lively tone toward Lydia as he rose to his feet and bowed low toward her. As he did this, he waved his hand in a slow sweeping motion across his front. It was a cordial greeting indeed and thoroughly unexpected.

Lydia had an immediate aversion to the presence of the man, for in her mind she dismissed him as a representative of the "enemy." She felt unable to speak, yet she stared at him, lured by his odd and foreign appearance.

He was an elderly man, a gentleman. His garments were expertly tailored and arranged just so, though not in any style of dress that Lydia had seen before. The man's silver hair was *large*, rather like a mane, being parted in the center, poofed high into the air, and then falling with generous wavy curls that flowed down onto both shoulders. His coat, rather shaped like a humorous, conical dress that extended to the knees, seemed well suited to the cold climate, it being stitched of heavy linen, dyed black, and fitted with animal furs of red fox, which made a soft, well-insulated lining. This fur extended out from the ends of both sleeves, surrounded the hem at the bottom, and ran up the center of the front all the way to the top, where the collar was covered by a shiny and over-large, peach-colored, satin bow tucked tightly beneath his clean-shaven chin.

Below the knees, his legs were warmed by black, skin-tight woolen stockings, which stretched down to his perfectly polished pointy-toed boots. His hands were clad in black, leather gloves. In one he held a fine, walnut walking stick, and in the other, which had another bit of the peach-colored ribbon tied to the wrist, he held his hat, most unusually shaped—three corners, made of fine, black felt with a lush, curly, white feather affixed to the front.

Lydia remained silent, continuing to study the odd-looking man. Her swirling stomach made her vision spin.

The stranger straightened and walked over close to Lydia as he eyed her up and down. She knew she wasn't much of a sight to him at that moment. It had been more than a month since she'd bathed and longer still since she'd combed her hair. Furthermore, the animal skin that she wore over her dress for warmth was hardly attractive, having little more than randomly ragged holes for her arms and head, and itself being stained and filthy from her chores. And by now, her shoes, which had become well worn, were caked with mud from her labor, as was the hem of her dress, having been dragged about upon the ground.

She was feeling worse by the minute, severely ill, so she couldn't even force herself to smile—this despite knowing all too well that in the presence of her enemy it would be in her best interests to do so. Instead, she lowered her gaze to the ground, imagining only how pale and gaunt her countenance was, and dreading that her eyes had become sunken, dark, and sad.

The stranger turned back to Wonalancet and resumed his conversation. And though Lydia couldn't interpret what they were saying, it appeared to her as though they were engaged in some sort of transaction and that it was rapidly drawing to conclusion. She lifted her eyes toward the old Indian and wrinkled her brow in confusion.

"I sold you to this man," explained the sagamore in Abenaki, in a straight-faced, business-like tone. "You shall go with him now." He showed no sense of loss from the deal. Her departure meant to him no sadness. She might as well have never existed, she sensed, for all the trouble she'd brought to his daughter. For such, it appeared, had simply determined the end of her stay.

Though Lydia understood the message, the shock of yet another change alarmed her. She'd just begun to understand the ways of the Pennacook and learned to survive their daily routine. And now she would become the property of another enemy—an unknown one at that. How she might be treated worse filled her mind with a new sense of panic.

The Frenchman looked at her and removed his right glove and then extended his white and delicate hand toward the young English woman. A smile formed on his lips, accentuated by his curling mustache. He peered into her eyes and waited patiently for her to place her hand into his open palm. In that moment, his deep, brown eyes didn't cause her any fear, for they spoke only kindness. And so, as though her wrist had been lifted by someone else, like the strings of a marionette, she delicately placed her filthy, rough hand into his.

The Frenchman gently squeezed it and then turned to Wonalancet and bid him, "*Adieu.*" He ducked through the opening of the lodge and gently dragged the young woman along.

The two walked together between the lodges toward the southwest, down the path that led out of the Indian village and in the direction of the French establishment. And as they passed the last lodge, they advanced toward a carriage, a closed coach that had been parked there beside of the road. A dashingly clad coachman was standing by it tending to the horses—two strong, black Arabians.

As they approached, the coachman stopped his dressing of the animals, turned and opened the door of the coach, doffed his feathered hat, and bowed low. He said, "*Monsieur,*" as he looked at the man, and then, "*et Mademoiselle,*" as he eyed Lydia.

The French nobleman replied, "*Merci.*" Then letting go of Lydia's hand, he stepped up into the coach and sat down. He looked out through the open door and motioned for her to join him in the carriage.

Lydia's head was spinning, and she was weak and faint, flush from the nauseated feeling that was brewing in her stomach. She paused a moment and stared at the carriage. She'd never seen a conveyance so fine as this in all her days, even on her trips to Boston. The coach was black as coal yet polished to shine so bright that she could see her own reflection in it. And what she saw was horrible. Her appearance was squalid and feeble, her face skeletal from malnourishment, a shocking contrast to the stately and perfectly clean carriage. Even the horses looked finer than she did, with their hairs so shiny, stroked and combed in place, and with their harnesses buffed and exquisitely fitted.

"*Entre vous,*" the Frenchman patiently bid her from his seat, motioning kindly again for her to enter.

Lydia raised her hem and lifted her foot to place it up on the first step. But feeling woozy, she faltered, tilted back, and was about to tumble.

P. GIFFORD LONGLEY

Quickly the coachman grabbed her arm and firmly braced her. Then with his gentle support, she climbed up and entered. She studied his concerned expression as she passed him. She hadn't seen sympathy in many months.

Lydia sat back on the fine, satin cushion, immediately adjacent to the gentleman. She felt disquieted in knowing she was soiling the seat just by resting there upon it, and greatly worried how her odor must be offensive to him—for he had taken a perfumed kerchief from his pocket and was holding it to his nose. She hadn't experienced that feeling in a while: *embarrassment.* She looked up at the Frenchman and wanted to apologize for making a mess of his fine carriage. And though she couldn't possibly know what words to speak that might express her regret, she sensed that he already knew what she was thinking. He removed the kerchief, nodded at her, and motioned with his hand, somehow gently communicating his thoughts, *It's only a cushion. We can always cleanse it.*

The coachman climbed up to the driver's box, and with his whip, he gently prodded the animals to draw the carriage forward and onto the road. The black wheels spun down the grass and dirt track in the direction of the French settlement, the ride of the coach being cushioned by springs as it passed along the many ruts, smoothing out a wealthy man's ride. After about a mile, passing through the closely developed quarters of the trading district, the road led them away from the village and toward the open pastures beyond.

Peering from her window through the misty afternoon, Lydia watched as they neared a proud villa—a prominent manse that was set off by itself, well back from the road, with its faint outline visible like an apparition through the gloomy gray. The carriage conveyed them toward the entry to the estate, flanked both sides by stone piers—limestone, ground smooth, finely finished, hand-chiseled with a crest, a prancing horse and shield, and the letters *"LB"* upon the front face.

The carriage drove straight up to the gate and then passed through and onto a path made of cobblestones; the metal shoes of the horses made their loud *clip-clops* as they strode along an avenue, which was lined with sugar maples evenly spaced astride the way. Ahead, at the end of the drive, lay before them a court, wide across the front, establishing the face of the manor, and enclosed on the two sides by other buildings—barns or servants quarters, she presumed.

Straight ahead stood the mansion, two stories tall and constructed of the same limestone that had been used at the gate, beset with carved trim that formed pediments, decorative triangles above each window, and with horizontal rows of string courses and an ornate cornice that trimmed the roofline as it wrapped all around the building. Across the symmetric front were tall windows at each side on both of the levels and a large, grand entrance at the center with a portico supported by columns. Lydia had never seen a church, or even a public building in Boston, as fine as this, and she was in awe as they approached. In her dizziness, she wondered if her vision was but a figment of her imagination.

The coachman pulled the horses to a stop in the midst of the court, with Lydia's side of the carriage facing straight at the front of the villa. As she looked up and studied the windows, her eye caught a movement in one on the second storey. A drape pulled back. There stood a woman clad in a white robe, gazing down. Her face and eyes were calm and curious as she observed their arrival.

The coachman clambered down from his perch and opened the carriage door, extending his hand, waiting for Lydia to climb out and down. The young English woman reached out to him, weak and shaking. She nearly stumbled as she made her way out and then stood to the side, waiting while the gentleman disembarked.

Lydia stared up at the woman, yet transfixed there in the second-storey window, still looking down and studying her, watching. But being back upon her feet again must have been too much of a shock for Lydia. She became faint, and her stomach now was overly bothersome and swirling. Her head was spinning. And in the pensive uncertainty of the strange new surroundings, while having no more strength to control her body, she crumpled to the pavement, unconscious, sweated full with fever.

P. GIFFORD LONGLEY

The Frenchman cried out to his servants, who ran from the house and carried the frail, ill stranger inside.

Lydia awoke disoriented by her unfamiliar, yet magnificent, surroundings. Above her eyes was a fine, pure, white ceiling of plaster, perfectly illumined by the peaceful light of the morning. Her hands touched the smooth silk of a sheet. It seemed she was lying upon her back in a bed with warm covers over her body, and her head was sunken into a soft bolster.

She reached up to touch her face. Her skin felt smooth and clean, and her hair, which had been laid out to either side, was soft and combed. She stared down toward her feet, at her bed, which was white and clean. Beyond her feet she saw the bright walls of the room, patterned with faint, white flowers and curling stalks, delicately painted from corner to corner. A fireplace dominated the facing wall, with its marble supports and mantle framing a crackling fire; its glowing heat made the air of the room most fragrant and pleasant.

Tilting her head to her left, she admired the tall window, which extended from the floor to the ceiling, perhaps twelve feet high. The white muttons held large panes of glass, which colored, shaped, and refracted the northern light and the view beyond—past a court of cobblestones and up a long drive lined by young maples, the branches of which tenuously held onto the last few golden leaves of autumn.

Turning her head back and to her right, Lydia discovered she was not alone in the room. A woman was there in the corner, kneeling with her profile to her and situated before a pink, satin chair. She wore a white, linen robe with a shawl that concealed the side of her face, her head tilted forward. Her elbows rested upon the cushion, and her hands were clasped together. The woman was praying.

Suddenly insecure, Lydia instinctively pulled both her arms beneath her bedding, hiding under the covers. Reaching in, she felt her clothing on her stomach, which was embroidered and lacy. Curious, she lifted the bedding a few inches to look beneath. She was wearing a different garment, not her own dress. It was a beautiful hand-stitched nightgown—pure white and clean.

"The maids tended to you and gave you fresh, clean clothes," said a woman's voice coming from her right. Her words were perfect English, spoken with a lovely French accent. "I hope you are not offended."

Lydia turned to look at the woman. She'd risen to her feet and was standing with her hands modestly clasped together at the front of her waist. She recognized her as the one standing in the window.

"I...I suppose it *was* necessary," Lydia replied shyly. "I was...rather in a sorry state. I should be thanking you." An awkward silence persisted, and then she continued more self-assured. "And now, if you would instruct me, I should be getting up and doing my chores." Lydia pushed the covers to the side and began to raise her body, but being so weak, she couldn't restrain herself from falling back onto her bolster.

The woman came straight over to the edge of the bed, concerned. "Now, you have been quite ill and unable to eat. So you should stay right there while I get you some food. You will need to build up your strength." She reached down and with her soft, warm hand touched Lydia's cheek and forehead. "Yes, the fever is gone. I was deeply troubled for you, the last three days, since you arrived. But now it appears as though you shall be well."

Lydia looked up from her bolster at the woman, who was smiling down at her, kind and attentive. They studied each other's faces a moment. The woman appeared to be about thirty, still youthful and pretty, but plain, yet mature in her manner, very confident in her way. Lydia commented, "I'm afraid I do not know you."

The woman politely responded, "I am Jeanne. Jeanne Le Ber. And who might *you* be, young lady?"

"Lydia. My name is Lydia Longley."

"Well, I am very glad to meet you, Lydia," she said in a joyous tone, extending her hand. The two exchanged a gentle shake. "Now we shall prepare some food for you to eat that your strength might be restored." Jeanne bowed her head, turned, walked toward the door, opened it, and left the room.

Lydia couldn't help but wonder why she was being treated with such kindness.

After a little while, Jeanne returned with a tray of food: hot vegetable soup, warm bread, and tea. The hostess helped Lydia to sit up in her bed and tended to her as the famished young lady made fast consumption of the tea and broth.

Longing to enter into conversation, Lydia broke off small pieces of the bread to nibble them slowly as she spoke. "I hope to not be bothering you for long."

"You are no bother to me, my dear." Jeanne smiled. "Other than to see that you were doing so poorly when you arrived. It is indeed *easy* for me to wish that you were well and then to *help* in any way that I can. That is a part of my purpose here."

Lydia nodded her appreciation and asked, "Would you tell me where I am? Here … about this place?"

Jeanne looked around the room. "This is my father's house, Jacques Le Ber, whom you have already met."

"The man in the carriage?" Lydia asked.

"Yes."

"I'm afraid I did not know his name … I do not know French. I just knew he was my new master."

Jeanne looked at her puzzled and asked, "Your master?"

"Why, yes. He bought me from the Pennacook sagamore. And now I am his slave."

Jeanne rolled her eyes back, tilted her head up at the ceiling, and laughed.

Lydia felt embarrassed, dreading that she'd already said the wrong thing. Frowning, she begged, "I am so sorry. I should know better than to speak out of turn. Would you forgive me, Madame?"

Jeanne regained her composure and gently placed her hand on Lydia's to reassure her. "First of all, my dear, I am not married, and secondly, *you* are not a slave. My father has merely paid your ransom."

Lydia was stunned silent. She locked eyes with Jeanne's, measuring her. *Had she heard it right?* After a few seconds, Lydia's eyes swelled with tears, and her face became red. She began to cry.

Jeanne removed the tray and set it to the side. She sat down on the edge of the bed, leaned forward, and tenderly wrapped her arms around the young English woman, wishing to console her. She whispered words of comfort in her ear, "Yes, my dear. You are free to go at any time you so desire."

Held in her benefactor's embrace, Lydia's emotions finally released. She lost all control of body, heaving deep sighs and sonorous sobs. Jeanne responded, gently stroking her back with her warm hand. And after a long while, when her eyes were all cried out, Lydia began to wonder about her newfound freedom. *Where is it that I should go?*

JOHN AUGURY

July 1695

John had been living among the Kennebec for nearly a year. His thirteenth birthday had come and gone without celebration or even notice. The body of the boy was changing now, becoming taller, stronger, and his grimy face showed the development of light hair on his upper lip, the beginnings of a mustache. The clothes he'd been wearing at the time of his capture were fast becoming out-grown rags, though in the heat of July, he'd had no more occasion to wear his tattered shirt. In several ways, he had come to look like the Abenaki, always naked above the waist, bare legs and feet, his skin well tanned. Yet his sun-bleached hair, now shoulder length, and bright blue eyes clearly marked his distinction from them.

Taxous had shown a certain kindness to the boy since his capture, founded on the Indian's superstition and supported by a measure of trust, as the youth was always honest. He allowed John to come and go without suspicion, no doubt buoyed by his confidence that the boy really had no place to escape to. To him, John was set apart from the other hostages, willing to embrace life among the Kenne-bec, fearless of his new circumstances, physically able, and tough—a trait that was of utmost importance to the sagamore. This was one strong-hearted boy indeed, a true survivor, somehow special, though always serious. He hadn't seen John smile. Not even once.

John, a keen observer and a quick study, took to learning the language with seemingly little effort, benefiting from Taxous's good command of English and the sagamore's willingness to interpret. In that first year, the boy had learned to effectively communicate as he listened far more than he spoke and, as much as possible, remained in the background.

It wasn't so much that the young man feared interaction with his captors; to the contrary, rather he hoped to blend in and to become an integral part of his new culture. He cared not to be resentful of the past and resistive—not like some of the other hostages there, who had suffered terribly as a result. No, he desired to be accepted as someone belonging in the Indian village, if only for a time. But despite this desire there was something restraining him from fitting in completely, and it wasn't his appearance. There was something holding him back. He just didn't know yet what it was.

The summer season found Taxous and his people staying in the Kennebec village of Norridgewock, a village larger than its southern neighbors of Amaseconti, Kennebec, and Sagadahoc, which John had seen in his occasional travels with his master. There was a consistent pattern in the physical development of these settlements established along the river, where their crops abounded in the fertile soil, and with their dwellings situated on the upland, above the spring floods brought by the winter melt flowing down from the mountain headwaters in the north.

Norridgewock was a peaceful place, secluded from the outside world, with its enclave of native lodges surrounded by dense forest, lending it a sense of hidden protection. There John had begun to understand the native culture and to see with his own eyes how the families united together to survive the often-harsh New England climate. Dependent upon each other, they worked with singular purpose on the essential elements of subsistence: farming, hunting, and fishing. In this setting the captives were taught an unforgiving lesson as new members of this culture, thrust in with the labors of the rest. The rule was simple. Do your part, or don't eat.

Since their first arrival in Norridgewock a year ago, the captives had been distributed amongst the native population, bartered or sold to different households in the Kennebec villages, some to other places in Provincial Maine and Canada, the locations of which John didn't know. Several English who'd been captured in Oyster River lived there with Taxous's people. John would see them out and about, but, as he didn't know them, he would not speak to them. The only other English there known to John were his fellow captives from Groton—the last two who remained near Taxous: Lydia Lakin and John Shepley.

These two English captives were often seen together, an apparent encouragement to one another—perhaps even a bit more than that, as seen in the way in which they gazed at each other at times. Yet these two hadn't adapted as he had. John saw the resistance in them, keeping them at arm's length from the new culture—so evident in their persistence to maintain their English garb. *Maybe they are clinging to dead memories?* he wondered. Or perhaps they were just so set in their English ways that they couldn't let them go. They had been, after all, much older than he was when taken.

John could read their intransigence in their faces: their refusal to accept their lot as slaves of the heathen, their hesitancy to perform their chores, and their underlying hatred for their captors. John did agree the treatment they suffered at the hands of their masters was unreasonably harsh at times, but he was convinced that these two had brought their troubles upon themselves. Or at least made them worse. *They just need to be less angry*, he thought, *and less English.*

One evening, after John had returned from a successful hunt with Taxous and several of the other Indian boys, a celebration feast was arranged. A bonfire was lit in the center of the camp, and the entire village turned out to feast on the fresh cooked meat. During the singing and dancing, John sat by himself and to the side, enjoying his generous piece of roasted flesh. Shepley noticed him there and came to join him, with Lydia, like a fragile waif, quietly tagging along. John briefly looked up from his dinner at them both and nodded, acknowledging their presence, but then continued to consume his meal as he usually did: alone.

After a few moments of awkward silence, the two sat down. Shepley, determined to discourse, began, "I see you had a successful hunt."

John finished chewing, swallowed, and paused to correct the misconception. "Yes, *they* did. I was just along to help." He became quiet again as he chawed off another piece of the red meat from the bone. Then he licked his fingers with his mouth full.

Shepley stared at the piece he held in his fists and asked, "So what was it? The kill. A ... a deer?"

John chewed and swallowed fast, excited to tell what he saw. "No, it was a magnificent animal—a *moose*, taller than me. Its antlers were near four feet abreast." Full of spirit, John stretched his arms out to show how big. "I declare it was as stout as a plow horse!" He noticed a deep bruise on Shepley's face and then quietly went back to eating.

Shepley's curiosity continued unabated. "How did they kill it?" he asked.

John hadn't spoken to Shepley much in the last few months, but the stimulation, his diversion over the details of the day's adventure, broadened his interest to share some conversation. "Incon shot it with several arrows," he explained. "One went through the heart, and the animal went down hard. More than a *thousand* weight, the beast!"

"Did *you* shoot at it?" Shepley persisted.

John turned toward Shepley slowly. He lowered the bone he'd been chewing on and wiped his lips on the back of his hand. "They don't give me a bow. I'm just there to help track the animal, and once they kill it, to help them haul the carcass back here. There's more than a quarter ton we dragged back, plus the hide and the antlers."

Shepley's eyes sagged. His head tilted downward. He swallowed hard and clenched his jaw several times, which emphasized his malnourished sinews. The bruise on his cheek pulsed purple with blood as he spoke darkly, "If I held a bow ... or a gun ... or a knife, and I was hunting with these hell-hounds, I would surely take the first opportunity I had to kill one of them...these, my tormentors..." His voice trailed off in a murmur.

John stopped eating and gazed at his fellow captives, measuring their dismal demeanor. It dawned on him that the entire time he'd been speaking with them that Shepley and Lydia were starving—*right next to him, empty-handed*—while he was feasting aplenty. He would eat well because he'd learned to fit in. He understood the ways of the village—ways that wouldn't tolerate the weak, those that wouldn't help themselves. And though he'd used those very ways to make himself comfortable, taking full advantage of his quiet skill and strength, he couldn't forget the lessons that he'd learned from his father and mother, to be kind to those less fortunate.

At last he spoke, "Did either of you have something to eat?"

Their forlorn faces wagged wearily from side to side. In the long, dark shadows of the campfire, their eye sockets became empty, like black windows peering into desperate souls, making their emaciated heads appear as red-orange skulls, prophecies, portents of their dismal demise. That is, unless they changed their ways.

John reached across and handed the rib to Shepley. "Here, why don't you share the rest of this." It still had a fist-sized piece of meat clinging to it. "I've had enough. Besides, I'm tired and I think I shall go to bed."

John pushed himself to his feet and stared down at them both. Shepley smiled briefly in appreciation, while Lydia was already ripping at the morsel with her teeth. She attacked it like a ravenous wolf, many days without a kill. He was certain they would huddle pathetically together and gnaw the bone bare, then suck out the last trace of marrow. He recalled afresh what it'd been like to have been that hungry.

Several weeks passed and another hunt was arranged. Taxous and his son, Incon, assembled a group of boys to join with them, including John and another English of his choosing. John suggested Shepley to the sagamore, hoping the hunt to be a positive change to his fellow captive's routine, an opportunity for him to earn and receive better victuals. Taxous was at first reticent to John's selection, for he'd formed a low opinion of Shepley. But looking the boy in the eye, he consented to his choice, as he had an uncanny trust of him.

In the afternoon, the troop of ten set off, led by Taxous at the front with the sagamore's cousin, Walambais, at the rear. After fording the shallows of the Kennebec River, the band climbed the banks on the far side and continued up an Indian trail that led to the north, passing through country that was heavily wooded. The group traveled light, with the Indians carrying only their weapons and a day's provisions. They reached their destination, Lake Wesserunset, before the onset of evening. There the group bathed in the cool waters to refresh themselves from the ten-mile hike.

The preparation for the hunt was all new to Shepley. He watched the others with interest yet separated himself, seated a short distance away on a grassy bank overlooking the lake. John hoped Shepley wouldn't do anything foolish, like run away. He noted that Taxous was keeping his eye on him. But John also knew his fellow captive was observant, wise, and motivated. Shepley wouldn't jeopardize Lydia back at the village, who most assuredly would feel the sagamore's wrath if he attempted anything—the unspoken guarantee of Shepley's cooperation and attentiveness to the tasks.

When they finished their swim, the natives walked up out of the lake and stepped ankle deep into a field of muck situated in the shallows, near to the western shore. There Taxous and Walambais dredged up handfuls of umber mud and rubbed it onto themselves. Incon and the other boys joined in, covering their skin with the dark, gooey sediment. John approached the edge of the group and stood a moment, feeling the warm lake bottom ooze up between his toes. The English boy reached in and tentatively scooped up a handful of the mud and sniffed it. He began to dab it here and there on his shoulders and arms. With his finger he wiped a streak on each cheek.

As John applied the mud, he carefully observed the manner by which Taxous prepared himself—always with a purpose in mind, no

P. GIFFORD LONGLEY

wasted effort, no wasted time. He refocused, intending to maintain the same degree of efficiency. But not everyone there felt the same way about getting down to business—at least not the whole time.

Incon, occasional prankster, picked up a large stiff clump of the goo and fashioned it into a ball. He turned it over and over in his hands to make it nice and round, all the while with a sly grin forming on his lips. When he was satisfied with the size and shape of his clump, he suddenly turned and hurled it at one of his native friends, who took the great splat across his chest. Retaliation from the target was the immediate reaction. Predictably, the other boys were happy to join right in, hurling more clods at each other, laughing loud, having a grand time playing with the slime. And all the while that the merriment persisted, the white boy stayed quietly at the fringe, somehow managing to avoid the messy splatter. But that wouldn't last for long.

Incon reloaded and set his aim again at one of his friends. The young native leaned back and launched his brown missile with extra force. But this time he missed his intended target. The ordnance sailed over and found a different victim, striking John square in the face.

The sagamore's son grew still, disappointed with his faulty aim and shocked he'd mistakenly struck the reticent English boy. The others quieted from their ruckus. They all watched together, waiting to see what the unknown captive would do. Even Taxous paused to see what would happen.

John was stunned by the mud. *How could something so squishy feel so solid?* His face smarted from the hit. Yet no one could see his expression of pain, hidden behind the clump. He reached his hands up slowly and swept some of the matter from his eyes.

Facing downward, he blinked several times, trying to clear his vision. Through his muddy lashes, he stared down at the field of muck, shiny from the thin layer of lake water over the top, mak-ing a smooth, black-brown mirror bearing his reflection. He was a humorous sight, wearing a big turd for a nose. He couldn't help himself when his cheeks filled with air, and his lips exploded with a comic, "Pshaw!"

Several of the Indian boys who heard him giggled...if only tentatively.

John reared up and glared at them with angry intensity. His eyes shone like a hot blue beam, panning around the group, staring at each one as they again grew quiet. He hung his head back down and returned his gaze once more to his own silly reflection. How could *anyone* find his present appearance less than *hilarious?* He burst forth a hearty laugh.

And as though he'd permitted them, the Indian boys joined with him in loud and hearty howling. The mucky mirth resumed as the grimy juveniles splashed around together in the goo and once again lobbed more gobs at each other. Now he joined them, forming and firing accurate missiles of his own, greatly enjoying himself.

John stopped for a moment and looked over at Taxous, seeing that the sagamore had been studying his every move. Then presently he grew quiet as did the others. Each resumed their necessary ritual in business-like fashion, covering their skin with the mud. It would be getting dark soon. They needed time for the mud to dry before the cool of the evening set in. Then the boys crowded around John and helped to coat him in the areas he couldn't see or reach. Together they smoothed the material onto his back until at last he was finished and all of his white skin had been covered.

John turned toward Shepley, still seated alone on the shore among the tall grasses. He scooped up two handfuls of the stuff and carried it over to him. He held out his hands to his fellow captive. "Here, you'll need to cover your face and arms with this."

Shepley stared up at him without moving. But as John remained insistent he finally raised one hand and took a bit of the sludge. The newcomer raised it doubtfully to his nose. He jerked his head back with a sour expression, having had a good whiff.

John chuckled as he explained, "The game can smell you coming from a mile away. But not if you don some of this."

Shepley wrinkled his nose, with no intent to rub it on.

"It doesn't smell so bad after it dries," John explained. "Besides, it takes the shine off your white skin...so you can blend into the woods."

Shepley at last took two fingers of the goo and wiped a small bit on his face. He quipped, "Why don't you rub some of this *dung* into that shocking, bright hair of yours?"

The idea gave John a start of instant appeal. He stepped back out into the field of mud and picked up more handfuls. He slopped it onto the top of his head, pulling the sludge down through his locks, stretching them long and stringy and dark, dripping down onto his shoulders. Self satisfied, he returned to the shore and stared again down at Shepley. "How do I look now?"

Shepley sized him up. John stood naked except for his breech-clout, drab and slimy from his feet to the top of his head. You would never know he was English except for the bright, blue eyes that peered out from his snuff-colored face. He muttered his sarcastic appraisal, "Just like one o' them hell-hounds."

After their preparations were complete, the band divided into two groups. John went with the one led by Taxous, and Shepley went with the other led by Walambais. The groups parted ways and went to different sides of the lake, positioning themselves amongst the thickets lining the shore. There they would wait in hiding for morning when the big game would come down to the water's edge to drink. John made himself a bed of leaves and lay down to rest with the other boys as it grew dark. Soon he fell fast asleep.

Before the sun came up, John became aware of movement. Incon, who'd been near his side all night, was awake, crouching with his bow raised and arrow set.

Fling! Fling! Fling!

Incon had let his arrow fly, as had several of the other boys. And before John had even time to sit up to see the targeted game, it was running away from them, headed deeper into the gloom. He glimpsed only the backside. It was a bull moose. Its massive hooves pounded and shook the forest floor as it flew from them, tearing up great clods from the trail with each swift and powerful stride. But it didn't run as an animal merely startled. Rather, it raced as one hit, fleeing for its life, for one or more of their arrows had hit their mark.

Quickly the band was on their feet and chasing after their prey. If they could just hold to the trail of the wounded animal, they could easily follow it and finish the kill. But they had to act fast or the beast could get away. And if they lost this one, they might have to wait yet another day for such an opportunity. Thus they proceeded with the earnest hope that there would be plenty of fresh meat again in the village that night.

Taxous took the lead with the other four boys in his group following, though with his swiftness, he forged out well ahead of the youths. The moose had cut a trail through the underbrush that was easy to find as it hurdled its half-ton frame through the thickets, knocking over small trees and shrubs, breaking off branches, and tearing up the soft mulch with its hooves. And after they'd tracked the grand elk about a mile, the sun was nearing the horizon so that the brightening sky shed forth its light to show more details of the animal's flight. John paused to examine the ground and noted the unmistakable drops of blood along the leafy track.

Incon, who was with him, noticed it too. He spoke to him in Abenaki, "It won't be long now." The Indian smiled with anticipation. They pressed on together in the pursuit.

After another mile, the trail grew less obvious. John could only assume that the animal had stopped running, as there were no more broken branches and the path had become smoother, harder to detect. Nevertheless, the trail of blood persisted to lead them along. John wondered if the animal hadn't been wounded severely enough and if it might yet get away. At the same time he marveled at the strength of the beast and its unflagging will to live.

By now, the band of trackers had strung itself out along the path as they slowed to avoid missing the subtle clues. John fell in after Incon, and he turned to look behind him, but he could only see one of the other boys, a dozen rods to the rear. Up ahead, Taxous was nowhere in sight. Apparently he'd crested the trail, which was ascending up a long rise. The sun had risen now, and yellow beams of light filtered down through the hardwood canopy, making the telltale crimson stains glisten on the fallen oak leaves. Surely their game couldn't be that much farther ahead. *It can't keep going while losing so much blood.*

Incon was the next to arrive at the crest in the trail. The boy stopped and stood very still. He had his eyes fixed dead ahead. The youth rigidly held his bow at his side. And as John caught up with him, he thought he could see that the young Indian was *shaking*.

When John reached the crest, he came alongside the sagamore's son, transfixed by the Indian's quivering profile and wondering what was wrong with him. Something seemed to be holding him there— an invisible force, like icy hands clutching at his throat. He seemed to be unable to move any farther.

Incon slowly twisted his muddy face toward John, staring with tortured eyes bulging from their sockets. He faced forward again and whispered with dread a single word. *"Malsum!"*

John had heard of the Indian legend of "Malsum," the twin of the Abenaki's creator god, the embodiment of evil in the form of a wolf. But that was just so much superstition to him. He should turn to see the sight for himself, to see what was so fearsome to his companion.

Before their feet, the forest floor fell away into a bowl, walled in on three sides by craggy rocks and tall pines. At the center of the depression, just twenty paces distant from them, stood the dark, tawny beast that they'd been pursuing, with its long head facing away and hanging low. The moose was breathing heavily. Several arrows sagged from its left side, from which dripped a line of blood. Taxous stood near to the front of the great animal. In one hand, he held his knife and the other his tomahawk. But the sagamore's gaze wasn't fixed upon the wounded moose; rather, his attention was focused beyond and toward the rocks that lined the bowl. For it was there that lurked a pack of wolves above and around him, each with their teeth bared, snarling down, measuring Taxous and the moose, making ready to pounce on them both!

John expected Incon would quickly raise his bow to fire at the pack, but the Indian boy remained motionless. Why was he spellbound by the scene, unable to move, unwilling to help his father? They were all in peril, not just Taxous! There were stories about wolves, great packs of the fearless carnivores attacking whole bands of men in the woods, their shadow kingdom, and devouring them there.

The English boy could no longer stand by, idly watching. At last he reached for Incon's hand and seized the bow. The Indian's limp grip simply let him take it. Then he retrieved an arrow from Incon's quiver, set it on the nocking point, and surely stretched the bow-string with his left hand as he raised his sight past the feathers and along the shaft toward the tip. He was a skilled marksman, as he'd practiced many times before at home, and he knew precisely how deadly the weapon was that he held in his confident grasp.

But where should he aim first? He must be efficient. He must be wise. He must quickly show deadly force in order for them to escape the ravages of the pack.

He scanned the pack to find his target. He should shoot the biggest wolf, the strongest one—their leader. But which one was that? The choice was confusing. They all looked so fierce, much larger than any dog he'd ever seen. But they were handsome beasts, dark gray on their backs, white on their bellies, ears straight at attention, their muscles tensed, fur bristling, growling, low, ready to leap.

Several lurked behind the rocks, and there was no clear view of their hearts, his lethal target. He quickly scanned from right to left, and spied their leader—the powerful one, perhaps one-hundred-fifty weight, ears tattered from many a valiant and violent fight, perched forward on a boulder immediately before Taxous.

John pulled his drawing hand back taught to the anchor point and set his sight on the face of the wolf. Its golden-yellow eyes glowed vicious. He lowered the angle a half-inch to find the heart, visible there just above the top of Taxous's head. And in that brief instant before he released, he remembered Shepley's woeful words. If he would just now drop his right hand another inch he would be aiming directly at the center of his captor's back … and from deadly close range. *Who knows but that God has put me here at this moment to exact my righteous revenge? Who can stop me? Surely not Incon, timid with fear.* But could he shoot the man in authority over him—a man given that authority by forces greater than himself? Could he shoot his master in the back?

Suddenly the wolf sprang forward at the sagamore. John let the arrow fly. It was a clean release. The shaft pierced the air and penetrated deeply into its mark, true in the heart of the wolf.

The animal whelped and fell limp on the ground at Taxous's feet. Two of the other boys who'd since scurried up the hill to witness the event screamed victorious at the sight. Their shouts startled the rest of the pack and caused them to scamper up and over the rocks. They left out of sight.

Taxous snapped his head around to see from where the arrow had come, spying John lowering his bow to his side and his own son standing beside him, empty-handed. The sagamore quickly regained his focus to the dangerous task yet at hand, firmly clenching his knife and tomahawk as he turned and faced the massive moose.

The great beast was by now exhausted. The ground beneath it was drenched with its blood. It eyed its foe, heaved one last heavy breath, dropped first to its knees, then fell over dead.

The sagamore relaxed and gave a deep sigh as he dropped his weapons to the ground. He spun toward the English boy, smiled broadly, raised both arms high, and shouted a fierce cry of victory. "John Aw-geh-ree!"

As though they'd all been directed, the other boys joined him in the cries, "John Aw-geh-ree! John Aw-geh-ree! John Aw-geh-ree!"

Incon, full of smiles, grabbed John by the shoulders and shook him joyfully.

John felt strange being the center of their attention and praise. He hadn't experienced that in a long time and didn't know how to react. Expressionless, he became reflective, wishing he could simply withdraw and be left alone.

Taxous walked up to the English youth and proudly placed his hand upon his shoulder. He smiled at him in respect, while the other boys slapped him firmly on the back. John gazed up at the sagamore as his muddy face revealed an ever-so-tentative grin.

Afterwards they butchered the moose and placed the hide and large cuts of meat on sleds that they'd fashioned from saplings. They dragged their loads back to the base camp beside the lake. It was about midday when they arrived, and the other group was already there waiting, having returned without a catch. With the early hour, they decided that they should return to Norridgewock that day, but not before they first bathed to remove their silty camouflage.

As they came up from bathing and stood knee-deep in the lake, Shepley came over to John, mindful of the great kill and curious about the good cheer and new camaraderie he saw emerging between the English boy and the others. Quietly he observed, not wishing to draw attention to himself.

While they stood there together, Incon splashed over to John, pointed in his face, smiled, and shouted, "John Aw-geh-ree!" Several of the other boys repeated the same thing and then looked at John and grinned.

Shepley measured John's happy face but couldn't figure it out, and so he had to ask, "Why are they calling you that?"

John shrugged at the question. "I dunno. I've heard Taxous call me that before. I guess he can't say my name. You know, maybe 'Lon-geh-lee' is too hard to pronounce in Abenaki and sort-of comes out like 'Aw-geh-ree.'"

But Shepley, well educated, knew better than that and sought to correct him. "Haven't you ever heard of an 'augur?' *Augury* is a real word. It means 'good omen.'" Shepley shook his head, confounded. "What happened out there?"

John explained briefly what had transpired.

Shepley's brow wrinkled with incredulity as he glared at him. "You? You shot ... *the wolf?*"

John stood silent and glanced down at his image, which was shining in the water, reflecting to himself on how he'd been a "good omen" to the sagamore. Then he lifted his blue eyes back toward Shepley and gave him a confident nod.

TURNING

Sunday, August 4, 1695

When Lydia awoke in the morning, she had no idea how important this day would be to her. For certain, this was the Lord's Day, and that normally did carry with it a heightened sense of purpose, as it afforded a time to attend church to seek relief from her burdens, to pray and ask for God's help. She'd been attending the Catholic Mass with Jeanne for many months, and though the knowledge of her attendance there would surely have offended her family, especially Grandmamma, she had found some comfort there. After all, she didn't understand most of what was said, what with the mass being conducted in Latin. So she was confident that *their* religion could have no detrimental effect. She was merely glad to be able to enter a building that was so obviously devoted to God and to pray there, in her own manner, before the foot of the cross.

When Lydia was dressed and ready to depart, she went to Jeanne's room. Peeking through the ajar door, she saw the woman kneeling before the open window, head tilted forward, hands raised and clasped together, praying as was her constant custom. The packages that they'd been assembling all week were set just inside the room, near the door, ready to be taken. Carefully, so as not to disturb

Jeanne, she pushed the door open, tiptoed in, and began to lift one, intending to take it down to the carriage.

"Here! We shall take them down together," said Jeanne, who had risen and was already walking over to help with her arms happily extended. The smile on her lips seemed broader than usual, and there was an extra radiance in her expression that was positively endearing.

Influenced by the ever-respectful manner of Jeanne, Lydia tilted her head forward to curtsy. "Thank you for permitting me to help you with this," she said.

"You are welcome, my dear. But you need not thank *me*, for it is *God* who has brought you here to this place at this time to help with His work. And these fine vestments now surely bear His mark, placed there by the many talents He has bestowed upon *you* and which have so burst forth from your skilled hands."

Lydia blushed.

Jeanne continued. "*Really*, your use of the blue and purple thread was so unexpected and so *beautiful* in its simplicity!"

Lydia demurred, "Those are merely my favorite colors."

"Indeed, now *mine* too. So ... shall we be going?"

The women gathered the packages into their arms, carried them down to the carriage, and then rode off for the chapel.

After mass, the two women returned to their coach, retrieved the packages, and carried them across the lawn to a long building situated in the back—a stable that had been converted to a school for French and Indian children. The headmistress of the institution, Marguerite Bourgeoys, kept a modest apartment there, and it was by reason of an appointment with her that they'd come.

"Sister" Bourgeoys, as she was called, being also the founder of the local convent, the Congregation de Notre Dame, greeted them at the door and invited them both inside. Lydia had met the kind, elderly woman several times before, as she was a dear friend of Jeanne, who often visited the school.

But before they could even sit down, Marguerite, wearing a smile that spread from ear to ear, gushed with her usual high energy in

French, which Lydia struggled as always to apprehend. She caught only about every third word and wished the woman would slow down and enunciate. Lydia used whatever other senses she could to try and comprehend what was being said, studying the woman's body language and expression. And so it was apparent that the Sister, though very proper and cordial, was most excited to be receiving the gifts. But she did not display any manner of selfishness; rather, she expressed appreciation at participating in the joy of discovering something new, revealing a genuine anxiousness to see what they'd made.

Jeanne handed Marguerite the first of the packages.

The silvered saint hurried to untie the bow, her eyes wide with excitement, like those of a child opening a Christmas present. She first pulled out the priest's tunic, a long white garment, and stretched it out to examine the front and back, feeling the fine linen with its delicate blue and purple stitching that ran around the hem, the ends of the sleeves, and made for a square image of a breastplate embroidered on the chest. "Ooh!" she cooed. "*Si original et si beau!*"

Lydia interjected with a pinch of pride, her French a bit ragged, pointing out that there also was a matching stole.

Marguerite acknowledged and then pulled out the long strip of white satin fabric, which had tiny silver bells stitched to its ends and crosses embroidered on the front, utilizing the same blue and purple thread. "*Très joli!*" she exclaimed as she continued to examine the stitching, pulling it up very close to her face.

Jeanne leaned forward impatiently, taking the vestments from Marguerite, redirecting the older woman's attention to her. She spoke quickly, "*Et j'ai aussi quelque chose d'autre pour vous, ma Soeur.*"

Lydia looked to Marguerite. Marguerite's smile only broadened. She nodded her head and scanned the other packages as she made a quick rejoinder, motioning to be given another present.

Jeanne shook her head. Her friend's lovely face was drawn in earnest. Lydia only caught, "*Non, ma Soeur,*" of Jeanne's answer, meaning, "No, my sister."

Again, Lydia turned her attention to Marguerite, who abruptly paused and set the garments down. Quickly the sister spit out more French as her brow creased in confusion.

Jeanne impatiently repeated herself, interrupting, "*Et j'ai aussi quelque chose d'autre pour vous, ma Soeur.*" This time Lydia caught the words *quelque chose d'autre*, meaning "something else." Now Lydia's brow creased. There yet remained packages that hadn't been opened, or was Jeanne referring to some other gift?

Jeanne's statement began a flurry of French from both women. Lydia's ears raced to keep up with the conversation. She could see that Jeanne had succeeded in changing entirely the subject, but she hadn't understood near enough of what they'd just said to make any sense of it.

Marguerite leaned forward to listen, and grew noticeably more reserved. Finally, she asked, "*Est-ce que vous êtes certaine, mon enfant?*"

Certaine—she asked if Jeanne was certain. Lydia whipped her head around to study her friend.

"*Oui,*" said Jeanne in a hush as she lowered her eyes. A calm moved over her, smoothing the lines in her troubled face and easing the tenseness in her shoulders. She lifted her gaze once more and looked steadfastly at the sister. She continued resolutely, "*Oui, Jésus m'en est témoin.*" Lydia understood the last phase clearly to mean "as Jesus is my witness."

The sister considered carefully what she'd heard and posed a more conclusive question. "*Bien … alors, que faisons-nous ensuite?*"

Jeanne offered in a matter-of-fact tone, "*Si vous avez un peu de papier, je le copierai pour vous.*"

Lydia deduced that Jeanne had asked for paper, apparently to write something, but what, she didn't know. This entire meeting had become to her too strange, and now she felt insecure, as if she'd been intruding in a private discussion.

Marguerite rose up and placed her hand on Jeanne's shoulder and smiled. "*Venez donc avec moi, ma petite.*" Then the sister turned politely toward Lydia, and while pointing at the teapot on the table, she spoke slowly and more clearly, offering her hospitality. "*Nous tarderons quelque temps, mon enfant. Il y a du thé… là, sur la table. N'hésitez pas à vous installer et vous en servir. Vous êtes comme chez vous."*

Lydia apprehended that the two would be leaving the room and that she was expected to remain until they returned… and drink some tea.

Jeanne rose up from her chair, and the two Catholic women passed through the doorway that connected into the large classroom adjacent to the apartment, pulling the wooden leaf shut behind them.

Lydia pondered all she'd just seen and the little of what she'd heard. It seemed cryptic. What could possibly have been *so important* that her and Jeanne's months of work had so readily been set aside—set aside as if it had been of such little matter?

She sat quietly alone and consumed several cups of the tea while she waited, trying to be patient and speculating as to what might be taking place in the adjacent room. But at last her curiosity proved too powerful. She got up and tiptoed over to the doorway, wondering if she might be able to overhear something. There were voices beyond, in the next room, though these were muffled and couldn't be distinguished. She studied the pine door and noticed a small opening down at the latch. Crouching, she peeked through.

At the front of the classroom, she spied Jeanne seated at a desk composing some document with Marguerite at her side. Just then a knock was heard at the other entrance on the opposite side of the room. The sister walked over, opened the door, and greeted there a visitor, a gentleman, and invited him to enter. The man appeared to be on some official business, as he carried with him a small leather satchel. Lydia studied the man carefully as he greeted Jeanne, sat down beside her, opened his case, and retrieved several items from it. When Jeanne had finished writing, the man took to making some notations on her document, and then, after dripping a bit of candle wax onto it, he set his seal. Then he abruptly arose, gathered his things, and departed.

Lydia, seeing that the business was apparently concluded, feared she'd better return to her chair. But seized by her curiosity, she lingered there another minute, long enough to witness Jeanne kiss the hand of the sister and then as she bowed low before the large cross mounted on the wall. And as she did so, she placed her right hand to her forehead, then deliberately moved it downward to her heart and then lifted it to her left shoulder and finally over to her right before rising.

In a moment, the door of the classroom swung open. Jeanne stepped through and straightway addressed Lydia, who was seated and waiting in her chair as though she'd been there all along. "Shall we go now?" she asked. Sister Bourgeoys stood behind her in the opening, holding the official-looking parchment in her hands. Neither of the women gave any further notice toward the packages that they'd brought, left there on the floor.

Lydia set her empty teacup back down on the table and looked up with a smile of innocence. "Any time that you are ready, I am as well."

The two women said their good-byes to Marguerite at the door and then walked quietly over to the carriage. Lydia was a flood with questions but kept these to herself, not daring to impose herself into Jeanne's personal business and realizing that any such queries would be considered rude. She just assumed, and hoped, that Jeanne would tell her what had just taken place ... when she was ready, of course.

As they were entering the coach, Jeanne spoke to Lydia, "I should like to make a special visit before we return to the villa. *Est-ce que ça vous derange?*"

"Of course not. As you wish," Lydia replied as they climbed into the carriage and sat down.

Jeanne turned and instructed the chauffeur, "*A la croix, s'il vous plait.*"

As they were driving away from the chapel, Lydia turned to Jeanne. "Did I hear you say that we were to go 'to the cross'?"

"Yes, that is right."

"How splendid!" Lydia remarked, wearing a look of cheer. "I have seen it but from afar and would love to go to the top of the mountain to behold the view."

P. GIFFORD LONGLEY

"Yes, the view is magnificent," Jeanne foretold. "But you shall see that for yourself when we arrive there."

It was a fine Sunday afternoon with a warm, cloudless sky. The summer air was fresh and not so humid as it was prone to be in Groton. Lydia leaned back on the satin cushion and tilted her head toward the window as they rode along, with the breeze brushing her cheeks and pushing back her hair. The smoothness of their fine ride did not betray their speed.

She turned a glance toward Jeanne, who sat beside her very still, eyes forward, giving a sense that the woman's mind was somewhere else, in a place far away. Lydia could tell that Jeanne wasn't ready to speak about the meeting. Neither of them uttered another word the whole way.

The coachman steered their carriage up the track to the top of Mount Royal as the path curved through the trees, winding like a wide spiral as it ascended slowly toward the peak, some seven hundred feet above the village below. There they stopped at the edge of a meadow, a clearing that had been made in the forest atop the knob a half-century before. At the far edge of the clearing stood a lone wooden cross, beyond which the grade dropped steeply, thus creating a fine overlook, which afforded wide views toward the eastern horizon.

Lydia stepped out from the coach and down to the ground. Then she turned her back to the horizon, watching Jeanne climb down after her, studying the woman's eyes as she descended—eyes that were looking beyond Lydia toward that horizon—deep brown irises that reflected an image, the image of the cross.

"May we go closer?" Lydia asked her.

"Yes. Indeed."

Jeanne stepped past Lydia and continued forward with resolve, lifting the edges of her robe as she gathered speed and ran through the tall grasses and the lacey, white wildflowers. Lydia followed after, trying to keep up, looking ahead at the cross, which loomed ever larger as they approached it.

The cross was of a tremendous size, much larger than Lydia had expected. Hewn from a massive tree trunk, it had a heavy cross bar notched and pegged in place more than fifty feet above their heads. The base of the cross was braced by heavy boulders, piled there to restrain it against the wind. Lydia now realized that it hadn't been meant to be a scale replica of Christ's execution tree; rather it had been erected there, on that rise, standing as a symbol to be seen from many miles away.

At the foot of the cross, Jeanne crouched and prostrated herself flat upon the ground, with her arms extended straight out and her face downward. Lydia had never seen her do that before. Normally the woman only knelt when she prayed. But this seemed to be a special place for her friend, and so she accepted the heightened sense of the occasion and continued to walk along by herself, past the cross and over to the edge of the precipice, treading very carefully out onto a ledge of exposed and weathered granite.

Before Lydia's gaze was a spectacular sight. Jeanne had indeed been correct! The view was unobstructed over the tops of the trees farther down the mountain, a view that spanned from the far north on her left and swept forward, toward the east, and then around to the mountain ranges in the south on her far right. She'd never been up so high before or experienced such a vantage to the world below, and she felt a sense of exhilaration, a dizzy giddiness, as though she were flying. And from this great height she saw many things below her that were familiar. But this new perspective clutched her curiosity and fueled her imagination as she tried to distinguish those things below, things she'd only ever seen before from the ground.

Immediately beneath her she recognized the French enclave, cleared out from amidst the woods, decorated with its tiny buildings that had been laid out along the grids of streets, bustling with ever-so-tiny people and horses moving to and fro. Further on, she spied the Indian village, distinguishing there the primitive teepees and lodges. Beyond the village, the path led down to the river, now more than a mile distant, with miniature canoes traversing its curves toward a vast bay in the far north. From there, she traced the tree-lined watercourses, which turned from the river's eastern banks and bent back to the right where they coursed up and through the wide center of the scene—these being fed from their sources high up in the mountains in the south on her right, mountains that stood majestically with their craggy tops absent their snow cover and set bare against the horizon like a jagged flint. At last she imagined what lay on the other side, beyond the mountains—New Hampshire, and still, farther south, Massachusetts, from where she'd come. So there it was, laid out before her like a clear, crisp map—her journey there, so plain to be seen and understood.

As she was positioned there, admiring the view, Jeanne came up alongside her. "Have you seen our villa below?" she asked as she pointed to the spot, set apart from the rest of the community, with its rolling acres of fine farm land, the tree-lined drive, and the glistening limestone edifice that had been Lydia's home for nearly a year.

"Yes, I see it … in its entire splendor! Your *wonderful* home."

"No. It shall be my home no longer."

Lydia jerked herself around to face her friend, worried. "Are you leaving St. Marie?"

"No. I am not leaving." Jeanne eyed Lydia's worried expression tenderly, as though she had expected it. Jeanne's gaze moved to the cross. She let the peace enfold her and took a deep breath before turning to Lydia once more. "I have decided to part with everything. This afternoon I gave my portion of the estate to Sister Bourgeoys to help the poor, to build a new chapel for Notre Dame, and to construct a modest apartment there where I shall go to live … that I may enter the convent and serve my Savior the rest of the days of my life."

Lydia grew quiet as her eyes drifted away. After a long moment she asked, "And when shall this be?"

"I suppose it will take some time for my portion of the estate to be transferred and for the construction of my apartment to be complete—perhaps next year, sometime in the spring."

"I see … "

Jeanne gently lifted Lydia's hand, patting it as she did so. "My dear, I do not want you to worry about me in the least. And you should not worry about yourself either. I will gladly arrange for you to stay at my father's estate for as long as you desire. Please consider it your home. And, of course, I shall like for you to come and visit me any time that you would like to. Perhaps we could even sew and paint together?"

"Yes, I … I would like that," said Lydia pensively. She kept looking away. An odd jealousy descended on her, as though she'd lost a friend, a friend who cared more for someone else. She suddenly remembered her isolation among the Pennacook, the awful days with no one to speak to, no one to share her thoughts.

Lydia took a short breath and turned back at Jeanne, "Maybe … Maybe I could …" She stopped herself. Her face went white.

"Yes? Maybe you could what?"

Lydia stared at Jeanne a moment as her color returned. "Nothing. I don't know what I was thinking." She smiled awkwardly, shook her head, and stared back out at the scene. Internally, she castigated herself. *Just because Jeanne has been so nice to me is no reason to turn my back on Mother and Father and their faith. I'm English!*

Suddenly uncomfortable with herself, Lydia thought about returning to the villa. She wanted some alone time to think.

The two stood with the warm sun at their backs, still gazing out over the wide scene. A gentle breeze swept up from below, over the treetops, and brushed against their faces.

Jeanne interrupted the silence. "I am so glad you came over here to this edge to look out. Whenever I have had the joy to come up, I have come here to the edge and placed my feet in that *very spot* where yours are right now. And each time I have looked down at the world as it spreads out below my feet, beholding with all clarity the many places from where I've come and recalling the paths and circumstances that led me here. And each time I then found myself turning my body around and placing my back to that world." She deliberately paused, turned, and then continued as she raised her hand up to point. "Then I lift my eyes up to this cross and see the place to where I now must surely go."

P. GIFFORD LONGLEY

As Jeanne finished speaking, Lydia had also turned and was now peering up at the cross fixed high above her head. Then she glanced back out at the scene below her, pondering from where all she'd come and the many circumstances that had led her there to that spot, fully recognizing for the first time that none of those circumstances had been of her own choosing. She turned again and stared up at the cross, for the first time embracing the thought of leaving her old world behind forever, while at the same time wondering, wondering where it was that she might be led to next.

HOSTAGES

Wednesday August 13, 1695

Jack pressed forward through the crowd and drew up alongside of Jonas Prescott. After patiently awaiting his turn, he at last took the deposition from him and held it in his own hands, nervously shaking, as he carefully examined the text:

In the month of July 1694 there was a gathering of the Indians at the said new Fort Amasequonti and preparations to go forth to war, and two or three days before they intended to set out, they kild and boyld several dogs, and held a feast, where was present Bomaseen & Warumbee with divers others, of the chief among them, they discoursed of falling upon Oyster River and Groton; and Bomaseen was to command one of the company, & the day before they intended to set forth, myself with ffour Indians more were dispatched away to Canada with a letter from the Fryar and were upon our voyage thither and back again about ffour days and brought down about two barrels of powder, shot proportion-able & some fire armes. About the time of our return, the Indians came in after the mischief done at Oyster River & Groton, and in perticular, I saw Bomaseen in his canoo, which was

well laden, there was two English captives, some scalps, and
a large pack of plunder brought in that canoo, and Bomaseen
two or three days after his return home went away to Canada.

Hezekiah Miles (alias Hector)
[his mark]
Given before me at Boston
May 31, 1695
William Stoughton
Lieutenant Governor

Jack lowered the document and sighed. After more than a year, this was the first bit of eyewitness testimony, the first evidence of precisely who may have conducted the raid on Groton. No request for a ransom had ever come. The silence had been almost too much to bear. And yet, this document, though it was most informative, did not contain any sort of conclusive message or direction. He lifted it again to pour over it more carefully, longing for a clue of satisfaction.

As the crowd began to disperse, Jack returned the copy to Jonas and asked, "Is … is there nothing more than this? This document is now more than two months old. I … I do not understand."

Jonas became defensive. "Jack, I do not know what I could possibly impart that might satisfy your thirst for news. We are at war … and … and communication is simply interminable. And because of this, I must not feel that the lack of a detailed report is any indication of a bad result. No. On the contrary, I must remain confident that the news will come … the demand for their redemption. However, you shall just have to wait. Like the rest of us." Jonas turned away abruptly, placed the document into his bag, and made ready to leave.

Jack reached out and firmly grabbed Prescott's arm, turning him back. "I've grown weary of waiting. I find myself becoming an old man … helplessly watching as events drift along without my involvement, without my action. I have become a rueful bystander to a contest apparently played by no one!"

Prescott thrust Jack's hand away with a scowl.

P. GIFFORD LONGLEY

Jack fixed on his angry expression, instantly regretting his words. "Jonas, I hope you do not think me critical of you, or anyone else in the council or the militia. I … I … " He stopped himself and paused to gather his thoughts. He needed to start over.

Jack placed his hand on his chest before continuing. "You see, my problem is wholly within myself. My dissatisfaction is within *me*. I mean … I labor each and every day at the business and on the farm, and I wake each morning wanting of nothing. I consume a satiating meal, and sleep each and every night in my soft, warm bed … and am able to do any fine thing that I so desire, whenever I choose to. And all this time I think that Lydia, Betty, and John have no such rest or repast, that they are dragged about by their captors, tormented by those heathen, and made to suffer in the worst of ways … while I am so free and so blessed … and so … so … *comfortable*." Jack hung his head and stared at the floor, whelmed by his sadness, standing heartbroken, suddenly feeling his age. His once-proud shoulders slumped.

Jonas set his bag down and turned directly toward Jack. He studied Jack's disturbed expression as he strained for the right words, contemplating his own position as selectman. No one appreciated the burden that he'd carried for the families, those with loved ones yet missing—a burden that had steadily become more cumbrous upon him, heaped with the guilt of having nothing meaningful to report to them. Everywhere he went in town he saw them. It was impossible to avoid their anxious faces, fielding their woeful queries, seeing their ever-present sorrow, and discerning their dissatisfaction with his work—his efforts, his tireless pursuit of bulletins to their benefit. He knew he was doing smartly for them, but then again, none of the missing were members of *his* own family. If it had been his nephew and nieces taken, wouldn't he feel completely frustrated with the results as Jack now did?

At last he spoke gently and from his heart, "I am at a loss, Jack. Tell me … *tell me* what more I should do."

Jack thought quietly to himself for a moment, for he hadn't expected being put to task—not in the same way he'd just done to

Jonas. Then an idea flashed into his mind. "Do you suppose I might be able to have an audience with this Hezekiah Miles... or Hector? I wonder, perhaps he could give a physical description of the captives he saw. There were at least two. Surely then I could know more... That is, where my brother's family might be."

Jonas had known Jack far too long to bother to talk him out of getting involved. He knew if he suggested, "Suffer this matter to the officials and to the militia," that Jack would view such as feigning and wouldn't quit or back away. The man was, after all, one of the original proprietors, a pioneer, one who had openly served the town and who would graciously lend aid to another in need... not one to sit idly by and watch others do all the work. Besides, as he thought about it further, speaking directly with Hector was indeed a splendid idea. At least it should do no harm. He reached up and placed his hand firmly on Jack's shoulder. "Can you come with me this Friday?"

Jack lifted his head and shoulders as the weariness ran away from his expression. "*Yes*," he replied without even knowing where to.

Jonas proposed, "I'd planned a trip to Boston on another matter. Perhaps we can get permission to question this Hector. I understand he is yet detained there with other prisoners of war."

Jack felt a sudden sense of relief as he stretched out his hand to grasp Jonas's. The two men shook heartily. Jack walked away refreshed with a new sense of hope.

Monday, August 18, 1695

When Jack and Jonas arrived at the Boston jail, they learned from the warden that Hector had been freed nearly a month before. Hector hadn't been considered by the court to be an enemy. He'd been found *not* to have aided in the attacks on Oyster River and Groton. The native had only been involved in commerce—his livelihood as an independent trader—having himself been detained by the Abenaki on suspicion of being an English spy. And based upon the testimony of several witnesses who knew the man and vouched for his good character, Hector had been confirmed as being a "friend

Indian." So they turned him loose with the hope that he might remain a source of information as he resumed his business exploits up to Maine and back. Then after revealing this information to Jack and Jonas, the warden disclosed the Indian's address where he dwelt in Saugus. They set off straightway in search of him.

Saugus lay northeast of Boston, about eight miles up along the coast. It was a village familiar to Jack, being just below Lynn, where he'd lived two decades earlier, during and after King Philip's War, having found refuge there as Groton lay in ruins. Those years, now distant in his memory, had been bittersweet times for Jack, seeing there the birth of his fourth child, but suffering the loss of Hannah, his first wife, and then enduring the estrangement from Father, but all the while enjoying the support of many old and trusted friends— friends from his childhood days there in the place of his birth. But, all things considered, his life had long moved past the trouble of those times, and he was now only returning out of want.

They found Hector's home in the low-lying part of town, down by the Pines River. It was situated on a promontory—a small crag of rock and sand that was set well above the flood stage—which afforded remarkable views out over the tidal grasses toward the ocean that lay just a half-mile distant. The Indian's house was a simple structure and didn't look like much, being little more than a shack. But it was well-kept and clean, though frayed by the ocean gusts and grayed from the harsh sun, as there were no trees at all around to protect or obscure it.

From a defensive perspective, the openness gave the place a certain advantage to its owner, being accessible only from the west by means of a long, narrow strip set higher than the flanking marshes; and this made it easy to guard and, in this instance, to see from there the two men as they approached on horseback, riding deliberately out to visit him in the afternoon sun. By the time that they arrived at the house, Hector was standing in the doorway to greet them, pipe in one hand and loaded musket in the other.

Hector was past middle age, with a receding hairline and skin that was well tanned but wrinkled with many lines. The little hair he yet had was black as coal, falling to his shoulders and adorned with copper strands and shells, this framing a clean-shaven face. His outfit was half-English and half-Indian. He wore a fine, white, linen shirt that covered his sturdy torso, and below the waist a breech-clout, apron, and new moccasins upon his feet. As the men drew near, he placed his pipe in the corner of his mouth and took a firm hold of his musket with both hands across his front, making himself ready to address them. "Ye gentlemen lost?" he mumbled as the pipe went up and down with each word.

Jonas responded, "We seek Hezekiah Miles."

The proprietor rotated his musket to his side. The barrel now faced forward, ready to raise at them. "And who might ye be?" he asked with caution.

"I am Jonas Prescott, and this here is Jack Longley."

The Indian squinted into the afternoon sun and angled the barrel up a few inches. "And how comes ye lookin' fer Hezekiah?"

Jonas quickly and directly explained their purpose. "Jack here, his brother's family was massacred in Groton, and the Indians took captive three of the children. We purposed to find Mr. Miles to see if he were able to inform us as to who might have committed this doleful crime and perhaps describe where those children might be."

The Indian carefully examined their faces another moment, but being an affable sort, he lowered his weapon and took the pipe from his mouth. "I be Hezekiah Miles, but most folks call me Hector, fer some reason. I shall gladly tell ye what I know. Why don't ye come inside?" He smiled at the men and then added, "Jus' leave yer weapons on yer saddles."

The men dismounted and lowered the reins to the ground to let the animals graze on the salt grasses beside the path. They followed the native into his home.

The interior of the shack was all in shadow as they entered—but for the beam of daylight that followed them in through the open door and painted a sharp line across the clean plank floor. Two tiny open windows situated in the wall opposite the entry hardly helped with the light, yet those apertures permitted a kind easterly ocean

P. GIFFORD LONGLEY

breeze to sweep through, which kept the temperature inside pleasantly tolerable. Jack's eyes strained to adjust to the darkness as he looked around.

From the inside, Hector's place was larger than expected, being filled with many items and stores piled in the corners, placed on shelves, and hanging from the walls. There was a tall stack of beaver pelts, a half dozen oil lanterns, several pairs of boots and moccasins, blankets, leather goods, belts, pouches, bags, hats, linen shirts, women's dresses, canisters of powder, oil, tea, and tobacco. Jack assessed the value of the goods and understood that the windows had been sized for security—not nearly big enough for a man to squeeze his shoulders through. He turned and examined the door, the weakest point of defense. It was some three to four inches thick, secured with a set of four stout, wrought hinges, and there was an impressive pair of locks.

He then looked around and studied the décor. A large stone fireplace dominated the windowless left side of the abode. In the corner was a cot, which had a crucifix mounted on the wall above one end. The only other furniture in the space was a square English table in the center—like new, chestnut-colored wood, stained, and perfectly polished, surrounded by a handsome matching set of four back and arm chairs. These seemed so oddly fine to be there in an otherwise austere dwelling. Jack stared for a moment at the chairs, admiring them, thinking how he might copy the design.

Hector immediately took note of his interest. "Ye like them chairs? They're fer sale ... fer the right price."

Jack said nothing, and instead refocused to their purpose for being there.

Seeing now the serious expressions on both men's faces, Hector quickly changed the subject. "Yes, well ... why don't ye gentlemen have a seat, and we can get right down to yer business? But first, I'm gonna get me some tobacco. Either ye care fer some?"

The men nodded their appreciation to his hospitality as they sat down. The host retrieved his goods and joined them as they pulled out their pipes, stuffed in several pinches of the Indian's tobacco—

the best according to Hector, imported from Virginia—and then they lit up from the flame in the elegant oil lamp, which he kept burning on the table. Soon the little cabin was filled with the intoxicating aroma of their smoke.

Jonas at last began. "We read your deposition … dated May the thirty-first."

Hector nodded. "I figgered as much. That was an unfortunate sitiation fer me." He noticed Jack's worry-lined face and winced. His choice of words wasn't the best. He quickly redirected his attention to their concerns. "But fergit about me. What is it ye'd like to know?"

Jack leaned across the table and asked directly, "I understand you saw English prisoners."

Hector's recollection was clear and instantaneous. "Yes. But I only seen two of 'em with mine own eyes."

"I was hoping you could describe them. In case I might know them … or even that they might be my brother's children."

"Well. There was a boy and a girl. They was pretty bruised up. But I still remember their blue eyes … *real pretty* blue eyes. And I was fairly certain they looked like each other, like they be brother and sister, especially with that hair of theirs."

Jack leaned closer in agitation and asked, "Blonde?"

"No." He shook his head. "Orange. I mean jus' like a turnip."

Jack slumped in his chair.

Just that quickly Hector saw no further point to the discussion. The men had obviously been seeking after someone else. Feeling suddenly awkward and convinced he'd nothing more to interest them, he rose to his feet and abruptly pushed his chair back. "Now, gentlemen … I do have business that I mus' to be gettin' to."

Jack leaned forward and raised both elbows up onto the table. In an animated fashion, he sunk his face down into his palms, greatly disappointed.

Realizing their intrusion now and being respectful to their host, Prescott stood and looked across the table at the Indian. "We do appreciate your time, Hector, and we shall be leaving now." He

P. GIFFORD LONGLEY

reached his hand out and placed it on Longley's shoulder. "Come on, Jack. We should get going."

Jack muttered under his breath, "I just don't know when we're going to be able to pay that ransom..."

Hector came right back to attention. "Did ye say ransom?"

The woeful man tilted his head and lifted his eyes toward the Indian, distorting his face with his hands, shamelessly exposing his dejection. "I've been trying to figure out how to ransom them. But I just don't know who to pay."

The Indian pulled his chair back toward the table and once again sat down. He never had been one to turn down a good business opportunity when he saw one. "I might," he suggested.

Jack raised his eyes with unexpected promise toward the man, sensing at last they were getting to something good. Jonas sat back down, leery of what he was about to hear.

Hector prepared to address the men as his eyes searched around the room. He drew in his breath and reflected. "I am Cowasuck, born of the people of the dawn. I know these men—what drives their hearts and turns them to kill...and kidnap. I used to be at their side, givin' their deeds my hearty approval, joinin' in their raids, darkenin' these fingers with the blood of hate."

He raised his hands and turned them over to look at them, paused, and then glanced over his shoulder toward the object on the wall above his bed. He continued with a calm confidence, "But I'm not one of 'em no more." He lifted his hand and pinched his nose between his forefinger and thumb, grabbing a hold of the bit of scarred flesh between his nostrils. He stretched it down, revealing a hole where a nose ring had once been. He concluded, "Yes, I can help ye."

Jack noted for the first time the scarred septum, a ragged remnant of a pagan practice.

Prescott interposed with doubt, "We have no idea where they are...the hostages. No ransom demand has been made. No message sent to this colony, as we are at war."

But Hector would not be discouraged. "The Abenakis' fear yer militia and yer prisons, where many of our brothers been hanged. They'll send no courier down to the Bay…cuz they been double-crossed by English too many times. Ye must send a courier up to them…to pay yer ransom fer ye."

Jack brightened. "And *you* would carry the ransom to Maine…to redeem my brother's children?"

Hector looked gladly at Jack. "*I would.*"

"And you would bring them back?"

Hector hesitated as his eyes tilted downward. He'd had many business dealings with the tribal leaders turn difficult in recent times. He hedged, "I will pay yer ransom to the man, the one what took 'em, and to no one else. But whether he permit me to bring 'em back straightway I can't say. These men, they don't think or trade like ye English. They play a game … needful to be regarded in the eyes of their people, to show *they* are in control. But I … I would do my best to bring 'em, or to have 'em returned by some other means."

Jonas's eyes narrowed in suspicion. "How much would you charge to be our courier?"

Hector deferred, "You know this dangerous work…even for me, an Abenaki."

"How much?"

"They suspicious of me and me's dealin's with ye English."

"How *much?*"

"Five pounds," at last he proposed.

"*Five pounds!*" exclaimed Jonas.

"Per person. That's five each."

Jack quickly did the calculation. Fifteen pounds was more than he might earn in an entire year. But he didn't hesitate to interrupt the two. "I'll pay it. I can give you the money."

Jonas snapped across at Longley, astonished. "*Jack!* That's on top of the ransom. What? Another twenty each? That's *seventy-five* pounds! I pray thee, *how* are you going to come up with that?"

"I'll raise it."

"And how do you know we can trust this Indian. We may give him your fortune and *never* see him again."

Both men turned and stared at Hector, who had been quietly calculating the magnitude of the transaction. The Indian grew serious. He knew they were wise to question his integrity as they'd only just met him. Yet this was where the deal would be struck—or not.

He looked toward Jack but addressed them both. "I don't want yer bag o' silver pieces that mus' be paid to the *thieves*. I tell ye that I myself been ransomed from amongst 'em." Again he glanced over his shoulder at the cross on the wall. "And I *swear* by Him what ransomed me ... I'll pay the price fer yer brother's children." He rose to his feet and stuck out his hand, looked Jack firmly in the eye, and waited, holding forth his promise of service.

Jack rose and clasped Hector's open palm and held it as he stared into the Indian's dark eyes—eyes filled with images, haunting remembrances of war, pillaging, destruction, and murder. But he saw no malice remaining, rather only endless regret and ponderous pain, pleas for forgiveness, and a newly healed and deeply repentant soul, a soul longing for opportunity to make amends.

The Indian smiled. "I go again to Maine mid-September."

"And you shall have the payment," promised Jack.

They shook.

Jack and Jonas then said their good-byes, stepped outside, mounted their horses, and departed for Groton.

Saturday, September 13, 1695

The two riders sat on their steeds, leaned back, and halted in the shade of the trees that grew before the edge of the marsh, gazing out along path that led down to the promontory. They stared at Hector's house in the distance, poised in the open sun with the crisp, green-gray ocean horizon beyond it.

Each rider had a bag slung over their saddle, heavy with silver. They studied each other's expression, their hearts whelmed by the great fortune they carried—carried to be placed into the hands of a stranger, a heathen convert, a businessman. Yet it wasn't too late to change their minds and to find some other means.

The last month had been a whirlwind of activity. No new information had come, but Jonas's appeals to the government in Boston and to certain wealthy individuals in the colony sympathetic to their plan had indeed helped to fill their bags. He had also shared the idea with the families in Groton to see if they might have interest to participate in the transaction. But only two other families had trusted in the effort and pitched in with their contributions: John and Mary Lakin had raised funds for their daughter, and Reverend Hobart, being compelled by the story of the apparent faith of their intended courier, had dug deep into his own resources to purchase his son's freedom.

The Longleys were well suited with the proceeds of William's estate, held in trust by Middlesex County awaiting disposition by the trustees on behalf of the three heirs yet in captivity. And Jack himself had bestowed some from his own savings, as had his sisters. Jonas, realizing that poor John Shepley had no family left to redeem him, had felt moved himself to subsidize the young man's bounty. Together they'd raised ten years of wages—the price to free six hostages.

As they sat unannounced in the shade at the edge of the woods, they watched Hector come out from his house and walk back and forth down to his canoe, loading his goods and making ready to depart.

"Do you trust him, Jack?" asked Jonas.

"I feel like I have to."

"You don't sound very certain."

Jack offered, "I've had a lot of time to think about this. And if you were to try and analyze it even longer, I don't think you could ever feel that this was a sure thing or a solution that would guarantee the right result. No. Reason would tell you this was a poor idea. But then I consider the alternative, which, as of today, is to do nothing. That surely doesn't endear itself to me. No. Some things that you do, you just have to do by faith. Then trust in Providence."

P. GIFFORD LONGLEY

They watched Hector continue to load the canoe, very business-like, very neat.

Jack continued. "In a way, I feel like I was drawn here to meet him. I neither think it a mistake nor an accident that I came here that day with you ... nor even that I find myself again here at this moment."

"You *sure* you want to do this?"

Jack just smiled. He kicked his horse forward as Jonas followed, riding out from the shadows of the woods and into the open, down the path between the marshes and out onto the promontory.

Hector stopped his preparations and looked up from beside his canoe, having detected their obvious coming. He stood still as he became convinced of their purpose and watched their approach. The Indian courier could see full well that these men had placed their trust in him. It was proven he would be carrying a vast sum to ransom the hostages. And now, with the fullness of this realization, he suddenly hoped that he hadn't made a terrible mistake by extending his offer to get involved.

DECEPTIVE SWITCH

March 1696

Skulking to the left of his opponent, John skillfully sidestepped on the frozen earth, crouched and balanced on his toes, turning and ready with his bare arms outstretched. Both grapplers now circled round each other, angling for advantage, ready to lunge out and grab, eyeing every movement of the other, looking for first opportunity, wiry and taught, shirtless in the cold, their breath condensing like great clouds of smoke in the morning air, the last gasps of winter.

The crowd formed a circle and pressed in around them, excited, having anticipated the match all week, the many native boys murmuring amongst each other. Several made wagers, but most just presumed who would be the victor. Several men as well had turned out to watch the sporting spectacle, a right of passage, interested in seeing the next generation's leader emerge—the sagamore's son, who'd never lost a fight.

And then there was his opponent, this growing white boy, the little-known captive, yet he'd put away every one he'd faced—some most impressively with his unconventional style. But still, Incon was his elder and soon to be his proven master, more muscular, more experienced, especially with a knife, though no such weapon was allowed in this contest. Other English prisoners were there to watch, as was Shepley, but this minority kept itself quietly to the fringe. The Indian was the clear favorite, and Taxous was there to watch his son vanquish his opponent and bring pride to his royal bloodline.

An eternity of seconds passed, and still both warriors remained aloof, skulking in their endless slow circles, unengaged, protective of their own positions and wary of the other's first move. And then the chanting started, first one boy slowly clapping rhythmically and murmuring the name of his choice, then joined by another and yet another as the sound began to swell. "Inc-con ... Inc-con ... Inc-con."

With their words of encouragement, confidence began to swell in the breast of the sagamore's son. He lunged and missed. The white boy was too keen and swift, artfully using his extra height and longer reach to advantage, cunningly showing his leg and then pulling back just in time, keeping perfect balance, ready to catch his overanxious opponent as he passed him by. But the more experienced grappler withdrew at the last second—he'd hesitated—and fell back into his ready crouch, still circling in the frosty breaths.

Several more in the audience joined in the catchy chant, pulling for their favorite, longing for some action, swelling louder in its slow and steady pace. "Inc-con! Inc-con! Inc-con! Inc-con!"

Pressure began to mount on the young native leader. He must strike. All eyes awaited his usual stunning dive and vicious lunge. With cockiness, he reached again, but John easily withdrew, so skillful and uncatchable, resuming his energetic crouch and dance. And again the Indian tried to attack, and once more he flailed and swept only the air. Frustration was building in the crowd. They'd come for action, yet all they'd seen was elusive dance and unwillingness of their favorite to commit.

Finally Incon saw an opportunity and charged. He lunged and seized a tenuous hold of John's leg with only his fingertips. The white boy bent forward over his attacker's shoulders, pushing back, poised on his other toe, stretching straight the taken leg behind him, so strong, so unwilling to yield it.

More in the audience joined in the clap, glad to see the grab, thirsty for the fall, louder, faster, stomping with their feet, up and down the frozen ground; they raised their sound in unison. *"Inc-con! Inc-con! Inc-con! Inc-con!"*

The native drove ever forward, curling taut his calves, his opponent countering every move, circling backward, skillfully balanced. The Indian from beneath reached ahead, pushed undaunted, with his fingertips yet grasping behind the knee, straining, driving his shoulders forward round the circle, stretching hard and pulling.

But the knee wouldn't yield.

John leaned his full weight on the back of his opponent and pressed the shoulders downward. With his left armpit, he clamped and crushed the native's neck, twisting it, ready to snap the spine. With his able right hand, he shoved the head of the Indian straight down *hard*, face forward into the earth. In the same fluid motion, he pushed himself erect, bouncing backwards away, smiling down, still dancing on his toes, and then crouching again and ready to continue. This was to John a game he'd longed for. Incon was his friend. And he was having fun.

The chanting faded when Incon went down. The Indian stumbled quickly back to his knees and then to his feet, stunned. His vision twisted, blinking from his impact with the earth. With the back of his hand, he wiped the frozen mud and blood from the corner of his mouth. The quieting crowd watched unexpected. This taste of blood was different—as was this opponent. He hadn't been so felled before and had no palate for it.

A native comrade from the crowd yelled in French, *"Hé! Incon ... Punir cet Anglais!"*

He regathered his composure and resumed the crouch, huffing, his nose now running with blood, angling his body and edging forward again. He drew toward John, arms outstretched, ready for another strike.

John measured him, getting a better look at the blood running down from his friend's nose and mouth and eased up to console him. "Listen, I'm sorry about that ... "

And in that vacant second, Incon didn't hesitate to move, kept coming, lurched ahead two quick steps, and grabbed the white boy just above the waist, pressing forward, intending to drive him unawares flat onto his back.

But John was ready. He'd practiced the move before. At Incon's point of contact, he planted both feet. He fell, using Incon's momentum, tucking his head and shoulders, rolling, inverting, kicking his powerful legs skyward up and over his opponent, landing on top, his knee into the Indian's sternum. The breath of the dark one exploded upward in a volcanic vapor as he lay completely still with both shoulders flat upon the frozen earth.

The crowd hushed.

Incon lay motionless, stunned, unable to breathe. He was already defeated.

John rose to his feet, himself surprised by the apparent easy victory. He looked round the circle, seeing the now familiar native faces staring back at his with their mouths gaping, amazed by his show of skill. But he made no smile and felt no pride. He only stared each back.

And in the quiet he looked down at Incon, eyes anxiously wide. The poor young man was gasping to restore his air. John reached down and gently touched his chest, slowly lifting his hand as though commanding it to heal, to raise his lungs to refill with air, the restoration of life. The Indian puffed out a small vapor and then breathed in a deep gasp; his face relaxed, just as if his vacated soul had returned to his flesh.

John graciously seized his friend's hand and pulled him to his feet. Incon staggered to regain his balance and, more importantly, his composure.

And then the new chant started, beginning with a single voice and slow clap. "Awe-gree … Awe-gree … Awe-gree."

John spun to see the lone inflection. It was a native boy smiling with admiration, persistent with his chant of respect as others round him stayed silent. John felt embarrassed, but the boy wouldn't stop. Another next to him relaxed his gape, reluctantly smiled and joined, followed by a third, and then the sound swelled and spread all round the circle, the clapping, stamping, building celebration. "Awe-gree! Awe-gree! Awe-gree! Awe-gree!"

The victor turned from the vanquished and stepped away and toward the center of the ring with his head spinning midst the praise, eyeing the happy chanters as they boldly called his new name. He looked modestly outward from the ring to the spectators beyond and there saw Taxous, the mighty leader, his master, now surprised but tilting his head forward and offering his respect. John stepped instinctively toward the sagamore, the crowd pressed back and divided the circle to make a path to allow their new hero through.

And in that instant, Incon looked up from the back of the ring. He saw the English boy walking away from him and enjoying the adulation that had at first been meant for him. He staggered erect and stepped to one side, grabbed a shoulder of one of the crowd, reached to the witness's chest, and rudely seized hold of the knife that dangled there. It was a coward's move. He knew the fighter's code and that John held no knife.

Overwhelmed by his jealousy, he disdained the fearsome penalty for what he was about to do. The white boy was no friend. He had to pay for shaming him. And besides, who would dare to punish him, the son of the sagamore?

He placed the blade in his strong right hand and stepped forward. He raised his arm and quickened his step; he felt the strength resume in his loins as he made ready for the leap to strike a deadly cut.

With his back to his new enemy, John continued to stride forward toward Taxous in slow motion, stepping between the celebrants, his ears filled with their joyous praise. Several reached out to congratulate him, continuing their chant of honor. And that was when he saw it in their faces—a reflection in their eyes, the vision of flight, like the shadow of a great eagle gliding darkly down, its razor talons extended.

Instinctively he ducked his head and lowered his right shoulder.

Incon sprung on him, knife downward thrusting at the middle of John's back. But the white boy's spin was timed near perfect, and the blade caught only the top of his right shoulder, scraping several inches down the back of his arm.

And with his countermotion already set, the white boy spun adeptly to his left, grabbed first Incon's right wrist with his left hand, landed his right elbow firmly to the face, rotated over the top, grabbed and spun Incon to the ground hard upon his back. He completed the circle and landed again on top with his knee at Incon's throat.

John easily tore the knife from the hand and rolled the stunned Indian over to his chest, pressing his full weight now on Incon's back. He grabbed the black hair, yanked it upward with his left, and with his right hand, he pressed the blade at the Indian's throat. He paused before completing his rehearsed move and stretched the hair taut.

Gazing up the divided path, he found the feet of Taxous, and then scanning up the sagamore's body to his oversized head, he stared straight into the eyes of his master.

The crowd turned toward Taxous to see his instruction. He was the author of the code. The sagamore hesitated, apparently still try-ing to absorb the shocking display—what he'd just seen *from his own son*. He knew everyone was watching their leader to see what he would do. If he changed the rules now, he would be cast as selfishly motivated and weak. He must be consistent. *He must do the right thing.* And so he sternly forced a grin as he nodded his righteous affirmation to the code … and gave his consent.

And then there was John, ready and authorized now to exact his own rightful revenge, to take the life of one so precious to the murderer, the one who'd taken so many that were precious to him. He twisted and pulled the hair up taught. Incon groaned from the torture as John's blood ran down his elbow and dripped onto the victim's back. But holding the blade there, he troubled over what he was being permitted to do. *Surely Incon's disgrace is punishment enough! He has become like a brother to me. How can I take his life?* Again he looked up at Taxous, who watched him as he held the knife there. The sagamore was waiting for him to use it. Yet John knew he must do the right thing.

P. GIFFORD LONGLEY

Still pulling at the hair, John bent forward and placed his lips at Incon's ear. He whispered in Abenaki the word for "peace." He would give to Incon the power to end the fight.

Incon stayed silent with his neck twisted in agony. The young Indian was ready to die, for his pride would not permit him to yield.

"Peace!" John whispered yet again.

Incon kept his lips sealed tight.

"Say it, *damn it!*"

Incon opened his mouth, and his chest heaved out short breaths of vapor as foam and blood dripped from his teeth, and then the word at last came out. "*Kwaskuai...*"

John relaxed his hold and dropped his opponent, who fell limp. He pushed himself to his feet, now breathing hard, with his arm dangling, the blood running down his wrist onto the knife, dripping down his leggings and onto his moccasin. He stood erect and raised his eyes, looking toward Taxous to see his reaction. But the sagamore had already turned and was walking away, disengaged, ashamed of his own son, headed away from the crowd, out of the camp, and down toward the river.

That same day brought a visitor to the Kennebec winter camp, a native who lived among the English but who traveled and traded throughout the vast Acadian Peninsula with both the French and Abenaki. The man was neutral in the conflict, only coming there on business. He cared not whose money he earned, and at last being free to range the upland rivers around Moosehead Lake, which had only recently given up their ice, he brought with him many fine things in his large canoe, things desirous to native and European alike.

Taxous had come down to the river alone and noticed the peddler there stationed at his goods, no doubt unwilling to leave them to enter the camp, guarding them with his watchful eye. The merchant knew it would not be long in the morning until the natives came down to their canoes. And so it would be there on the banks where he would conduct his enterprise.

The peddler was surprised to see the sagamore approach alone. He knew right away he was a leader on account of his fine dress, robe, and royal apron, and his imposing stride. He was fairly certain that the impressive man drawing near was the one he'd heard about, the very one he'd come to see.

The merchant waved at the leader and called out a friendly greeting, "*Kwai!*"

But Taxous made no response and just continued to step forward, staring downward, pretending to examine the goods neatly displayed by the trader on the beach.

The peddler studied the powerful Indian with a sense of foreboding, relieved that he carried no club, no tomahawk, for he knew the legendary violence of this man. Cautiously he addressed him, "If ye don't see anything ye like, I can get it fer ye."

Taxous paused and stared at the man, purposefully making the visitor feel uncomfortable and acting as though he'd not granted him permission to speak.

Yet persisting to remain friendly, the trader introduced himself with a forced smile. "I'm Hezekiah Miles. But most call me Hector."

Taxous muttered in Abenaki, "I know who you be."

Hector expressed his surprise as the conversation continued in their native tongue. "You do? I ... I can't say as I remember meeting you before."

"Bomaseen told me about you." Taxous groaned disparagingly. He cared not at all for weak Indians, those who dealt regularly with the English and who had so willingly abandoned the proud ways of the Abenaki. Hector was known for this.

"Oh ... Bomaseen. I haven't seen him in more than a year. W-what did he say about me?"

Taxous offered no response.

Hector fidgeted at the sand with his moccasin. "And what did you say your name was?"

"I didn't."

Hector felt a chill of apprehension run down his spine as he quickly deduced he was engaged in a contest of wits, and he hoped

P. GIFFORD LONGLEY

not to be outsmarted. He was certain now of whom he was speaking with, yet sensed he should play along and pretend otherwise. Perhaps he could use this knowledge to his advantage? In any case, he should quit wasting time and get down to business.

"Well, listen, I was intending to get a message to the great leader here. He's *highly respected*, only I don't think I can make it up to the camp on account of my wares being spread out here. I had planned to quickly conduct my trade and then to move along right away. I have a piece of paper here. Could you take it to the sagamore for me?"

Taxous, now suddenly engaged, watched with interest as the trader retrieved the small parchment from his purse. Hector handed it to him and explained, "This message is for Taxous."

Taxous, himself literate, seized hold of the document and rolled it open to read. But Hector dared to continue with the game as he stretched out his hand to retrieve the note. "That message is alone for the Great Sagamore!"

The big Indian stepped back out of his reach and scowled at Hector, undeterred. He lowered his eyes and read the document to himself:

> *Be it known that Hezekiah Miles (alias Hector) is hereby vested with authority on behalfe of certain families from ye Towne of Groton, in ye County of Middlesex, in ye Province of Massachusetts Bay to negotiate, redeeme, and make for safe passage home of ye following hostages taken from said Towne on July 27, 1694:*

> *Lydia Longley*
> *Elizabeth Longley*
> *John Longley*
> *Lydia Lakin*
> *Gershom Hobart*
> *John Shepley*
> *September 9, 1695*
> *[Signature and seal]*
> *Jonas Prescott, Esq.*
> *Selectman*

Taxous rolled the scroll up in his fist and measured the face of the trader before he spoke. "I'll see that he gets it."

The sagamore *was* interested in the ransom, but it was time for him to return back to attend to more important matters. He would destroy the document later, as it made no mention of any sum. Other offers would surely be forthcoming—more serious offers that came with a price, a good high price. He turned and took several steps.

Hector suddenly felt as though he was losing the contest even before it had begun. The man he needed to see was walking away from him, and he might never see him again; neither would he be able to conclude the exchange. He called out, "Listen, aren't you interested in hearing about the ransom?"

The sagamore stopped walking. The mention of money was the key. He should wait and hear a bit more. He might agree to negotiate with the peddler for a while and, in the process, expose the defector for all his weakness. But a better thought occurred to him. Facing away, he asked, "Do you have the money *here*? Today?"

Hector hadn't expected such a direct question so soon. "Yes..." he fumbled. "Well, some of it, that is." His voice straightened. "I have the rest in a secure location."

This was better than he'd thought. He knew the man was lying. The money was already there—*all of it*. Taxous turned. "How much have you got?"

"I have enough for a few hostages."

"And how much would that be?"

Hector felt a knot form in his throat as though his airway was being constricted by a snake. He pressed ahead, "Well, I suppose it all depends on how much a hostage is worth... you know... uh... to a great sagamore like Taxous."

The big Indian could see the peddler knew with whom he was speaking, reading it in his delusive eyes. And he could see that the pathetic man imagined he was the better negotiator. The face of the English-sympathizer suddenly disgusted him. He turned to depart.

"Five pounds," the trader blurted out after him.

Taxous stopped in his tracks and stared down at the ground, keeping his back to the merchant. He wondered if he could rob the man, as weak and as foolish as he seemed.

Succumbing to the tightening squeeze, Hector quickly appended his offer. "That's five ... for *each* hostage."

The big Indian turned and brought his eyes to a simmer. He raised the parchment in his clenched fist and quickly stepped forward and down toward Hector, approaching to a distance that was entirely too close. And then he scowled down as he barked out his fetid breath in the man's face, "It cost a lot of Abenaki blood to purchase those heretic slaves! I think if I told the *Great Sagamore* that amount, he might be very insulted ... perhaps even *angry*."

The trader shrank back to a more comfortable distance. "You must forgive me. I hope you understand that I am in a difficult position here. And just as it says on that piece of paper in your hand, I am here to negotiate ... on behalf of others ... *not for myself, of course.* As I had no intention of paying too low a price, something that would dishonor my very own people."

Taxous sickened at the thought. *"My" people? The traitorous lout!* He folded his arms and waited for the better offer and wondered where the money was stashed.

"I am prepared to offer you ten pounds each. That's sixty pounds. I think you will agree that *is* a lot of money."

The sagamore stroked his chin and smirked. "To some people that would be a lot, but we are talking about the value to a *great sagamore*, not just to anyone in the Nation of the People of the Dawn."

"Indeed you are correct. And once again I find myself in a flawed position. And of course you would know that ten is not my final price ... rather fifteen. And that is a considerable sum to *any* leader in Acadia."

Taxous squinted at Hector. The sleazy huckster imagined he could sell or buy almost anything and always come out on top. But that's all it was: *imagination.* This was no real contest at all. In fact, it was becoming a tiring game.

He replied, "But Taxous is not like 'any other leader' in Acadia. Some would even say there is *no one greater* than he."

Hector had reached the end of his budget, and he feared that if he tendered full price that the negotiation wouldn't stop there but keep going higher and into his own wages. He hesitated as Taxous awaited the next bid, then he gambled, speaking uneasily, but from his heart. "I can only give you all that I have myself—the full price given me for them. Twenty pounds each. I have no more." He lowered his gaze and dared not to engage again the face of the sagamore.

The game had gone on long enough. "Twenty?" asked Taxous as he appeared to mull the sum and slowly force a grin. "I think that is a price that the *Great Sagamore* would feel honored with."

Hector felt relieved, imagining his victory. But the negotiation wasn't final yet, and so he continued. "Now, as for the transport of the hostages back to Massachusetts, I have sworn that I shall make every effort to bring them with me. Do you think Taxous would permit them to come with me today?"

The sagamore frowned cleverly. "I cannot say. Taxous will do what Taxous will do."

"Yes … of course." Hector scratched his head as he grimaced and dared to be more direct. "Now, before I can pay you that considerable sum, I shall like to go and see these hostages for myself." He took a half step forward and up the bank.

Taxous stuck out his hand and curtly clamped the man's shoulder, squeezing it to the point of pain. "I think you are forgetting something," he said. "The sagamore will not trade unless he sees first the silver."

A sense of sudden dread swept over Hector, yet he held his position. "But you must understand that I am bound to return these hostages with me and that I must see them."

Taxous stared firmly down from his high position. He stood like an imposing statue, fixed high above the little peddler, who leaned before him, with his feet set lower down on the sloping bank. The sagamore withdrew his hand, re-crossed his arms, and flexed his ample muscles. He clenched his jaw several times, which caused the sinews to pulse in his cheeks, and these glistened like hardened bronze in the morning sun. All that he had to do now was wait for the huckster to show him the money.

Time was clearly on his side in this transaction. As he patiently waited, he glanced down at the objects to his right, distracted by them. Several brass lanterns were set out there atop a stack of goods, fine items that caught his interest. He picked up a lantern and raised it to his face to examine the shiny metal. He turned it round in his hands and twisted the knob for the wick, and as he did so, he peered through the globe, staring at the peddler standing silently before him. The rounded and irregular hand-blown glass refracted and distorted his pathetic expression—the weak man who so openly now could be seen as dreading what he was being made to do.

Hector wished he had a hold of his musket. At last, he raised his hand up and spoke. "Now you just wait right here while I go and get it from my canoe." He spun around and took several anxious steps out into the water, toward his vessel, which was near to him, half-beached.

Taxous didn't hesitate to make his move. He followed right after, leapt high into the air, and drove the lantern down hard onto the back of the peddler's head. The glass shattered into many pieces as Hector crashed forward with a loud splash and then lay completely still, crippled, face down in the shallows.

The sagamore hurried, swishing knee-deep out to the end of the canoe. The man's provisions were there, together with a musket and two large saddlebags. He lifted the leather bags, which were heavy with clinking coins. He considered his impressive haul as he carried them over and dropped them onto the sand. But suddenly an odd sense of insecurity came over him. He bent and greedily guarded his new fortune, peering about for spectators.

No one was on the beach in either direction. But turning over his shoulder, he faced up the bank and spied there a lone onlooker, someone peeking out from behind a tree, a young man. It was the crestfallen Incon, curious, an eyewitness to the transaction.

Taxous glanced down at Hector. Blood was running from his scalp as he lay lifeless. He needed to finish him off, to silence him. Regardless, he knew he had to quickly get rid of the body before more came along and asked too many questions. He could make up some story to scam his foolish son about what'd just happened, but it would be harder to fool everyone else. It would be so much easier not to have to—to keep the matter unknown to others. *Say… Maybe I can involve Incon with the kill?* That would silence the boy and seal the secret.

He motioned and called out to Incon, who ran down to the water's edge as he explained, "Here, this man tried to swindle me. Help me lift him."

The two raised Hector from the water and placed him into his canoe. He was still breathing but unconscious and wet in the cold.

Taxous reasoned out loud, "These no-good English-sympathizers. Spies, I tell you, bringing evil on our people. He does not deserve to live."

Incon measured his father's expression. The sagamore's eye was twitching. Sweat beaded on his bronzed brow in the cool air as he bent over the wounded peddler, avoiding his son's gaze. The throbbing of Incon's own face measured out the silence as he surveyed the scene and quickly seized the opportunity.

"Do you think this scum is worth the trouble? Perhaps he would be worth more alive? Carrying somehow the message of fear and terror to others who might consider swindling *you* and our people."

Taxous was startled by the idea. The peddler would surely never come back to the Kennebec after this. He'd be too afraid. That would silence him enough and at the same time increase his own fearful legend. Why hadn't he thought of that? He looked with interest at Incon. Maybe there was hope for his weak son after all.

"Yes," the boy continued, "he could wear a sign, a mark, so that anyone greeting him can see it and be forewarned."

Taxous nodded in agreement. He drew his scalping knife from the sheath and bent over the peddler, hissing, "*The heretic.* He is a traitor to his people. He is no friend! Now let him wear this mark for the rest of his days." He gouged a bloody cross into Hector's forehead.

Incon watched with impassive interest, a barely visible smile curving the corner of his mouth. The two of them then worked together and pushed the canoe from off the beach and out into the shallows, and then they shoved it into the current. Slowly it drifted downstream and away from them.

Taxous remarked, "How often do the waters cleanse us from the *filth* of life and wash away our problems?" They stood watching for several minutes until the vessel rounded the bend and left out of sight.

Father and son stepped up from the water and onto the bank.

Incon glanced down at the saddle bags left there but thought he'd better not ask what was in them. He spied the small parchment, the ransom note, lying beside them and cleverly bent to retrieve it. "What's this?" he asked innocently as he rolled it open and studied the handwriting. The young man didn't know how to read.

Taxous reached out and gently took it. "It's just a bill of materials ... for ... these goods here ... that I ordered, but we shouldn't be needing it any more since we now have them." Taxous smirked as he took the parchment and shredded it into tiny pieces and then tossed them into the current, watching them slowly float away downstream.

Incon stared up at his father. He envied his skill at deception. It came so easy to the sagamore.

But now this matter was apparently over, and Incon's heart suddenly darkened as there lurked a matter far more important that had to be resolved. He was weighed down by the terrible burden of his disgrace. Yet, as awful as it was for him to speak of it, he felt he should wait no longer to address it. "Father, I ... I disgraced myself and you today."

The sagamore turned away from the river and now gave Incon his full attention.

The young man's tears formed in the corners of his eyes as he continued. "I no longer feel worthy to be called your son."

The topic of the conversation made Taxous feel uncomfortable. "Yes," he spoke conclusively, "you were weak."

Incon's tears were flowing now. "Yes, Father. I should not have violated the code. I should not have cheated."

"Cheated?" A look of surprise filled the sagamore's face. "You think I feel ashamed because you *cheated?*"

"But, isn't that so?"

Taxous glared down at his son, disgusted. "I am not ashamed because you *cheated.* I am ashamed because you are *weak!* Because you fairly lost the fight to a *slave,* who soundly crushed and embarrassed you, and did so with such flare and skill." A smile of passion formed on his face as he spoke at last the truth from the depths of his belief. "I tell you that boy has more heart and strength in him than *you* will *ever* have. Maybe I should make him my son in your place!"

Incon felt the full weight of his shame as he hung his head. What could he say now? *I was pathetic today! I deserve this chastisement... but... but... to have my position among the Kennebec stripped away? That is too much to bear! But it doesn't have to end this way. Surely my right of birth has to mean something. I have advantage here in my hands, and I can use it...*

He lifted his sincere and tear-filled eyes toward his father and spoke with purpose. "You would choose a foreigner over your own flesh and blood to rule your people?"

Taxous felt a cold shiver run down his spine, a shiver that threatened his spirit, like a knife held to his throat. He stared aghast at Incon. The boy was more perceptive than he'd ever imagined, for Incon had seen it happening—Assiminasqua's error all over again— *and he hadn't!* He silently bemoaned his own foolishness.

Taxous shook himself. And for a moment, he examined his thoughts and desires with a degree of honesty that he hadn't felt since he was a young man. What a burden it had been to live his life the way he had, ever manipulating and forcing the outcome of events to his favor, shaping his decisions—and those of others too— ever in a manner of falsehood, struggling for advantage. How different his life might have been if Father had only trusted him more and given to him what had rightly been his. Then surely he would have had the full honor of all the people and the admiration of the many, admiration he deserved. That would have been the key. But he did not have to let the same thing happen again. Now *he* was the one in control.

He reached out and gently placed both hands on his son's shoulders, speaking kindly. "I shall indeed set things right again for you, my son." He turned and pointed toward the river. "These same waters that just took away my problem shall also take away your source of shame…Tomorrow, on the Equinox, when the sun shall rightfully return—a sign that you shall be restored to preeminence."

Incon looked up at the golden orb as it rose steadily higher in the sky, suddenly hopeful, anticipating his restoration. He could sense now that whatever deception his father was yet planning would surely inure to his benefit.

PENTAGOET

The First Day of Spring, 1696

In the morning, the sagamore entered where John had been sleeping, carrying with him a handful of goods: clothing. He instructed the young man to put them on and to meet him down at the river. They would be leaving soon.

John sat up, peeled his blanket aside, and looked at the items: a pair of boots, leggings, shirt, and jacket. They all looked new. He stood up and pulled each piece out, turning it over front to back, holding it up to himself to see if it might fit. He tore off his old clothes—soiled and bloodied rags—and cast them to the side, standing there naked and filthy. How strange it felt to be putting on something new, and without so much as a bath. But it would be weeks more before the river would be warm enough to properly wash himself. Nevertheless, he set to donning the new garments.

First there was a fresh breechclout and then soft deerskin leggings. He pulled them on. They were a bit short but felt good on his legs, like he could run in them with speed. Then came the shirt, which was white linen with silver-colored, wrought metal buttons down the front. *Surely something of great value*, he thought.

He swung his arms into both sleeves and grabbed the collar and hiked it up to his shoulders. He winced, as the back of his right arm was still smarting from the wound. He raised the collar and craned his neck to look inside. The dressing hadn't dislodged. *It should need to stay there several more days*, he thought. And as he adjusted the shirt and began to button it, he pondered again the bout the day before. The garments must surely have been his reward for winning.

He bent and picked up the jacket. It was made of deerskin, light in color, with ornamented stitching on the back. He wondered who'd made the exquisite item. Surely it would have taken weeks to have worked the leather, soaked and de-haired it, brain-tanned, stretched and suppled it, then cut and assembled the pieces, matching them just so, and then completing the stitching. He happily pulled it on. The shoulders seemed snug at first, and the sleeves were a bit short, but this lack of perfection couldn't permit him to say no to such an attractive gift. *Perhaps it might stretch a bit*, he reasoned.

At last, he sat down to pull his boots on. But as he placed his right foot into the first one, he felt an object there and took it back off to peer inside. Reaching in, he retrieved a sheath made of black-tanned leather, which had a long strap wrapped around it several times. In the sheath was a white whale bone handle, which he then pulled forth to reveal a silver, precision blade. He sat there stunned, eyeing the exceptionally crafted object. He weighed it in his hand, feeling the balance. It was the finest scalping knife he'd ever seen, and this one was apparently his very own.

Mindful of the instructions of Taxous, John pulled his boots on, hurried outside, and stepped briskly through the camp with his head erect and arms swinging as he headed toward the river. The natives stopped and stared as he passed them by, and he smiled broadly back at them, a spectacle, proud of his new outfit. The knife dangled like a trophy from his neck. It swayed back and forth with each big stride.

As he approached the riverbank, he spied others already there with Taxous, a group of warriors. Shepley and Lydia Lakin were there as well, the two of them standing close and speaking to each other, as was often the case. Her back was to him as he approached.

She was wearing a new outfit, azure in color, with her feminine form accentuated by the stylish skirt. It had never occurred to him before that she was actually quite attractive. He found himself staring—that is, until he saw Shepley watching his approach. He seemed to be guarding her, no doubt perturbed by John's gawking.

John quickly redirected his gaze up at their faces and, remembering how fine he himself looked, strode straight up to the two of them, so taken with himself that he hadn't even noticed Shepley's new garments. He grinned broadly and pronounced a cheery, "Good morning!"

But Shepley only frowned and grunted.

"*So.* I see you're dispirited this day," John retorted.

"No, just another fine day..." Shepley muttered sarcastically, "*here in hell.*"

John turned round and studied the others. Several of the warriors were coming and going, loading up the canoes with supplies. It was obvious they were about ready to depart—half a dozen canoes but not too many provisions. "Looks like a short trip," he surmised.

Shepley spotted John's new knife and smirked out his usual sarcasm, "So why don't you go ask where we're going...*sachemo?*"

John knew Shepley could be abrasive at times, and he didn't bother to answer as he tucked the sheath inside his jacket. Still, he did wonder where they were going. And why were Shepley and Lydia both there? It didn't make any sense to him.

After a few more minutes, the provisions were fully loaded and the band was assembled. The fifteen then entered their canoes and headed straight upstream, with Taxous leading the way and John kneeling in the middle of the same vessel, paddling with the rest of the natives.

The melt had only just begun, the river marginally swifter than normal. The near-frozen waters were sharp and clear and formed a sight glass of sorts, revealing the rocky bottom in all its brilliant colors. Thus their crystal highway offered not so much resistance as they pulled forward against it on their six-mile journey upriver to the lake. Before noon, they were out upon the vast Moosehead, navigating between the islands with their heading set east-southeast.

The sun had just passed its zenith in a cloudless sky when they arrived at the opposite shore, aided there by a warming southwesterly that pressed at their shoulders. From there, they worked their way up through a narrow, swampy passage, along by the Prong Pond, which was set in the shadows of the Scammon Ridge. The impressive hillside yet wore snow on its northern faces, the white cover lying beneath the bare maples, rooted in its slopes. This scarcity of trees stood erect like the silvered, short morning hairs on an old Englishman's scalp.

They beached their canoes at the little muddy pond—the point at which they could paddle no farther—and portaged up a gentle slope toward a gap in the range, a gash that divided the steep, icy crag to their right from the little knob on the left. They clambered over snags and frozen hassocks in the trail, carrying their goods and vessels up amidst the shadow, through the narrow pass, and then downward by the sun-thawed track beyond. There they found the new headwaters to their journey, these familiar to the natives, but foreign to the three captives who'd never been this way before: a mountain pond with deep, black waters yet bound with sheets of white ice lurking in its shady edges. The mucky path led them to a sunbathed beach, where they set their vessels again in the water, reentered them, and resumed the paddling, pressing ever onward to the south across the open water, wasting no time.

After several miles, the placid surface narrowed toward its outfall: a mountain stream that twisted down the foothills, having carved a narrow canyon there over unrecorded time. And so they floated down its early current, which pushed them along swiftly, feeling their timing fortunate as in just a few weeks this passage would become a roaring and ferocious torrent fed by the April rains and swollen melt.

The mountain stream swept them ever onward, southeast through the gorge, between the upright, weathered faces of granite strata erected on both their sides, in some places standing more

P. GIFFORD LONGLEY

than three hundred feet above their heads, rising like an awesome cathedral to grant them sanctuary in the wilderness. John marveled at the wall that was on his left, examining the few gnarly evergreens that tenaciously clung to the soil-filled cracks situated high above in its sheer faces. He imagined these bits of green, how they had been so inhospitably cast there as seeds—not of their own volition, but rather thrown over the edge by some stormy blast and sprouting right where they fell, being fed by the droppings of the mourning doves that cooed in the sunny perches above them. And so they stretched their twisted branches upward, striving for the light and summoning all of their hope.

The right wall of the canyon told an entirely different tale, completely devoid of life—the shaded rocks encased there by the cathedral's massive pipe organ of icicles, the frozen bluish stalactites, dripping and glistening, soaring up the mighty face, yet impotent in their silence. Atop the canyon, the balsams on both sides stood straight and tall, being well fed and swaying in an abundance of light, but oblivious to the struggles of their siblings beside them in the crevasse, which clung there to the rocks, feeding on the dung, hoping for the light, yet still fortunate they'd not been entombed in the ice or even swept away, the intrepid, somehow subsisting and surviving the test.

The flotilla passed on from there along and through the canyon for many miles, the sharp turns and jagged projections obstructing longer views ahead and behind them. In the mid-afternoon, they approached a tall mountain ridge, an imposing wall that lay directly in their path and which was bisected by their watercourse with its broken cliffs crumbling from the left and right; fallen boulders tumbled down a thousand feet to the banks of their rivulet. That such a tiny stream, which now bore them along, could have cleft in two this mighty barrier was a matter of astonishment to John.

And leaving at last the mountains to their backs, they continued their journey and followed the course as it turned due east near on toward sunset, when the stream drained into the western edge of a long thin body, the Lake Sebec. There they quickly set up camp beside the shore, lit their fire, and rested for the evening.

With neither time nor the intent to hunt or fish, the trail provisions made up their meal, and there was a good abundance of them for all in the traveling band. The three English captives sat together on one side of the fire to consume theirs, left alone by the Indians.

Curious to this fact, Shepley observed, "Isn't it peculiar how things have changed?" He eyed Taxous and the others, who were engrossed in casual conversation amongst themselves.

"How so?" asked John.

"See how they pay us no mind?" said Shepley.

But John only grunted and then chawed on his piece of dried venison, slowly savoring the salty meat with its grainy texture. He felt a sense of comfort and acclimation with the troop, and so the observation hadn't seemed to him so remarkable.

And then like a flash, a thought came to Shepley as he smirked and revealed his notion. "I can see now what the hell-hounds are up to."

Taken by the comment, the other two stopped eating and awaited his explanation.

"They're gettin' rid of us. I'm certain ... And these new clothes— they just want us to look like we're worth somethin'."

Lydia interjected excitedly, "Do you think we've been ransomed?" Her eyes suddenly brimmed with hope—hope that had been so presently lacking in her life. And her cheeks, no longer pale and gaunt as in her starving days, filled with color as a smile brought beauty to her expression.

"No ... ," sighed Shepley in gentle reply to her, but then he aimed his drollness toward John as he retorted, "And it's a good thing for you, boy."

John raised his attention toward his comrade.

Shepley continued as he twisted his face and altered his voice. "Yeah, before some young Injun skulks into yer lodge at naht and *slits* yer throat!" Shepley simultaneously scrunched a distorted grin as he formed his forefinger into an imaginary knife and drew it up along his own neck as though slicing it.

But John hadn't been worried in the least about Incon. He wasn't a threat. Though Shepley's suggestion *was* disquieting—the idea that he might be taken away from his new life, perhaps sold. This thought produced in him a sudden jolt of disappointment, as things had just started to go really well for him. He swallowed his meat and wiped his mouth with the back of his hand. He measured the face of Shepley, illumined there by the flickering glow of the campfire, showing him to be self-assured and full of reason. *Maybe Shepley is right*, John considered. *But, then again ... probably not.*

Shepley leaned back with his piece of meat and waxed philosophical, almost comical, "Yep. I'd say a big change is a comin'."

And amidst the uncertainty regarding the true impetus to their journey and the possibility that Shepley had indeed been correct, the three presently grew quiet as they finished their meal and then, like the rest of the camp, bedded down for the night.

In the morning, the trip continued eastward, with the travelers enjoying the persistent fine weather, pushing out across the narrow wedge-shaped lake toward the point, the swift outflow, headed downriver, south and east again, through the wide flatlands, converging with, then carried along by the strong current of the Piscataquis. The paddling stayed easy, pulling slightly ahead of the flow, steering and guiding with speed, sometimes more thrilling in the steeper drops amidst the whitewater. Past noon they drained into the southward roll of the wide Penobscot, and the sense that it would not be long before they arrived proved quickly true. They circled the last few bends by mid-afternoon and came upon Passadumkeag, their intended destination.

Passadumkeag was the largest village of the Penobscot people, whose territory encompassed the vast region of central Maine. This place was known to be the home of the Great Sagamore, Madockawando, the elder brother to Taxous. They'd apparently come looking for the renowned man, but they soon learned that he wasn't there at present. So instead, they would spend the night, enjoy a fine meal, and rest amongst their brothers. They would depart in the morning to go and find the man.

When they assembled on the beach early the next day, Shepley and Lydia were curiously no longer with them. John dared not to be so direct as to ask why the two weren't coming, but Taxous, sensing his concern, surprisingly volunteered that John would be seeing both of them again, and soon. Yet he could only wonder what that meant.

They resumed their mission southward, and before noon, the mouth of the mighty Penobscot spewed their tiny armada out into the vast bay with the ocean fanning out before them, far beyond the islands. A stiff westerly smacked at their sides and raised a heavy chop that threatened to swamp their vessels. The flotilla stayed in close, hugging the eastern bank as they crawled along toward the south, all the while with the breeze off the frigid waves chilling their progress. After several hours of struggle, they came by a point of land marked by a stone fort, broken and lying in ruins. They rounded the bend past the fort there and landed on the beach, the gravelly shore dotted with many small boats and alive with human movement. They had reached their goal, the French and Indian settlement of Pentagoet.

They pulled their canoes up to the top of the slope, well above the high tide mark, scrambling with their feet upon the loose and weathered granite pebbles, like so many marbles precariously strewn there by a child. There at the top, Taxous instructed John and his men to wait for him while he went off in search of someone. The sagamore walked away, swallowed into a crowd of other Indians that were arriving there on the beachhead, the numbers of visitors swelling as though assembling for war.

In this idle moment, John's curiosity was drawn toward the ruined fortress. He wondered how its massive stones had been thrown down, imagining the violence, but the silent stones were unable to reveal that the English had once pounded the battlements from their warships in the harbor for days on end, and then, after the

P. GIFFORD LONGLEY

occupants had fled for fear of their lives, they'd seized the unmanned guns, turned them in against the walls, and blasted the last of all that stood. But the English hadn't remained there; they'd allowed the peninsula to fall back into the control of the French. How surprising it was to John that such a prominent position, with such superb and commanding views overlooking the harbor, could be left so ruined like this and not rebuilt.

After quite some time, Taxous returned, bringing with him a Frenchman, not a soldier or a nobleman but rather appearing more like a trader, and a successful one at that, a powerful looking man, though short in stature. The two stopped several rods distant from the group and continued their conversation with each other, out of range of their hearing. A transaction of sorts seemed to be underway between them as John noticed the man hand a small purse to his master. At last the sagamore pointed to John to get his attention and then motioned for the young man that he should come to meet them.

Warily and wondering, the captive strode up to the two, anxious to figure out why he was summoned. As he approached, Taxous seemed to be smiling at him while the Frenchman intently examined him, sizing him up from head to foot, duly noting his strong and confident gait.

When John reached the men, Taxous addressed him tersely, "John, you wait here with Baron St. Castin. There is something I must get."

With no hand of greeting extended or formal introduction, these two stood waiting awkwardly beside each other, two Europeans, yet of clear unequal station. The Frenchman was a "baron," while John a slave, of obvious low import. In addition, culturally speaking, he and the Frenchman represented opposite sides of the war. No, there could be no sense of cordiality between them. So John, the captive slave, in obeisance to his master, simply stayed as he was told, insecurely enduring such close proximity to the Frenchman, a stranger, the enemy.

The baron remained silent and aloof, hardly heedful of Taxous as the sagamore walked away, focusing instead upon the others who were there round about him, coming and assembling. He restlessly folded and unfolded his arms and breathed heavily, tapping his foot, as though he'd been forced to stand there to tend to the big Indian's interests, like he'd been interrupted from his own concerns, pried away from some other more important matter or business. Still the Frenchman turned and looked up at John, managing a brief smile on his rugged, bearded face.

Taxous's path away from them took the Indian along the top of the beach to his canoe, where he retrieved a small bundle that was wrapped in a brown blanket. He brought it straight back to them. The sagamore eyed John the whole time he returned, wearing now an expression that seemed so oddly foreign to his purposeful persona, a look that John had never seen on him—a look of *sadness*. He came straight up to the young man and extended to him the bundle as he spoke, "Here. This is yours."

John reached out tentatively and took it, saying, "I don't understand."

The sagamore spoke simply, "You stay here now."

John seemed not to comprehend. "You mean for today?"

"No ... I mean ... I sold you ... And now, John Aw-geh-ree, now you go with this man." The big Indian had apparently concluded his transaction and with the same degree of speed and efficiency as he always had before. But, contrary to his manner, he hesitated before he left. The pause hung in the air as hope leapt in John's eyes. But again, and true to his pattern, he seemed to remember his first intention. He turned, and walked away with his usual and purposeful stride, heading toward the Kennebecs where they stood waiting beside the canoes, ready, as always, to commence with his next duty.

Halfway there, Taxous stopped, turned back toward John, and made brief eye contact with him. The sagamore's thin lips twitched, as if to form words. But didn't. Instead he straightened his back and redirected himself forward and away from them, resuming his fast pace until he rejoined the others. In a matter of minutes, the Kennebecs pushed their canoes back down into the waves, entered them, and paddled away, headed in the precise direction from whence they'd come.

John stood stunned. His former master had actually departed and left him there—just when he'd thought he'd figured the man out, having learned so many lessons while serving him. He'd learned to survive and had even begun to prosper in the presence of the man. But being left there now—*sold*—this made no sense. Hadn't Taxous favored him? Hadn't Taxous grown to trust him? Wasn't he of value to the man? Value? Oh, what is value? What is *his* value? Was it just to be a slave? A commodity to be sold to another? And that was why he now was there? Hadn't he just become the new property of the Frenchman? A stranger? The enemy? The unknown enemy?

In the urgency of his confusion and the necessity of his new situation, John quickly refocused his attention on that which was important. He'd survived the cruelty of an unknown enemy before. He mustn't forget that which drove and guided his manner: the even keel of a wise and observant spirit—and cooperation. Yes, cooperation at all times. Such was essential to avoid punishment. In a matter of mere seconds, he solemnly turned toward the Frenchman standing beside him, seeing there that the man had been curiously studying John's reaction to what had just transpired.

Castin gazed up at the face of the tall, handsome boy. "Ye act like ye mees sze snake. Heh?" he asked.

John blanched. "No. No, sir. I would not wish to offend my new master."

"Mass-der?" inquired the Frenchman.

"Yes … I have been sold to you … Haven't I?"

Castin tilted his head back and laughed. "Haw! Haw! I am not ye mass-der. Szat iz me fadder-een-law, Madockawando. Come, let us go and szee heem." Wearing a sneering grin, he leaned up and said something intended to be in confidence between them. "He's a man not much like hees brodder."

The Frenchman smiled broadly, and then in a friendly gesture, he reached out and firmly clamped John's right arm just above the elbow…precisely where he'd been wounded. It throbbed from the squeeze, but John didn't flinch or show any pain, knowing full well his rank and value and being too experienced in manners and relations to draw any negative attention to himself. The two then turned their back to the harbor and headed toward the Indian village, parting the crowd as they left—the crowd that whelmed the muddy field astride the rubble of the fort.

As they went along, Castin confidently strutted, making eye contact in a pleasant manner with the many natives, most of whom seemed to recognize him, smiling and tilting their heads to him in respect. It became apparent to John that the man beside him was someone of worthy character, perhaps even of great importance.

They crossed the field and came to a low, two-story stone and wood dwelling that stood beside the ruins, apparently recently built, oddly situated there as the lone permanent structure on the edge of the native settlement, set before the many teepees and lodges that were behind and beyond it. Before the front of the house was a small court of cobbles, which they stepped across as the Frenchman stomped his feet, for it was a place to kick the mud off his fancy, black boots. Castin then led him straight up a few steps to the entrance and held the door open for John to enter in.

The two stepped inside, and the baron closed the door behind them. John waited for his eyes to adjust to the dim interior of the little cottage. He saw that they stood alone in the corner of a square room. A stone fireplace was there aglow with embers, which filled the place with fragrant smoke. The walls, floor, and ceiling were all of wood, blackened already from the soot of too many a heavy downdraft. The pair of small windows on the front of leaded-glass seemed to be losing their battle to illuminate the space. The modest room was filled with furniture: a long wooden table and a number of chairs in the center, and a pair of sideboards with pots, pans, and utensils stacked on them. They were in the kitchen.

Castin removed his sword and pistols and set them to the side; then he stripped off his fine beaver hat and coat and hung them by the door. "Heer, Jean." He reached out and motioned for the young man to set his bundle down and to remove his jacket.

The Frenchman watched John attentively as he doffed his coat. He spied the knife that dangled from his neck. Castin hung the garment up and then reached one of his large and hairy mitts, taking hold of the sheath in the palm of his hand while squarely examining John's face from close range. "Szats quite a knife. May I?" he asked.

John didn't hesitate. He innocently reached up and lifted the strap from around his neck and handed the item to the man.

Cradling the sheathed weapon in his burly hands, the Frenchman grasped the bone handle and drew it slowly from its case, turning and admiring the blade, which glinted like a polished mirror. He touched the edge with his thumb. "Nice an' sharp. Ye ever use szis?"

"No. It was a gift."

"A geef?"

"Yes. I won it … I suppose … in a fight."

"Ye suppose? Ye mean ye don' know?"

"No. I *know* I won the fight. I just don't know why I got the gift. I assume it was for winning."

"An who gave ye szis geef?"

"Taxous."

The Frenchman lunged at John. He seized him firmly by the throat with one powerful hand. With his other he pressed the tip of the blade into John's chest as he blurted, "Ye lie!"

John stared wide-eyed down at the man. "No, sir. I have no reason to lie. I swear to God! Take the knife if you want it. I have no need of it."

The Frenchman relaxed his grip, dropped his hands, and backed away a step. He reached down to his belt and purposefully drew out another knife, remarkably similar to the first. He turned it over for John to see—same bone handle, though the blade was a bit dull from use. "I bought me knife from an Indian trader. He pass-sed szrew szese parts lass fall. Haven' szeen heem since." He put his knife away and continued. "Tell me bout szis fight. Ye fight wisz knife?"

"Yes. Well … no. The fight was wrestling. I never used the knife."

"Ye won?"

"Yes. I pinned my opponent."

"Um hmmm..." The Frenchman waited to hear more.

"He didn't like that I beat him, I suppose. He pulled a knife on me and tried to stab me in the back." John turned his shoulder to the man. The dressing had oozed a bit through the fabric, and there was a crimson stain on the sleeve. "I ducked, but he got me in the arm. Then I knocked him down again and took the knife from him."

"An szen... ye tried to kill heem wisz eet, eh?"

"No! The code said I should. But I didn't think it was the right thing to do. So I didn't."

"Sze code? Hmmm... Ye shewed heem mer-zie, eh?"

John nodded forthrightly, but then his face filled with uncertainty.

The Frenchman stared up at the young man's blue eyes, clearly weighing him. He made a decision. He resheathed the knife and handed it back to John, smiled, reached up, and patted him on the good shoulder. "Szere isz someone I'd like ye to meet. Come wisz me."

The Frenchman walked over to the side of the fireplace and passed through a small doorway that led to the next room, with the top of his head barely clearing through the low opening. John needed to duck to follow him.

They entered the parlor, where the ceiling was just over six feet, mere inches above John's head, with the tops of his hairs touching it. The young man felt as though he had to tilt his head sideways to avoid scraping it. An old man was seated there in a high-backed chair, relaxing before a warm fire in the back-to-back fireplace, smoking a pipe, and apparently reading some papers—and presumably having overheard all of the recent exchange in the room right next door.

Seeing them step in, the man lowered his reading. He rose to his feet, took the pipe from his mouth, and smiled to greet them. He was a big man, about the same height as John, but very thick across the chest. His pockmarked face was pale from the long, cold winter spent indoors, and his high cheekbones made the distinct profile of an Indian. There was a scarred hole in his septum from which dangled a round, silver nose ring. And though he was very rugged and fearsome-looking, he was at the same time quite handsome.

The Frenchman addressed the old man and introduced the guest, "Fadder, szese heer is Jean Augury."

John stood quietly before the man for a long, awkward moment.

"What's the matter, young man? Can't you speak?"

John straightened. "Yes. I can speak, of course. I ... I apologize. I suppose I was wanting of what to say."

The Indian then cordially introduced himself. "I am Madockawando."

John bowed respectfully. He stared at the papers in Madockawando's hands, wondering what was written on them.

The Indian noted John's interest and asked, "Can you read?"

"Yes, sir, my father—my parents—they taught me how to read and write from a young child and to cipher, as well."

"So, you are not a bastard orphan?"

John was greatly disturbed by the question. "No, sir. I lived with both my parents until they were killed ... near on to two years ago."

Madockawando made no response and instead studied John's face. A moment of silence followed that made John feel even more uncomfortable.

The Frenchman then interjected as though completing a private conversation that had occurred between he and the sagamore some time earlier. "He speaks sze truth. Heer. Look." He grabbed John's shoulder and spun him round to show the stain to the Great Sagamore. "Eet wasz only self-defense."

The old Indian's inquisition then suddenly turned threatening. "So ... you had no purpose in your heart to take the life of Incon?"

Like a great veil had been lifted from his eyes, John perceived at last that Taxous had besmirched his character. He'd made up some story about him to justify why he was selling him to Madockawando—no, "getting rid of him," as Shepley had so perceptively calculated. Flush and biting his lip, he confidently shook his head in a clear negative response to the question.

Madockawando then grinned knowingly. "I would not put it past my brother to stretch a story to suit his purpose." He stuck his pipe back in his mouth and took a deep draw.

The old Indian and the young man studied each other quietly. The elder sensed John's confidence and courage. John perceived the sagamore's honesty and thoughtfulness, something he hadn't been exposed to in a while.

Madockawando withdrew his pipe and blew a great puff of smoke out of the corner of his mouth. "Are you hungry, John?"

John smiled modestly and nodded, fairly whelmed by the hospitality of the question.

"Then you should join us for supper."

The Indian turned to the Frenchman. "Jean Vincent, *le prendre à sa pièce*." Then he addressed John. "Follow the baron, and he will show you where you will stay."

The Frenchman turned and left the room, heading through the opening back into the kitchen, explaining as he went, "Szer iz room upstairs," as John trailed along after him. At the front entrance, he bent and retrieved John's bundle and then entered an opening into a dark and narrow stair that spiraled steeply up to the second floor. At the top of the steps, there were four doors that led from the hall into the bedchambers. He opened one and stepped into a vacant room, which was lit by a small window located just above the floor line. There was a narrow bed in the tiny room, pushed back against the side and tucked under the edge of the roof. "Ye can szleep heer fer sze nex' few days," he said.

"Yes. This is fine ... *fine indeed*," said John, nodding his appreciation and feeling now a sense of wonder—wonder as to why he was being treated with such kindness.

The Frenchman stepped over toward the door to leave. "Ye can rest a beet now an szen come down an help wisz sze chores. *N'cest pas?*" He looked down at the brown bundle in his hands and then firmly tossed it to John, who made a perfect catch.

"Thank you," said John, fairly disbelieving his present good fortune.

The Frenchman paused and pointed to John as he corrected him, *"Merci."*

John understood, bowed, and repeated, "Mer-zee."

The Frenchman smiled pleasantly and turned as he retorted, *"Très bon. De rien!"* He closed the door behind him and clopped away down the hollow steps.

Left alone in the room, John examined the empty bed. He bent low under the rafters, set the bundle down on the floor, and then lowered himself into the soft mattress, adjusting his weight and pressing down into it with his fingers, measuring the comfort.

After a moment he turned his attention down to the bundle on the floor beside his feet, curious as to what Taxous had tied up for him in the dark, woolen blanket. He bent and pulled it up onto his lap, untied the knots, and cast the cords aside. The blanket had been wrapped around some object several times, so he unrolled it on the bed. At last, he exposed the lone content: a black felted hat, which lay there upside down. It had a white satin lining and a wide brim that was crushed and crumpled from being wrapped up. But he recognized it right away. It was Father's hat.

Forgetting where he was, John stood straight up with it, bumping his head hard on a rafter. He groaned as he grabbed his scalp, crouched low, and stepped over to the highest part of the room. He stood straight and examined the hat.

It was dusty and tired-looking. He brushed it off, slapping it against his leg. But that didn't make it look much better. He gingerly unfolded the brim and smoothed and stroked the surface with his fingers trying to restore its shape. He turned it upside down and raised it with both hands, holding the lining up to his face, breathing in deep through his nose and hoping it might yet smell of Father.

It didn't.

He stood very still holding the hat, silently weighing it with his hands, his mind wandering over the eighteen months he'd spent with Taxous, the harsh, cruel times, remembering all the forces that had been arrayed against him—and which hadn't defeated him. He had adapted. He had found the nourishment he needed for his body, and he'd built his skill and strength. And in all his circumstances, he'd learned to maneuver through the challenges, even the lies, having done so with success. He had survived. And there he was—*alive*. He remembered again who he was: the last surviving son of William Longley.

He stared lovingly down into the lining of the empty hat, fully focused on whose it was. Then slowly and purposefully he raised it up past his face, righted it, and placed the garment atop his head. It rested there high on the top of his hair. He reached up and grabbed the brim and pulled it down snug onto his dome.

The fit was perfect.

And wearing Father's hat now, John felt deeply moved to grief. So he cried in the privacy of his room for a good long time, all the while wondering what tomorrow would bring.

APPENDIX

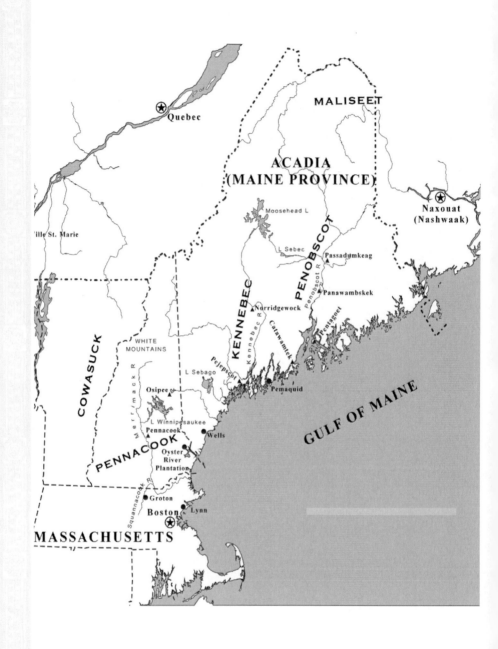

Northern New England and Maine (Acadia), 1694-1698

P. GIFFORD LONGLEY

SOURCES

The characters, places, culture, events, and times indicated in this book were developed for the story based largely upon information available in the public historical record, which, sadly, isn't free of conflicting accounts, scribal errors, and variants in name spellings (not at all unusual for the seventeenth century). Also a number of sources on the Internet were consulted, too numerous to include here (and URLs are too likely to change). And though there is a great deal of information available on the Internet, such was found to contain numerous conflicts and errors, yet not so much as to suggest that the basic aspects of this story are not possible as depicted.

The most reliable information that the author found came from personal visits to the actual sites and a careful review of the oldest books and documents, especially town clerk records and those found in the Massachusetts State Archives, where public records predating the existence of the United States are available on microfilm—images of original handwritten documents.

The reader would find the documents below to be among those that are the most reliable.

Longley Family Documents & Records:
[Longley] Crisp, Joanna. *The Last Will and Testament of Joanna Crisp*. Middlesex County, MA Probate Record #5320, 1698

Longley Family Documents & Records (continued):

Longley, William. *The Last Will and Testament of William Longley.* Middlesex County, MA Probate Record #14335, 1681

Longley, William, Jr. *Longley Family Estate Inventory.* Middlesex County, MA Probate Record #14336, 1694

Longley, John. *John Longley Guardianship.* Middlesex County, MA Probate Record #14337, 1697 & 1700

Longley, Anna [Hannah]. Essex County Massachusetts Depositions, Vol 3, page 34, 1663, age 16

Longley, John. Essex County Massachusetts Depositions, Vol 3, page 25, 38 & 46, 1663, age 23

Longley, John. Essex County Massachusetts Depositions, Vol 8, page 124, 1681, age 42

Longley, Mary. Essex County Massachusetts Depositions, Vol 3, page 32 & 34, 1663, age 19

Longley, Mary. Essex County Massachusetts Depositions, Vol 3, page 32, 1661, age 19

Longley, William. Essex County Massachusetts Depositions, Vol 2, page 284, 1663, age 47

Longley, William. Essex County Massachusetts Depositions, Vol 3, page 26, 1661, age 48

Longley, John. Middlesex County Massachusetts Deponents, 1691, age 53

Longley, Cicely. Middlesex County Massachusetts Deponents, 1691, age 40

Additionally, the author reviewed a number of histories on the seventeenth century to collect information on non-family characters, places, times, and period culture. Among the sources found to be the most enlightening were those written in the nineteenth century by authors particularly diligent in their research, as their data suggests a high degree of consistency with the oldest public records extant. The works listed below are among those deemed by the author as most reliable, helpful, and relevant.

Histories of New England and Acadia:

Brown, Craig J. *The Great Massacre of 1694 - Understanding the Destruction of Oyster River Plantation*. New Hampshire: Historical New Hampshire, Vol. 53, No. 3&4, The New Hampshire Historical Society, Fall/Winter 1998

Parkman, Francis. *Count Frontenac and New France under Louis XIV, vol. 2 of France and England in North America*. 1877; reprint, New York: The Library of America, 1983

Schultz, Eric B. and Tougias, Michael J. *King Philip's War - The History and Legacy of America's Forgotten Conflict*. Woodstock, VT: The Countryman Press, 1999.

Histories of Groton:

Butler, Caleb. *History of the Town of Groton Including Pepperell and Shirley*. Boston: T.R. Marvin, 1848, 1st Edition

Green, Samuel A, MD. *Early Records of Groton Massachusetts - 1662–1707*. Cambridge: John Wilson & Son, University Press, 1880, 1st Edition

Green, Samuel A, MD. *Epitaphs from the Old Burying Ground in Groton Massachusetts - 1662–1707*. Boston: Little Brown, & Co., 1878, 1st Edition

Green, Samuel A, MD. *Groton During the Indian Wars*. Cambridge: John Wilson & Son, University Press, 1883, 1st Edition

Green, Samuel A, MD. *Groton Historical Series*. Cambridge: John Wilson & Son, University Press, 1887, 1st Edition

Histories of Groton (continued):

Hurd, Hamilton D. *History of Middlesex County, Massachusetts with Biographical Sketches of its Pioneers and Prominent Men.* Philadelphia: J.W. Lewis & Co., 1880. 1st Edition

May, Virginia A. *Groton Plantation - A Plantation Called Petapawag - Some Notes on the History of Groton Massachusetts.* Groton: Groton Historical Society, 1976

Histories of Lynn:

Lewis, Alonzo, and Newhall, James R. *History of Lynn, Essex County, Massachusetts, Including Lynnfied, Saugus, Swampscott, and Nahant.* Boston: J.L. Shorey, 1865, 1st Edition

Lindberg, Marcia Wilson Wiswall. *Early Lynn families including Lynnfield, Nahant, Saugus and Swampscott : genealogical study from the earliest settlers through the Revolutionary War.* Salem, MA: Higginson Book Co., 2004

Longley Family Histories and Genealogies:

Bent, Gilbert O. *Who Begot Thee.* Wisconsin: The State Historical Society, 1903, 1st Edition

Green, Samuel A. - the several books listed above in "Groton Histories" contain accurate genealogies and many of the family details recounted in this work, among them a court deposition of the captive, John Longley, briefly recounting his life among the Indians.

Longley, Robert Dalton, *Longley Family - Some Descendents of William Longley, Born In England 1614.* North Anson, ME: Ideal Print Shop, 1952, 1st Edition

Mower, Walter Lindley. *The Sesquicentennial History of the Town of Greene, Androscoggin County, Maine: 1775 to 1900, with Some Matter Extending to a Later Date.* Greene, ME: private publication, 1938

Skeate, Elinore F. *The Longley Family Genealogy.* Groton, MA: available at the Groton Historical Society, database file, 2008

Made in United States
North Haven, CT
21 February 2023

32924878R00143